He stumbles to a halt on emerging from the undergrowth. The Draconis Constellation appears so low in the night sky he imagines that if he were on higher ground, he might reach up and pluck the winged beast's eye.

Just as he's contemplating the significance of the constellation's dominance, a thunderbolt illuminates the mist-shrouded plateau with a foreboding staccato glow. In that same heartbeat, a temple appears out of the eddying mist. A temple he would have sworn on all he held sacred hadn't been there before the flash.

The temple, standing sentinel-like upon a raised earthwork and consisting of a semi-circular ring of pillared arches and an inner ring of smaller stones, is already being eaten up within the mist inching its way across the plateau.

He senses a malevolence about this mist.

And then he sees it: The mist is moving against the breeze.

He draws his sword, touching the sliver of iron set within the pommel to ward off evil.

Mouthing a prayer to Xavius, Father of the gods, to watch over him this night, he starts for the temple.

Girlish laughter sounds from somewhere within the temple.

Scrabbling up the earthwork, he races through the outer ring into the temple. He catches sight of a girl in a long flowing dress with tumbling auburn hair skipping barefoot about a crude effigy of a winged dragon.

Kingdom of Conscience

by

Mick O'Shea

Tales of the Xavier Seven, Book One

Kingdom of Conscience

COPYRIGHT © 2022 by Mick O'Shea

Cover Art by *The Wild Rose Press, Inc.*

The Wild Rose Press, Inc.
PO Box 708
Adams Basin, NY 14410-0708
Visit us at www.thewildrosepress.com

Publishing History
First Edition, 2022
Trade Paperback ISBN 978-1-5092-4429-4
Digital ISBN 978-1-5092-4430-0

Tales of the Xavier Seven, Book One
Published in the United States of America

Dedication

For Tasha and her enduring encouragement and patience.

Prologue

He stumbles to a halt on emerging from the undergrowth. The Draconis Constellation appears so low in the night sky he imagines that if he were on higher ground, he might reach up and pluck the winged beast's eye.

Just as he's contemplating the significance of the constellation's dominance, a thunderbolt illuminates the mist-shrouded plateau with a foreboding staccato glow. In that same heartbeat, a temple appears out of the eddying mist. A temple he would have sworn on all he held sacred hadn't been there before the flash.

The temple, standing sentinel-like upon a raised earthwork and consisting of a semi-circular ring of pillared arches and an inner ring of smaller stones, is already being eaten up within the mist inching its way across the plateau.

He senses a malevolence about this mist.

And then he sees it: The mist is moving against the breeze.

He draws his sword, touching the sliver of iron set within the pommel to ward off evil.

Mouthing a prayer to Xavius, father of the gods, to watch over him this night, he starts for the temple.

Girlish laughter sounds from somewhere within the temple.

Scrabbling up the earthwork, he races through the

outer ring into the temple. He catches sight of a girl in a long flowing dress with tumbling auburn hair skipping barefoot about a crude effigy of a winged dragon.

A thought flashes through his mind in tandem with the lightning: the girl is Princess Rhiana of Abador. He has never before set eyes on Abador's sole heir; yet instinctively knows it is the princess.

He is advancing toward the inner ring when the laughter suddenly morphs into frenzied high-pitched shrieks. He sets off at the run, calling out to let the princess know she isn't alone.

The words choke in his throat on seeing rivulets of moon-glossed blood oozing from the markings etched within the stones.

Within that same eyeblink, the rivulets erupt into cascading torrents, and writhing serpents appear within the blood-sodden earth.

A cloying sulphuric stench fills the air, and an unearthly jarring reverberates about the temple.

The sword slips from his grasp on seeing the effigy coming to life.

He sinks to his knees as the winged beast fixes him with its slit-yellow gaze.

Chapter One

The Abandoned Keep

Lucian shot bolt upright, instinctively scrabbling about for a sword that wasn't there, when a familiar yelp served to wrench him from his befuddlement. It was Lykka. He gratefully wrapped his arms around the wolf allowing the succor to wash through him until the nightmarish slit-yellow eyes finally faded from his mind. He didn't trust his legs to support him, so sat trying to piece together the fragments of his day before he'd fallen asleep within the keep.

The box-shaped keep sat atop a raised earthwork surrounded by the weathered remains of the four-foot-high palisade. The keep had once served as a coastal fortification.

Lucian's grandparents lived outside of Kalimar; a small village situated upon a promontory located a few miles from Abador's northeastern coast. Kalimar translated as bountiful land and more than lived up to its name. It was fertile farming land with an abundance of wildfowl and fish that Lucian helped his grandfather trap and net in the tidal creeks.

To the west, where the land gradually rose to Bokran Tor, there were apple orchards and fields of maize, barley, and wheat. To the east, there was clay and limestone that could easily be quarried and fetch a good price at market. His grandparents also raised goats and chickens. All in all, it was a good life.

Although Lucian rode his filly, Kia, every afternoon, he'd never before visited this stretch of coastline because it lay beyond a treacherous stretch of the marshland known to all as the Sucking-sands.

He'd promised his grandmother never to venture into the Sucking-sands. And nor would he have had it not been for Lykka charging into the marsh after a wild hare.

Lykka was his best friend and his constant companion. During one particularly intense summer several years ago, he'd taken to sleeping outside in a hammock. He remembered being disturbed from his slumber by his grandfather shooing at a wolf with a broom. Lykka had refused to leave, however. His grandmother had scolded her husband for not realizing Lykka was a gift from the gods to watch over Lucian. She'd chosen the name Lykka as it meant good fortune in one of Kracia's ancient tongues.

Lucian thought his grandmother the wisest woman in the whole of Kracia, even if she insisted the world was flat and precariously balanced upon the shell of a monstrous turtle.

Seeing Lykka disappear into the marsh, he'd leaped from Kia's back, hurriedly wrapped her reins about a thicket, and given chase after the wolf without a second thought for his safety. He had knowingly disobeyed his grandparents in crossing the Sucking-sands. For an anxious heartbeat, he feared the nightmare was a punishment sent by the gods. He quickly pushed the thought from his mind, however. The gods had guided his footing through the marsh, or

4

how else would he have made it through?

Lucian could see from the lengthening shadows that sunset was closer than he'd suspected. He cursed his stupidity for falling asleep as he knew his grandmother would be worried. And, of course, Kia was still tethered beyond the Sucking-sands. He grabbed up his leather water flask and gulped down some water before splashing more onto his face. He hurriedly poured some water into his cupped hand for Lykka before scrambling to his feet.

He made his way across to what remained of the keep's outer palisade. A fogbank was drifting on the incoming tide. He was puzzled as to why his quarterstaff was jutting out of the sand some thirty feet from the keep. Then he remembered hurling the staff in celebration after defending the keep against an imaginary Ardassian raid. His father had died defending their village during an Ardassian raid, and he hated the Ardassians with a vengeance.

It had been arduous work defending the keep against the imagined Ardassian horde, but not so tiring that he would fall asleep.

He saw his slingshot a few feet away. His grandfather had made the slingshot out of flax, hemp, and braided rope and taught him how to use it. He grabbed up the slingshot, slipped it inside his jerkin, and slung the goatskin water pouch over his shoulder before making his way down the keep's interior stairwell and out through the gate to retrieve his staff.

Lucian was heading for the dunes when he suddenly realized Lykka wasn't following. Glancing about him, he could only assume the wolf was still inside the keep. Unable to mask his temper, he retraced his steps until he was in sight of the keep and barked a command.

When Lykka failed to heed the summons, he knew something was amiss.

Lucian threw down his staff and hurried back to keep. Lykka sat rigid, gazing out to sea through a gap in the palisade. Following the wolf's gaze, he initially saw nothing but fog, but then something caught his eye. It was the faint outline of a ship within the mist. The vessel was making for shore. He'd always imagined smugglers or slave traders would seek out a secluded cove such as this. He felt giddy at the thought of it being smugglers going about their nefarious business, unaware they were being observed.

Lucian was still watching the ship when the moon emerged from the clouds to illuminate the shore. He rubbed at his eyes, fearing they were deceiving him. It was a Drakkar...a Galyak longship.

****

The Galyaks were a fierce warrior horde that lived beyond the Kolkan Steppes in Ursia Minor. Their whole ethos was for war. Boys were trained to fight almost from the time they could walk. Any male infants deemed too sickly to survive through their first winter were cast into a death pit. For centuries, the Galyaks were content fighting amongst each other, but then a warlord called Salah Khan proclaimed himself Werloga and united the warring tribes. Over the coming years, the Galyaks subjugated each of their neighbors in turn before then sweeping down through the Kolkan Steppes and across Ursia Minor, crushing every army that dared stand against them.

On reaching the Gidean Sea, Salah Khan

determined to conquer Kracia and set his vast army to construct a fleet of longships.

Kracia was made up of five kingdoms: Abador, Varnia, Belanos, Kavashar, and Barrati, which was separated from the mainland by the Strait of Horus. Anticipating Salah Khan would first seek to secure a land base, Prince Leonid of Barrati sent emissaries out beseeching Old King Obelus of Abador, Günter of Varnia, King Jarod of Belanos, and King Paulus of Kavashar, urging them to set aside their differences. Kracia was beset by intrigue and in-fighting, however, and his petitions had gone unanswered.

Salah Khan had launched his armada on the first favorable wind. Rather than face the Galyaks in open battle, Leonid chose to remain behind his walls. His doing so, of course, left Salah Khan free to land his vast army unopposed. The Galyaks hastily erected settlements along Barrati's eastern coast before busying themselves through the winter months fortifying their settlements and constructing siege engines and towers in preparation for a spring offensive of Leonid's walls.

With no means of replenishing their grain supplies, the Barratians were half-starved by the time Salah Khan began his siege. With his people dying from disease and hunger, Leonid sought a truce with Salah Khan offering a yearly tribute of gold, oxen, and wheat. In return for keeping his crown, Leonid also agreed to recognize Salah Khan as his thegn. All through that same winter, more and more longships arrived on Barrati, each filled with warriors eager to make a name for themselves in battle so that they may lay claim to a piece of land to call their own.

Spring duly came, and Salah Khan set his sights on

Kavashar, which lay on Kracia's south-eastern coast. King Paulus was a rather arrogant individual, and that had proved his downfall. Believing his army to be more than a match for a horde of savages, he'd launched an attack on Salah Khan's fortified strongholds and was easily defeated. Paulus was also allowed to keep his crown, but only in return for agreeing to pay a yearly tribute three times that imposed on Barrati. He was also forced to give his eldest son, Prince Flavin, to Salah Khan as a hostage.

Abador was on the brink of war with neighboring Varnia, but upon hearing Belanos, the smallest of Kracia's kingdoms, was holding out against Salah Khan, Old King Obelus led his elite Centaurian Guard into Belanos to force Salah Khan to withdraw his army. The Galyaks, however, still commanded vast swaths of land stretching from Kracia's south-eastern coast to the headwaters of the River Sulah. Salah Khan named his new domain Helägaland.

Günter of Varnia stubbornly refused to form an alliance with Abador and Belanos, however, as Salah Khan's siege engines were of no use against his mountain strongholds. And so, the Galyaks were free to grow ever stronger.

Old King Obelus died the following year. Sensing Abador's newly-crowned King Ocwan might not be possessed of the same warrior spirit as his father, Salah Khan had led his legions across the Sulah River.

Salah Khan's objective was to reach the River Zylos, which all but cut Kracia in two. Should Khan arrive at the Zylos unopposed, he'd be free to erect fortifications along the river's southern banks. If that were to happen, the Galyaks' supremacy could never be challenged.

The fates were to lend a hand, however. Günter was thrown from his horse while out hunting and died soon thereafter.

Despite risking an uprising among his people, Günter's eldest son, Prince Rhödos, readily forged an alliance with Abador on being proclaimed Wulvran and planted his wolf standard beside the rampant unicorn of Abador on a sloping plain overlooking the Zylos.

The battle had raged all day with Abadorians, Huskenbachs, and Galyaks sweating, bleeding, and dying in the crush of the shield walls; the glowering skies rent with the press of spear points, blades, and shield rims; the earth drenched in blood, sweat, and gore.

The Galyaks finally broke through the Abadorian/Huskenbach shield wall. Believing victory was now his for the taking, Salah Khan advanced with his Bloodshields.

The Bloodshields were said to be the fiercest of Salah Khan's warriors, their name stemming from draping their shields with the flensed skins of those they had slain in battle. King Ocwan was new to Abador's throne but was nonetheless well-schooled in tactics from studying the battles of antiquity. The collapse of the shield wall was merely a feint, however. As the Bloodshields came swarming over the rise, they were surrounded on all sides by the Centaurian Guard. Salah Khan and two of his sons died in the ensuing fight.

Strengthened by the Belanese army, Ocwan and Rhödos laid siege to the Galyaks' south-eastern strongholds, driving them back across the Strait of

Horus. Ocwan and Rhödos had hoped to rid Kracia of the Galyak threat once and for all. Their ambitions were thwarted by the onset of winter, however.

By the time spring came around, Rhödos was dead. He died during a murderous attack on his stronghold alongside his three brothers and his two sons. Rumors soon reached Abador that Agnar, Rhödos' cousin, was behind the attack.

Salah Khan's eldest son, Kirgus, now ruled Barrati. And with Agnar being no friend of Abador, an uneasy truce prevailed.

Chapter Two

The Galyaks

Lucian knew he should make for Bokran Knoll with all possible haste to light the beacon that would alert the neighboring villages of a possible Galyak invasion. With Agnar posing as big a threat to Abador as Kirgus Khan, beacons such as the one at Bokran Knoll had been erected along Abador's north-eastern coast and kept in a state of readiness. Something was telling him that he should remain where he was to determine the Galyaks' intentions. It could simply be that the Galyaks had made for shore because their longship required urgent repair.

He was straining his eyes to see if the Drakkar was listing when a horn sounded.

Glancing along the cove, Lucian saw pinpricks of dancing light: Men from a neighboring village? But if that were so, why hadn't they first ridden to Bokran Knoll to light the beacon to warn the other villages along the coast?

The Drakkar was approaching the surf now. Something was disturbing about the riders' casual approach. He suddenly realized these riders, whoever they were, must be in league with the Galyaks. His suspicions were soon confirmed when several Galyaks vaulted over the gunwale and started for the shore.

Lucian had slain untold imaginary Galyaks while defending his village from attack but had never thought to see them in the flesh. The Galyaks wading through the surf looked every bit as fierce as they did in his imagination in their horned helmets and bearskin pelts.

Lucian was still taking in the enormity of what he was witnessing when one of the riders suddenly wheeled his mount about and set off galloping toward the keep. A harried shout sounded, and all but one of the other riders came on. How could the riders know he was there? He was gripped with panic. To stay where he was meant certain capture or death, but dashing the bluffs was equally suicidal as the lead rider was almost at the tower and would easily catch up with him.

Slipping the slingshot from inside his jerkin, Lucian fished a stone from his breeches pocket. With his eyes riveted on the lead rider, he loaded the stone into his slingshot. If he could dislodge the rider and grab the horse before it bolted, he might yet reach the sanctuary of the Sucking-sands. He was about to release the stone when he saw the rogue was riding side-saddle like a girl. He now realized what was afoot. The Galyaks were here to collect the girl from the riders.

Whoever she was, Lucian knew he had to do something to help. He swung his arm around and released his stone at the rogue leading the chase. His hands were shaking, but his aim proved true. The rider suddenly threw up his arms and tumbled from his mount. This took the other rogues by surprise as they reined up, glancing this way and that. After a heated exchange, they continued after the girl.

Lucian was willing the girl on, but as she reached the bluffs, her horse reared up, throwing her from the saddle. The rogues were soon upon her. Although he couldn't be sure, he thought he heard the one that had dismounted mockingly address the girl as "Your Royal Highness" before dragging her to her feet.

The moon suddenly broke through the clouds to illuminate the scene. Lucian saw the man's head was completely shaved except for a knot at the crown. He felt utterly helpless as one of the other rogues arrived with the girl's horse, and Knot-head heaved her up into the saddle.

Knot-head climbed into the saddle behind the girl and seized the reins to her mount. He paused long enough to bark out a series of commands to his accomplices before setting off to where the Galyaks were waiting. The other rogues broke from their huddle, and Lucian's heart leaped into his throat as two of their number brought their horses around and started toward the keep.

Lucian reached into his breeches for another stone. His heart sank, however, on finding both pockets empty. He dropped to his knees and was fumbling blindly for anything that might serve his needs when the two riders separated. The time for making a run for it was long past, so Lucian hurriedly wrapped the cord of his slingshot about his left forearm, grabbed up his staff, scurried up the motte with Lykka at his heel, and retreated inside the keep. The gate was hanging from one hinge, but he managed to wedge it shut. With one hand gripping hold of Lykka, he pressed against the keep's thatch, all the while mouthing a prayer beseeching Xavius to watch over him and Lykka this night.

****

Lucian sensed movement outside. He was mouthing another prayer to Xavius when he heard the telltale scraping of a sword being drawn from its scabbard on the other side of the gate.

Then silence.

Lucian was straining an ear for any more movement outside when the gate suddenly flew off its remaining hinge with a resounding crash. One of the rogues appeared within the opening just as the moon slipped behind the clouds, plunging the keep's interior into semi-shadow. Knowing Xavius had heeded his prayer, Lucian lashed out with his staff, catching the rogue full in the face.

There was a crunch of bone, and the rogue dropped silently to the ground

Mercifully, the second rogue was nowhere to be seen. Stooping to grab the felled rogue's sword, Lucian charged out of the keep, hurdled the palisade, and charged through the bluffs as though all the demons of the Netherworld were at his heel.

Lucian soon arrived at the Sucking-sands. It was only then he realized Lykka wasn't with him. He wasn't overly worried as the wolf was capable of fending for itself. He was more concerned about attempting to navigate the Sucking-sands in the dark. Just as he was praying to Xavius to send a wind to part the clouds, an ululating shriek filled the air.

He instinctively lashed out with the sword, but his assailant had second-guessed him, and the sword and staff flew from his hands as he slammed to the ground. Before he knew what was happening, the rogue straddled him, pinioning his arms with his knees.

The moon had re-emerged from behind the clouds

to cast an eerie pall upon the bluffs.

Lucian instinctively recoiled on seeing the disfigured face looming over him. A ragged scar ran across the man's sightless right eye and cheek; the puckered skin gave the appearance of a lopsided grin.

"Does my face offend you, boy?" Scar-face growled, slapping Lucian hard across the face with the back of his hand. "How 'bout I takes one of your eyes?" the one-eyed rogue chuckled while plucking his dagger from his belt and angling the blade to catch the light. "Maybe I'll take 'em both," he said, resting the tip of the blade beneath Lucian's left eye. "Before guttin' you like a fish and leave yer stinkin' carcass for the gulls." His one good eye widened suddenly. "I knows what we'll do, lad. We'll let the Galyaks have you for sport. It's a bit of a sail back to their island, and havin' you will distract them from ruinin' what my Lord Nikobar has planned for the princess…" He cupped a hand to his mouth. "Oops, me an' my big pie-hole," he mock-intoned.

Lucian had heard Knot-head address the girl as *Your Royal Highness.* "So, she was a princess," he said more to himself.

"Not just any princess, lad." Scar-face grinned. "She's Princess Rhiana of Abador."

Lucian was aghast. "Xavius will cast you into Orbelium for this!"

Scar-face leaned in till their noses were almost touching. "He'll have to catch me first."

Scar-face got to his feet and slipped his dagger inside his belt before reaching down and grabbing Lucian's arm. "We'd best get a scoot on, or the Galyaks will miss the tide. And we can't have that, can we?" he added, giving Lucian a shove.

Lucian had already noted his staff lying a few feet away. Feigning a stumble, he collapsed to the ground again. Scar-face let out an oath and went to kick him. This was what Lucian had been hoping for. He grabbed Scar-face's boot and twisted with all his might sending the rogue off-balance. He grabbed up his staff to strike Scar-face when he sensed movement in the darkness. He could only suppose the other rogue had regained consciousness. Seeing Scar-face scrabbling to his feet, he gave him a hurried kick before turning on his heel and setting off through the bluffs.

The moon had again slipped behind the clouds by the time Lucian reached the Sucking-sands, but with Scar-face and the other rogue giving chase, he didn't even break stride. It was as though Xavius was guiding his feet through the sands. He was almost across when he heard a strangulated cry. He instinctively knew it was Scar-face.

Lucian's instincts were screaming for him to leave Scar-face to his fate. But if the girl he'd seen was Princess Rhiana, then he could use Scar-face's plight to his advantage. Using the tip of his staff to test the ground, he retraced his steps through the marsh.

Scar-face was already waist-deep, and his exertions were sucking him farther into the mire.

"Where are the Galyaks taking Princess Rhiana?" Lucian demanded.

"I had an inklin' you'd come back, lad." Scar-face chuckled to himself. He wrenched an arm out of the mire and held it up to Lucian. "Help us out, matey, and I promises I'll tell you all you needs to know about your precious princess."

Lucian took a hesitant step closer to Scar-face. "Where are the Galyaks taking Princess Rhiana?" he asked again. "I'd be quick about it if I were you, or I won't be able to save you."

"Not as daft as you look, is you, lad." Scar-face grinned. "My Lord Nikobar will feed me guts to the gulls if I goes tellin' you where the Galyaks are taking the princess. What we have here, matey, is what you might call an impasse. What I means by an impasse is—"

"I know what an impasse is," Lucian retorted indignantly.

The sands were up to Scar-face's throat now, forcing him to tilt his head back. "Course you do, a clever lad like you. The question you needs to be askin' yerself, matey," he spluttered, pausing to spit the foul gloop from his mouth, "is will you be able to live with yerself knowin' you had a chance to save your princess?"

Lucian knew he was a fool to trust Scar-face, but he was desperate to know where the Galyaks were taking Princess Rhiana so he could raise the alarm. He dropped down onto one knee to steady himself before extending the tip of his staff toward the one-eyed rogue.

Scar-face managed to pull an arm free of the sands and grab hold of the staff. Lucian was pulling Scar-face free when the swine's other arm suddenly broke the surface, a dagger clutched in his hand. He was drawing back his arm when Lykka came vaulting out of the shadows onto Scar-face's shoulders and snapped at his ear, causing him to drop the dagger.

With Lykka leading the way, Lucian set off through the Sucking-sands, leaving Scar-face's anguished cries echoing on the night air.

****

All was still when Lucian arrived home, but the cloying smell of tobacco lingering on the air told him his grandfather hadn't long retired to bed.

Lucian was halfway across the room when the old man appeared in the bedroom doorway.

Though visibly relieved to see Lucian alive and in one piece, there was anger in the old man's eyes. "Where in the name of Xavius have you—"

"Princess Rhiana of Abador has been abducted, Grandfather!" Lucian blurted out. "The Galyaks have her! I saw it with my own eyes."

Lucian's grandmother appeared at her husband's side; her gray-white hair was hanging loose about her shoulders. She'd draped a woolen shawl over her nightdress. "Oh, the gods be praised," she said, walking over to Lucian. "What's this about Princess Rhiana?"

"She's has been abducted by the Galyaks," said Lucian. "I swear! If it weren't for Lykka one of the brigands would have killed me."

"And where did you see this happening before your eyes?" his grandfather asked, his eyes narrowing with suspicion.

"In a cove beyond the Sucking-sands," Lucian said. "I know you forbade me to go into the Sucking-sands, Grandmother," he continued warily, glancing from one grandparent to the other, "but that doesn't change what I saw."

"We'll talk more about this in the morning, Lucian," his grandfather said sternly. "Now to bed with you. The nets will need untangling before we—"

"How can you concern yourself with nets and

tides?" Lucian gasped. "I tell you Princess Rhiana has been taken! The Galyaks have her." He glanced to Lykka as though the wolf might confirm his tale. "You must believe me!"

"That imagination of yours is going to land you in trouble one of these days, boy." His grandfather sighed wearily. "Come, mother. Let's get you back to bed; we'll be lucky not to catch a chill. This nonsense can wait till the morning."

"Princess Rhiana might be dead come the morning, Grandfather," Lucian pleaded. "We must set off for Abador now. We must tell of what has happened."

"Lucian, you must stop with this folly," his grandfather said irritably.

"But—"

"But nothing!" the old man barked. "What is it you intend on saying when you arrive at Abador's gates? You've never before laid eyes on Princess Rhiana, so how is it you're sure it was she? What you saw, my lad, was some unfortunate girl being carried off into slavery. She has my pity, but there's nothing to be done for her, so that's an end to it. Now come, mother."

Lucian's grandmother ignored her husband. "What makes you so sure it was Princess Rhiana you saw being taken?" she asked, wrapping the shawl tighter about her shoulders.

"Scar-face let it slip," Lucian said. "He's the one-eyed brigand who tried to kill me."

"Well, that settles it," his grandfather sneered, his tone oozing sarcasm. "I'll go saddle the horses. King Ocwan will be sure to believe you now."

"Shame on you, Willum Lansong," his wife scolded. "Have you ever known Lucian to lie?"

"Well, no…" the old man conceded reluctantly. "But, mother, if Lucian goes to the city with fanciful tales about Princess Rhiana and Galyak raiders, he's sure to end up in the stocks or worse."

The old woman fixed her husband with an icy stare. "That's as may be, but if Lucian remains here and says nothing and it turns out what he says is true, then I should imagine a week in the stocks would be the least of your worries."

"The gods preserve us but the madness is infectious," the old man retorted, mock-rolling his eyes. "You two can believe what you like. But I cannot accept a band of brigands could sneak into the royal palace unobserved, snatch Princess Rhiana from her private chambers, and get her out of the city without anyone being any the wiser."

"Rather than waste your breath mocking your grandson, why don't you make yourself useful and relight the fire," the old woman said irritably before turning to Lucian. "I know in my heart it was the Princess Rhiana you saw at the cove. I think we could use a mug of honeyed mead while we await the fire to die down so that I might see what the embers have to say."

****

Lucian sat huddled by the hearth, idly nursing his hot mead. His mind was still racing from everything that had happened, but the delicious fiery liquid was slowly soothing his unease. His grandmother's mug sat on the floor untouched, for she was engrossed with the glowing embers. All he saw when he looked into the hearth was a guttering fire in need of more kindling, but from the way her eyes sparkled in the firelight, the glowing coals were giving up their secrets.

By looking into the embers of a dying fire, the old woman could glimpse snatches of the future. The young women of their village would come and sit with her by the fire in the hopes of discovering the name of their future husbands or how many children the gods might bless them with. Some of these women came more than once, of course, while one woman in particular journeyed from a village many miles from Kalimar. Such was his grandmother's reputation. The woman's name was Varna, and because she'd traveled from afar, his grandparents always invited her to stay the night. Lucian looked forward to Varna's visits, for she always brought nice food and told the best stories.

Whenever Lucian had asked the old woman to reveal something of his future within the embers, however, she'd always say the time was not yet right.

Now, it seemed, that time was at hand.

"What do you see, Grandmother?" Lucian asked with a touch of impatience as Lykka padded across and lay at their feet.

The old woman didn't respond. Instead, she took a sip of her mead and closed her eyes while savoring its warmth. "It was indeed the Princess Rhiana you saw," she said at last. "And it was the Galyaks. They are taking her to the temple you saw in your dream."

Lucian had been absentmindedly running a hand through Lykka's thick gray-white pelt, but his hand suddenly froze. "Does this mean the temple I saw in my nightmare exists in the real world?"

"It exists." The old woman nodded solemnly. "It is dedicated to Gazankulu, the Dragon Lord of Orbelium."

Lucian remembered his grandmother explaining

how Mount Herros and Orbelium, the Netherworld where the souls of the damned suffered eternal torment, were like two sides of the same coin. "Was it Gazankulu that I saw, Grandmother?"

The old woman glanced up from the coals. "No, child. For no mortal can meet Gazankulu's gaze without being consumed in flames. What you saw was most likely a fire demon."

Lucian thought for a moment. "Scar-face said something about the Galyaks returning to their temple, so it has to be on Barrati…?"

"That I cannot say." His grandmother sighed wistfully. "I can only tell you that the temple stands on a plateau and is surrounded by water." She brushed a strand of hair from her face and returned her gaze to the embers, the dancing glow reflected in her eyes. "And I see the temple too clearly for it to be in a distant land."

The old woman got up from her stool and walked across the room to unfasten the leather curtain covering the window. "Come, tell me what you see," she said, lifting away the curtain and pointing a finger up to the night sky.

Lucian went to join his grandmother by the widow. He followed her gaze but saw nothing out of the ordinary among the multitude of stars peppering the night sky. "What am I looking for?" he asked, keeping his gaze on the night sky.

The old woman put her arm about Lucian's shoulders, drawing him nearer so that his view was in line with the tip of her finger. "Do you see the three stars forming a triangle over here?" she asked, drawing him closer to her. "This is known as the Winter Triangle."

"What is its significance?" Lucian asked her.

"The embers tell me you're to play an important role in Princess Rhiana's life," his grandmother replied. "I want you to promise me that whenever you sense impending danger, you'll imagine yourself within the Winter Triangle. Promise me you will."

Lucian was reeling. The very idea of his playing any role in Princess Rhiana's life, other than his delivering the news of what he'd witnessed at the cove, was inconceivable, yet his grandmother's gift, he knew, was never wrong. "I promise," he assured her.

"One of the stars making up the Winter Triangle is Sirius," the old woman continued. "Sirius is said to be the brightest of all the stars in the night sky. And Sirius is to feature greatly in your destiny."

"But how could a star feature in my destiny?" Lucian frowned, picturing the star falling from the heavens to crush some imaginary foe in his mind's eye.

"The embers do not explain, child; they merely reveal," his grandmother answered.

Lucian knew better than to question his grandmother's wisdom and continued gazing up at the Winter Triangle. And as he did so, he thought he saw Sirius twinkle as though introducing itself.

Chapter Three

Journeyeing to Abador

Lucian cuffed the sweat from his brow with the back of his forearm before sliding down from the saddle. He gazed about him in all directions before reaching for the leather water flask hanging from the pommel of his saddle. Lykka was playfully toying with a sand lizard within the dried-up riverbed snaking off into the distance, but seeing his master unslinging the flask distracted him from his torments. He had contemplated leaving Lykka behind when setting off for Abador, but his grandmother said she'd seen the wolf at his side in the embers.

The goatskin had been bulging when they'd set off soon after dawn the previous day but was now worryingly less than a third full. He quenched his thirst and sprinkled some water onto his upturned face before filling his cupped hand and holding it up for Kia before doing the same for Lykka. He'd spent a cold and uncomfortable night curled up in a hollow recess within the riverbed. Not even imagining himself within the Winter Triangle had helped because he'd been too anxious to light a fire for fear of giving himself away. He'd slept fitfully owing to the occasional scavenger picking up their scent. Lykka's presence had ensured none had dared venture too close, however.

Lucian slung the goatskin back over the pommel of his saddle before wearily scrambling up onto a rocky outcrop. Shielding his eyes from the sun's glare, he studied the range of hills on the shimmering horizon, groaning inwardly at the prospect of another day's ride across miles and miles of scorched emptiness ahead of him. It wasn't yet midday, but the heat was already unbearable. He'd promised his grandmother faithfully that he'd follow the coastal road to Abador. He hated defying her, but keeping to the coastal road would mean a lengthy three-day journey to reach the walled city, whereas cutting inland and traversing the outer fringes of the Eramian Wasteland would significantly reduce his journey time.

He consoled himself with the logic that every minute he shaved from his traveling time would help bring about Princess Rhiana's safe return.

The Eramian was a vast expanse of arid alkali desolation, stretching from the snow-capped Carpasian Mountains to the Kavashan border and from the Land of Helgos in the east to the headwaters of the River Zylos in the west. Winters were harsh, and summers fiercer still. It was known to all Kracians as the Wastelands. The Eramian was said to be the domain of the Gogolah, a malevolent sand fury that lurked beneath the surface, waiting to seize upon unsuspecting victims. Some believed the Gogolah to be nothing more than a tale that mothers used to frighten their children into behaving.

According to his calculations, Abador lay just beyond those iridescent hills. If he rode through the night, he reckoned he should be standing at the city gates by the coming dawn.

Should his reckonings prove erroneous…?

Pushing such thoughts from his mind, Lucian scrambled down from the outcrop. Abador did lie beyond those hills, and he would be standing at the city's gates by the morrow. In a purposeful show of self-belief, he reached for the goatskin again and mock-saluted the buzzards circling overhead.

The foul creatures had been tracking him all morning in anticipation of their next meal. Again, he prayed his navigational reasoning held. If not, the buzzards would surely be rewarded for their patience. He would have no one to blame should the creatures end up feasting on his flesh, of course, but the thought of Kia and Lykka ending up as sun-bleached carcasses because of his folly was too much to contemplate.

Lucian clambered into the saddle contemplating whether the buzzards were in range of his slingshot but decided to conserve his energy. Instead, he dug his heel into Kia's flank and set off beside the riverbed with his eyes dreamily fixed upon the distant hills. He'd barely gone a hundred yards, however, when Lykka suddenly set off along the riverbed in the opposite direction to which they were heading.

He turned in the saddle and was surprised to see a rider following his exact path. The rider was far off and little more than a shimmering blur of man and horse. Lykka was poised by the rocky outcrop; his gaze focused on the approaching rider.

Easing his slingshot from inside his jerkin, Lucian wrapped one end of the cord about the pommel of his saddle before sliding down from Kia's back. Making a casual show of inspecting one of the filly's hooves while gathering up a few stones, he surreptitiously slipped the stones into his pockets. He also satisfied himself that his staff would easily pull free from its fastenings should the need arise.

The rider was about fifty yards distant now. Keeping one hand on Kia's flank and within easy reach of his slingshot, he fished one of the stones from his pocket and placed it on his saddle.

Lucian was turning to face the rider when Lykka sprang out from behind the outcrop.

However, instead of challenging the interloper, the wolf playfully circled his horse.

****

The rider remained motionless; his face hidden beneath the hood of his dust-coated cloak. Just as Lucian was reaching for his slingshot, the rider pulled back the hood, revealing a weathered but friendly face framed by a tangled mass of dark-brown curls. The interloper had a broad forehead, wide mouth, and a short-clipped beard that accentuated a strong jawline. The corners of his mouth puckered as though he was about to share a joke.

"It's a fine-looking wolf you have there, my young friend," the rider said at last. "Though I must admit he gave me a start when he leaped out from behind the rocks."

This caught Lucian by surprise. Because wolves were generally feared, his grandmother had said they should say Lykka was a Varnian wolfhound. He'd grown so accustomed to saying this that he'd almost come to believe it himself. "You see Lykka as a wolf?" he gasped.

"I don't mind admitting I've encountered the occasional beast that I couldn't identify while on my travels." The interloper shrugged. "But I know a wolf when I see one.."

"You clearly have a way with animals, sir," Lucian said, "for I've never seen Lykka behave in such a manner with a stranger before."

The rider slid down from his horse. "Then allow me to introduce myself, and we'll be strangers no more. My name is Arvos."

"And I'm Lucian."

Arvos crouched to nuzzle Lykka's chin. "Mighty glad to make your acquaintance, Lucian," he said, getting to his feet. "Yes, and yours also, Lykka," he added hurriedly as the wolf jumped up at him.

Lucian was just as taken with Arvos's horse as he appeared to be with Lykka. "Your horse is a magnificent animal," he said, approaching the honey-colored stallion, his eyes taking in the pommel, grip, and cross-guard of a splendid-looking sword protruding between the saddle cloth and a splendid four-horn leather saddle. "I've never seen a horse like him," he added, running a hand through the stallion's white-fringed mane.

"Antares is an Arabash," Arvos explained. "I'll wager there's not another Arabash this side of the Gidean Sea. I got him from a Molovian trader. They know their horseflesh, those Molovians, I'll say that for them."

"'Antares'," Lucian said, savoring the name.

"Named him after the star," Arvos told him.

Lucian remembered the Draco Constellation from his nightmare and shuddered despite the heat. "You have the advantage, Arvos, for I know nothing about stars, I'm ashamed to say."

"Oh, I just heard the name once and took a liking to it, is all," Arvos said hurriedly.

Lucian sensed Arvos had given away more than he'd intended, something he'd have rather kept to himself. And given the war bow and the fact Arabash's nostrils were slit so the stallion could breathe more easily while charging at full pelt, Lucian suspected Arvos's story was an interesting one. "Kia's named in honor of the Goddess," he said, glancing over to the filly.

Arvos dropped to a crouch again. "And how did you come by your name?" he asked of Lykka while giving the wolf's ears a playful nuzzle. "If you were mine, I would have surely named you 'Valkyar'. What with the wolf being one of His symbols?"

Valkyar was the Abadorian God of War, and Lucian always called upon Him while defending his village from imaginary Ardassian raids. "My grandmother chose the name," he explained. "Lykka means 'good fortune' in her people's language."

Arvos fell silent for several heartbeats. "Can I ask what it is that brings you onto this road, Lucian?"

"I'm making for Abador," Lucian responded, glancing again toward the shimmering hills in the distance. "I always come this way whenever I have reason to visit the walled city. Is that where you are headed?" he asked, turning back to Arvos.

"It is, lad." Arvos nodded. "I can only assume it's a most pressing matter that takes you to the walled city, or you wouldn't have chosen such a foolhardy and hazardous route?"

"I can only assume your business in the city is equally pressing, Arvos," Lucian replied matter-of-factly.

Arvos threw his head back, roaring with laughter. "Forgive me, lad, but it was never my intention to pry into your affairs. I'm going to the walled city to seek an old friend." He reached across for his water flask, pulled the stopper free with his teeth, and took a long draft before holding it out to Lucian.

"I have my own," Lucian said.

Arvos walked across to Kia and plucked Lucian's flask from the saddle. "I'd say you've got more flask than water." He grinned. "And anyone as familiar with this road as you claim to be would have refilled their flask at the watering hole a few miles back."

Lucian was lost for words.

"Look, lad, it's no business of mine what's taking you to Abador," Arvos said, adopting a more conciliatory tone. "But a man doesn't last long out here without a steady supply of water, so what say we continue our journey together? If only to save you from ending up like that unfortunate creature," he added, nodding to a pile of sun-bleached bones farther along the dried- up riverbed.

****

The darkening sky was awash with crimson hues as the sun slowly slipped behind the Thalesian Hills away to the west. Lucian's naivety over the drop in temperature in the Eramian Wasteland after sunset had been cruelly exposed the previous night, but now he was luxuriating beside a roaring campfire. Nor was he overly concerned with who or what might be attracted by the flames or the aroma of the cured mutton roasting by the fire. Satisfied the mutton was sufficiently cooked, he set about dividing into two portions.

"I thank you for your generosity, Lucian," Arvos said, settling himself by the fire and accepting his share of the mutton. "'Tis a feast fit for King Ocwan's table and no mistake." He grinned, tearing a strip off the mutton and popping it into his mouth. "Before our running into each other, it was looking like a coin toss between buzzard or sharing Antares' oats." He grinned again, tearing off another strip of mutton and tossing it to Lykka.

"I'm beginning to wonder whether my grandmother saw you within the embers, Arvos, for she packed enough mutton in my knapsack for two," Lucian said, taking a bite from his mutton and feeding it to Lykka.

"I have to say I'm surprised your grandparents let you set out for Abador alone," Arvos replied, arching an eyebrow. "The Eramian Wilderness is no place to be without so much as a pig-sticker to defend yourself."

Lucian plucked his slingshot from his jerkin. "I can defend myself well enough," he said with a shrug.

"A slingshot is a potent enough weapon in capable hands, but—"

"And I usually hit what I aim at," Lucian added.

"Forgive me, Lucian, I was talking before thinking," Arvos said. "It's a shameful shortcoming that has landed me in plenty of scrapes over the years."

"My grandparents think I'm taking the coastal road to Abador," Lucian said. "I hate deceiving them, but taking the coastal road would have added another day to my journey."

A voice suddenly sounded in Lucian's ear.

"Put your trust in this man."

Lucian wheeled around, scanning the surrounding

31

darkness.

"Are you all right, lad?" Arvos asked, seeing the confused look in Lucian's eyes.

"Didn't you hear…"

"Hear what?" Arvos frowned.

The ethereal voice sounded again.

"*You must put your trust in this man, Lucian, for the fate of Abador is in your hands.*"

Lucian's mind was a whir. He'd certainly no appetite so fed the last of his mutton to Lykka.

"Are you Abadorian by birth, Arvos?" he asked hesitantly.

Arvos frowned again. "Why do you ask?"

Lucian waited to see whether the voice spoke to him again before responding. "I'm making for Abador because I saw Princess Rhiana being handed over to the Galyaks with my own eyes."

Without waiting for Arvos to offer a response, he revealed everything he'd witnessed at the cove. "It was Princess Rhiana. You must believe me!"

Arvos sat staring into the flames. "I mean no offense, lad, but what you say just isn't possible."

"That's what my grandfather said, but I know what I saw," Lucian insisted.

"I don't deny you saw some poor unfortunate being dragged off to slavery, but—"

"My grandfather said that also."

"But you only have this one-eyed rogue's word that it was Princess Rhiana," Arvos reasoned.

"Do you see that constellation up there?" Lucian said, jabbing a finger to the night sky. "The one that takes the form of a winged dragon?"

"I see it." Arvos nodded, following Lucian's gaze.

"It's the Draconis Constellation. My grandmother says it's the herald of impending doom."

Chapter Four

Abador

Lucian gazed out over the walled city of Abador in breathless awe. For an insane heartbeat, he believed he was looking upon a tantalizing mirage brought to life each morning only to vanish away again once the sun had slipped behind the curtain of night. He'd pictured its splendor in his mind's eye countless times, but for once, his imagination had failed him.

Abador sat upon a jagged promontory that was separated from the mainland by the fast-flowing waters of the River Isar, which came cascading down through the Thalesian Hills to form a natural moat around the city's towering walls before flowing out into the Gidean. The Isar served as the city's first line of defense.

Soaring above the walled city and visible for miles around stood the Colossus of Abador, a towering bronze statue of Valkyar. The Colossus was built in celebration of Valkyar's slaying of Gazankulu to cast the infernal Dragon Lord back into Orbelium.

The elevated plain allowed Lucian to see beyond the crenulated battlements into the city itself. His eyes immediately settled on the magnificent hexagonal-shaped Regius Colosseum. He knew of the Colosseum because of the Abadorian Games. And yet now he was seeing it with his own eyes, he was struggling to believe man capable of building such structures.

The Senate building was equally impressive with its marble-pillared portico and cantilevered roof. Lucian was too far away to see the wording, of course, but knew from his grandmother's teachings that the script carved into the triangular space betwixt the pillars and roof's apex read "Let justice prevail or the heavens fall." Beyond the Senate, built into the steep incline leading up the royal palace, were scores of white-stone villas topped with sloping, baked clay-tiled roofs, which he assumed to be the homes of Abador's wealthiest nobles.

The royal palace was built of Carystian marble and centered around a large peristyle courtyard. The palace's Feasting Hall, Lucian knew, also served as an audience chamber. To the rear of the Feasting Hall stood the multangular Regius Tower, atop which a crimson pennant bearing Abador's golden rampant unicorn fluttered in the gentle breeze. Beyond the palace stood the Temple of Xavius, and he could just make out the temple's cantilevered roof.

Lucian and Arvos were making their descent to the road leading to Abador's main gate when they were forced to come off the road to make way for a column of soldiers dressed in black livery.

"By Xavius' beard!" Arvos spluttered as they watched the column clatter across the drawbridge and pass through the gate into the city. "Unless my eyes deceive me, those men are Valessians. Things are far worse here than I was led to believe."

Lucian was surprised at this. Arvos hadn't mentioned his harboring suspicions about there being anything untoward going on in Abador. Not even when he'd revealed what he'd witnessed at the cove. He'd never heard of Valessians, but their being able to enter the city unopposed had unsettled Arvos.

"They're landless mercenaries happy to sell their swords to the highest bidder." Arvos gasped, as though he'd been able to read Lucian's thoughts.

By the time they arrived at the drawbridge, they found the gate manned by two more Valessians. Lucian knew these men couldn't have been with the column from earlier as their livery was immaculate.

Arvos drew to a halt. "Should we get separated, there's a tavern off the main square called The Dancing Bear." He eyed the two Valessians. "You'll come to no harm there. The landlord is loyal to Abador. But I advise you to be wary about who you speak to regarding what you saw at the cove."

Before Lucian had a chance to respond, Arvos spurred Antares toward the gate.

****

Lucian and Arvos had no sooner stepped onto the drawbridge when the two Valessians grabbed up their spears and came toward them. "Let's see your papers," the taller of two snarled.

He was a sullen-looking brute with a hooked nose. The second Valessian had a pinched face and beady eyes.

"Since when have Abadorians been required papers to enter their city?" Arvos replied coldly.

"Since my Lord Nikobar decreed it so," Hooknose said testily, eyeing them suspiciously.

Pinch-face stepped around Hooknose and peered at Lykka. "That there's a wolf," he said, taking a step toward Lykka and jabbing the butt of his spear at Lykka.

Arvos gave out an exaggerated sigh. "What is it with town folk? Why, it's obvious to a blind man that Lykka here is a Varnian Wolfhound."

Pinch-face scowled at Arvos. "I was raised in the country, so I ought to know what a wolf looks like. And that most definitely is a wolf."

"My friend is correct," Lucian said, pausing to take in the raven device on the Valessians' tunics. "Lykka is indeed a Varnian wolfhound."

"No one asked you, so shut your hole!" Hooknose retorted.

"But Lykka is my wolf…wolfhound," Lucian said.

"I don't care who the beast belongs to." Hooknose growled. "It isn't passing through this gate. Papers or no papers."

"But—"

"There was plague here recently." Hooknose scowled.

Lucian was all too aware of the deadly pestilence that had stricken Abador for months on end, claiming an untold number of lives. The city's hapless apothecaries had tried everything in their power, yet each passing day brought nothing but death and endless misery. A red cross was daubed on the doors of all the houses infected. It was said the city eventually ran out of red paint. The plague struck both high and low, eventually reaching the royal palace claiming the life of King Ocwan's only son, Prince Tarvel.

"And there would be plague here still if it wasn't for my Lord Nikobar," Hooknose continued.

"Who is this Lord Nikobar you speak of?" Arvos

asked.

"We're the ones who asks the questions round here." Pinch-face growled.

Lucian looked beyond the sentries to the gate. He'd expected to find Abador in an uproar over Princess Rhiana's abduction. For the first time since setting off from his grandparents' farm, he began to doubt whether it had been the princess. As Arvos reasoned, Scar-face could have been toying with him at the cove. There was only one sure way to find out…

"I must speak His Majesty King Ocwan," he said.

"Must you now…?" Hooknose chuckled.

"It is a matter of great urgency," Lucian continued, ignoring Arvos's pleading eyes.

"Be off with you," Pinch-face said.

"Not so fast," Hooknose said, eyeing Lucian with renewed interest. "What is it you intend on telling Ocwan?"

"King Ocwan to you," Arvos interjected.

"Another word from you, friend, and you'll find yourself on a charge," Hooknose said coldly. "You won't be so cocky then, I assure you…" He continued glaring at Arvos for several heartbeats before returning his attention to Lucian. "Let's hear what you have to say to *King* Ocwan."

"What I have to say is for His Majesty's ear only," Lucian said defiantly. "You must take me to him."

Hooknose stepped closer and grabbed hold of Kia's bridle. "Not until I hears what it is you have to say. Now get down off your mounts. Both of you!" he snapped, glaring at Arvos again.

Arvos made as though he was dismounting before suddenly swinging his boot at Pinch-face to send him tumbling from the drawbridge into the Isar's fast-flowing waters.

Hooknose was slow to react. Before he could bring up his spear, Arvos brought Antares about and rammed his boot heel in the Valessian's face, smashing his nose.

"Remember what I said about The Dancing Tavern," Arvos told Lucian. "Tell the landlord you are of the seven and wait there till I come for you. Now come on!"

Lucian didn't need telling twice. He spurred Kia through the gate and into the city.

****

Lucian had found The Dancing Bear tavern without too much difficulty, but arriving at the main square to find a team of carpenters erecting a scaffold had unsettled him. He'd done as Arvos had instructed and was greatly relieved when the landlord led him through to the stables at the back of the tavern without question. With Kia and Lykka secured in one of the stalls, the landlord had sneaked him down into the cellar. He'd no idea what "being of the seven" meant and wouldn't have known how to respond had the landlord asked him to explain further. He just wished Arvos would arrive soon.

Hooknose and Pinch-face would have raised the alarm by now, and soldiers would be scouring the city for them. Kia and Lykka were both secured in the stables, but the longer he remained at the tavern, the greater the chance he'd be dangling at the end of a rope from the very scaffold he was half-watching taking shape a few feet from where he was sitting. He didn't blame Arvos for his actions at the gate, but if he was arrested and it was Princess Rhiana he'd seen at the cove, he'd be surely put to death, and what he knew about the princess would die with him.

He'd been too caught up with the events of the day to think about food but felt his stomach lurch as the mouthwatering aroma of freshly cooked bread suddenly filled the cellar. It was the landlord arriving with the food he'd promised.

Lucian's pockets, however, were as empty as his belly. "I'm sorry, but I have no coin."

"And I wouldn't take it if you had, lad." The landlord smiled, handing Lucian a bowl of mutton stew and a wedge of warm crusty bread.

Lucian estimated the landlord to be around forty years old. He had a long face, shrewd eyes, and a high forehead with his hair swept back into a widow's peak.

"My name is Lucian, and I thank you from the bottom of my heart," Lucian said, his stomach flipping again.

"No need to thank me, Lucian." The landlord paused while perching himself on one of the ale barrels. "I'm Caleb. And anyone who is of the seven is a friend of mine. Are they here in the city?" he asked, offering Lucian a conspiratorial wink.

Lucian wasn't sure how to respond. "Is who here in the city?"

"Why the Xaviers, of course."

Lucian could only stare open-mouthed.

The Xavier knights were renowned throughout the whole of Kracia. Their full title was Knights in the Service of Xavius and Mount Herros.

Lucian had often imagined himself going into battle in a full-faced plumed helmet, flanged leather corselets embossed with the rampant unicorn of

Abador, and his crimson cloak billowing in the breeze. The Xaviers were believed to be invincible in battle owing to their having been forged in Arkan Sula's crucible.

Arkan Sula was an Elkai, born to a mortal woman and sired by a shape-shifting incubus through which he'd inherited the mystical powers allowing him to converse with the gods. He lived in a cave high up in the Elovian Mountains that were believed to be the foothills leading up to Mount Herros, home of the gods. He was beholden only to the gods and was free to traverse the land as he pleased, calling upon commoners and kings alike for shelter and sustenance.

The Elkai hadn't been seen for many months, however. It was said that Xavius had charged Arkan Sula with seeking out the long-lost Spear of Lixivior, the legendary lance with which Valkyar had pierced Gazankulu's black heart to condemn the Dragon Lord to the fiery furnaces of Orbelium for all eternity.

Lucian's grandmother had explained how the universe was shaped like an egg, with the world being a flat firmament cutting across the egg's center. Euphorium, she said, was arched above the world, while Orbelium lay below. She'd then explained the distance between Euphorium and Orbelium, saying that should a hammer fall from Euphorium, it would take nine days to reach the world, then continue falling for another nine days to reach Orbelium. When he'd asked her the meaning of eternity, she'd said that if a gull were to carry the sands making up Kracia's entire coastline across the Gidean Sea a single grain at a time, the time it would take the gull to complete its task would be but a mere heartbeat compared to eternity.

"Why would you think I'd know if the Xavier knights were in the city?" he asked Caleb.

The landlord eyed Lucian warily. "Because you said you were of the seven."

"That's what I was told to tell you," Lucian responded.

"Who was it that gave you the code?"

"My friend Arvos."

The landlord came across, suspicion in his eyes. "And how is it you know this 'Arvos'?" he asked.

"We met en route to the city," Lucian replied. "We got into an argument with two Valessians at the main gate. Before separating, he told me I should seek out this tavern and tell you I was 'of the seven'."

"What does he look like, this Arvos?"

The landlord visibly relaxed again on hearing Lucian's description of Arvos. "If Varos is here in the city, then the others won't be far behind if they ain't here already."

For Lucian, it was as though a veil had suddenly lifted: the sword, saddle, Antares, the stallion's flair holes, and the effortless way Arvos had dealt with the two Valessians at the gate. Varos was a Xavier knight. The others were Avicus, Kadian, Torian, Saynor, Èinor, and Yanek.

"I see from your eyes that the coin's stopped rolling, lad." The landlord chuckled. "I knew Varos and the other Xaviers would come to save Avicus."

The enormity dawned on Lucian for whom the scaffold in the square was being erected.

"His Majesty issued a proclamation declaring the Xaviers traitors for trying to bring about a war between Abador and Varnia," the landlord explained. "I don't believe it for a heartbeat." he scoffed. "Croatalus—he's the commander of Nikobar's guard—is boasting of being the one who captured Avicus. I don't believe that for a heartbeat, neither."

Lucian was so taken by surprise he almost spilled the broth.

"It's all that swine Nikobar's doing." The landlord spat again.

Lucian remembered the two Valessians at the gate speaking that name. Scar-face had also mentioned it at the cove. "Who is Nikobar?" he asked, setting the bowl at his feet.

"Nikobar arrived here while the city was in the grip of the plague," the landlord explained.

"The story goes that he secured an audience with His Majesty. He claimed he was an enchanter more powerful than Arkan Sula and told His Majesty he'd lift the plague in return for his being granted sanctuary."

Lucian remembered his grandfather returning home with the news that the plague had been lifted, but he was certain the old man had said nothing about it being the work of any mysterious enchanter.

It was as though the landlord had read his mind. "Oh, I know, lad," he said. "The bards would still have us believe it was Xavius himself that lifted the plague. But if it was Nikobar who lifted the plague, then why is His Majesty keeping it a secret? And no one has ever set eyes on this Nikobar to my knowledge since the plague was lifted. Nor has anyone seen His Majesty, for that matter. He hasn't so much as set foot outside the palace."

"Did the Valessians arrive with Nikobar?" Lucian asked.

"His ship was manned by the swine," the landlord explained. "No-good mercenary cutthroats, the lot of 'em. Nikobar said the Valessians were his personal bodyguard. What would an enchanter capable of lifting a plague need with bodyguards? Tell me that! Arkan Sula has no need of a bodyguard. I never thought I'd live to see the day when Valessians would be welcome here. They stroll about giving orders like they own the place."

Lucian considered revealing his reason for being in Abador but decided to await Varos's arrival. He also momentarily wondered how he might react to seeing Varos again now that he was aware of his true identity. "But what of our soldiers?" he asked instead. "The men of the Abadorian and Centaurian Guard should be in an uproar."

"The larger part of Centaurian Guard were already either guarding the passes on the Varnian border or the Kavashan coast," the landlord said. "The remaining cohorts left the city when the plague took hold. It was the sensible thing to do under the circumstances. I suppose a couple of cohorts will most likely be hunting down the Xaviers."

"Well, the Abadorian Guard then?"

"What's left of it." The landlord sighed.

"What do you mean?"

"Those of the Guard that refused to take an oath of allegiance accepting the Valessians into the army were dismissed from service," the landlord continued his sorry tale. "Those rogues that did take the oath received promotions. You haven't been in the city long enough to take note, I suppose, but the Crows and their confederates in the Abadorian Guard most likely

44

outnumber those troops loyal to Abador. Or if they don't, they soon will."

"His Majesty sanctioned this?" Lucian gasped, still struggling to comprehend what was happening in Abador.

"He signed the proclamation right enough," said the landlord. "Maybe this Nikobar is the enchanter he claims to be."

They were interrupted by the landlord's wife shouting through the trapdoor. "You needs to get up here, husband. We got Black Crows!"

"That's what we calls the Valessians, lad." The landlord chuckled mirthlessly as he set off for the stair. "You'll be safe down here right enough, so eat your food, and I'll come check on you in a while."

Lucian had little enough appetite following the landlord's revelations, but he tore off a piece of bread and used it to scoop some of the broth into his mouth, careful to leave the chunks of mutton for Lykka. Pocketing the mutton and leftover bread inside his jerkin, he scurried over to the stair in the hope of overhearing what was occurring.

The trapdoor was made of stout Abadorian oak, however, and he heard nothing but muffled voices.

****

The minutes seemed to stretch into hours, but eventually, the trapdoor lifted, and Caleb descended the stair.

"What's happening?" Lucian asked him.

"The city has been placed under martial law by order of Nikobar," Caleb explained. "The official reason is that Agnar's spies are loose in the city, but I suspect it's you and Varos they're searching for. All citizens are to be off the streets by nightfall and are to remain indoors until first light. And no one is to leave the city, of course. We need to get you to Lanum's forge. You'll be safe there…safer than here, at least."

"Who's Lanum?"

"He's a blacksmith and as loyal to Abador and the Xaviers as myself," Caleb explained.

Lucian was wracked with indecision. Varos had told him to wait at the tavern until he came for him, but Scar-face must have got wind of what occurred at the main gate and made the connection on hearing about a fair-haired youth being in the company of a Varnian wolfhound that may well have been a wolf.

The landlord grabbed his arm. "We need to get going, lad. There's a reward for you, and we have to assume someone saw you come here."

"But Arv…Varos said I should stay here."

"But you're not safe here no more. We need to get you to the forge."

"How will we get there without being seen?"

"One step at a time, lad," Caleb said. "Lucky for you, the cellar and stable are on the same level." He went across to the ale casks lining the wall, stopping at the last one. "Give us a hand with this."

Lucian went across and helped the landlord drag the cask away from the wall, revealing a ragged hole in the wall.

"I knocked through to the stable so I'd have a means of escape if I got stuck down here for whatever reason. You'll soon come to a grate which should lift easy enough. The tavern's closed now, but I'll go by the front door just to satisfy myself everything is as it should be."

46

****

Lucian soon arrived at the grate but sensed there was someone in there. He was peering through the openings in the grate when a yowl shattered the silence. Without thinking, he thrust the grate aside and sprang through the opening.

The three figures crowded at the opening to Kia's stall turned as one. Lucian immediately recognized Hooknose and Scar-face. The third was a squat brute with badly pockmarked skin.

Hooknose hurriedly moved to the door to prevent Lucian from escaping. As he came past, Lucian noted the bruised swelling around his eyes from Varos breaking his nose. The third Valessian remained where he was, still holding the pitchfork with which he'd been tormenting Lykka.

"I was hopin' our paths would cross again, matey." Scar-face leered, plucking the dagger from his belt. "But when I heard about what happened to Jodal here at the gate earlier, I knew the gods were smiling on me," he continued, indicating to Hooknose with a cock of his head as he slowly advanced toward Lucian. "Now, what we needs to know is the name of your pal from earlier." He brought the tip of his dagger to Lucian's right cheek, slowly tracing the blade toward his eye.

"Secure him," the one with the pitchfork yelled. "We'll take him to my Lord Nikobar."

"Not till I've finished!" Scar-face snapped. "You must have told your pal about what happened at the cave, matey. So if you gives us his name, I promise to let yer furry pal live."

"You would be wise not to risk my Lord Nikobar's wrath," the other retorted.

Scar-face kept the dagger tip pressed against Lucian's cheek before stepping away.

Lucian hurriedly cast his eyes across the hay-strewn floor for anything which might serve as a weapon. If he was to die here, he was determined he wouldn't pass through Galdoch's Cave alone. But all he saw was matted straw.

Hooknose grabbed Lucian's arm, wrenching it behind his back. "Where's that pal of yours?" he hissed, reaching for Lucian's other arm. "Garth and me's got a score to settle with him, so we have."

"Then why not settle it here," a familiar voice challenged.

It was Varos.

Hooknose shoved Lucian aside on seeing Arvos in the doorway. "Today's a day for prayers bein' answered, that's for sure." He drew his sword, motioning for Varos to come to him.

Sidestepping Hooknose's clumsy lunge, Varos grabbed him by the throat and pushed his head back, snapping his neck. He then grabbed the sword from Hooknose's dead hand and flung it at Scar-face, pinning him to a support beam in a single fluid motion.

Lucian was momentarily paralyzed by what was happening. So much so, he was only vaguely aware of the other Valessian making a dash for the door, but Varos grabbed him by the arm and ran him into the wall.

Chapter Five

The Quest

Lucian's hands were still shaking slightly, yet he felt strangely exhilarated. He'd already been made aware of Varos's fighting prowess at the city gates, of course, even if he hadn't known his newfound friend was a Xavier knight. But seeing how Varos dealt with these three Black Crows in as many heartbeats left him breathless. "Are they all dead?" he asked, wrenching his gaze from the droplets of blood dripping from Hooknose's sword.

Varos was crouched over the Valessian by the door, feeling for a pulse. "This one's still breathing," he said, getting to his feet again and approaching Lucian. "There's something I need to tell you, lad."

"That you're Varos of the Xavier knights…" Lucian said, trying to sound casual.

"My apologies," Varos replied. "I did consider revealing my true identity to you, but, well, you know it now."

"Are the other Xaviers here in the city?"

"My brothers are unaware of Avicus's plight," Varos replied. "I set off for the city knowing only that one of us had been taken and was awaiting execution. It was Arkan Sula who told me it was Avicus."

"You've spoken to the Elkai?" Lucian spluttered.

Varos hesitated before responding. "How much do you know about us Xaviers?" he asked.

"Every Abadorian knows the Xaviers are oath-sworn to serve Abador," Lucian responded.

"That's true enough." Varos nodded. "But although we are oath-sworn to serve Abador, we are soul-sworn to Arkan Sula. The Elkai spoke to me while I was en route to the city…Just as he spoke to you last night while we were camped in the Eramian."

Lucian was dumbstruck.

"It was no accident that we encountered each other in the Eramian," Varos continued. "The Elkai didn't mention you by name, but he told me I would happen upon a lad and a wolf."

"He…he said I should put my trust in you," Lucian stammered, struggling to comprehend what Varos was telling him. "That's why I revealed to you what I saw at the cove."

"I don't profess to know why the Elkai has chosen you, Lucian, but you were meant to be at the cove that night."

"So it really was Princess Rhiana?"

"From what I've managed to ascertain, she was snatched while out riding in the Thalesian Hills," Varos explained.

"She went out alone?" Lucian frowned.

"I'm as much in the dark as you on that." Varos shrugged. "I can't imagine the princess being allowed to venture beyond the city walls without an escort, but I wouldn't rule out the possibility. Not with everything else that's going on in the city of late. Like this curfew. I had to assume the Crows were looking for us, so thought I should come here to find you."

Seeing the Valessian by the door beginning to stir, Varos stepped across, grabbed up the pitchfork, and brought the butt down on the back of his head.

"This one was at the cove," Lucian said, indicating to Scar-face's slumped form. "They were taking me to Nikobar. He must be behind Princess Rhiana's abduction."

"It would make sense seeing as this Nikobar, whoever he is, was the one who actually issued the proclamation declaring us traitors," Varos said bitterly.

"For supposedly trying to bring about a war with Varnia," Lucian said, repeating what the landlord had told him.

"So I hear." Varos chuckled mirthlessly. He set off across the stable to the stalls. "Caleb has gone to fetch Lanum," he said, grabbing Lucian's saddle from the rail. "The sooner we get you to his forge, the safer you'll be. For a time, at least."

"But I must speak with His Majesty." Lucian gasped.

Varos halted from saddling Kia but remained in the stall. "Nikobar doesn't only have his Crows searching the city for us, lad. The Abadorian Guard are looking as well. You'll be arrested before you get within a hundred yards of the royal palace."

"You're forgetting we have living proof of Nikobar's deeds," Lucian countered, indicating to the Valessian by the door. "And revealing Nikobar's involvement in Princess Rhiana's abduction will surely—"

Lucian was interrupted by a rapping on the other side of the stable door.

Varos drew his sword but immediately relaxed

again on hearing Caleb's voice.

****

Lucian took up a position by the door while Caleb and Lanum dragged Scar-face and Hooknose into one of the stalls and covered them with straw. Varos had already left with Kia to see what he could find out about Avicus.

There was no need going to any lengths in hiding the bodies, of course, as the other Valessian was still breathing. Lanum had given the hapless Valessian another thump to the head with the pitchfork before dumping him through the grating where Caleb was waiting to drag him through into the cellar. When the Valessian came around, he would find himself bound and gagged along with Caleb and his wife.

On their being discovered, Caleb would explain about Lucian by saying how he'd given lodging to a youth who was visiting the city for the first time and had put him in the stable because his wife was a-feared of his wolfhound. He'd then say he'd gone to the stable to inform the youth about the curfew and had been struck from behind, and the next thing he knew he'd found himself in the cellar with his wife and a Valessian.

"Is your friend well-trained?" Lanum asked, coming over to Lucian.

The blacksmith was, without question, the largest man Lucian had ever set eyes on. His barrel chest was as broad as any of the ale casks in the tavern's cellar, while his thighs and forearms were the size of tree lumbers.

"Lykka does as I bid him," Lucian said. "Why do you ask?"

"He's a dead giveaway," Lanum replied. "The Crows are on the lookout for a lad with a wolf. We can hide him in my cart beneath some straw, but we'll never make the forge unless he remains still and makes no noise."

"Don't fret, lad." Caleb chuckled. "We'll make sure he'll be able to breathe."

"And you must put this on," Lanum said, reaching into the cart and handing Lucian a leather apron. "If anyone asks, your name is Rolf, and you're my new apprentice." He then wiped a hand along the inside of the cart and proceeded to smear Lucian's face, neck, and exposed arms with soot.

Lucian estimated dusk to be a couple of hours away, but the streets were mercifully near deserted. The few people they did encounter paid them little heed. The journey was nonetheless torturous, for Lucian expected to hear a shout of alarm every step of the way.

They eventually arrived at the forge. Having ushered Lucian inside, Lanum hurriedly pulled the door closed behind them and hoisted the bar in place. Lucian scooped the rags aside to free Lykka from the barrow.

The forge's interior was in near-darkness, illuminated only by the glowing embers in the kiln, but Lucian's eyes soon acclimatized to the gloom. He went and stood by the door so as to be out of the way, watching on as Lanum got the kiln going with a pair of bellows that looked almost lost in his hands. "You and your friend must be hungry," he said, glancing up from his task. "I know I am." He grinned, grabbing up a shovel to serve as a makeshift pan. Within no time, the delicious aroma of sizzling ham filled the forge.

Lucian was gazing about the forge when he espied

three stalls beyond the kiln. Realizing two of the stalls were occupied, he went across to investigate. He readily recognized Antares. The other stallion was a magnificent coal-black charger.

"He belongs to Avicus," Lanum said, coming across with the shovel loaded with succulent strips of ham.

Lucian plucked a strip from the shovel, gingerly tossing it from hand-to-hand several times before stuffing it into his mouth. Sensing Lykka's gaze, he grabbed up another strip and tossed it to the wolf before returning his attention to the charger. "What's his name?" he asked Lanum, running his hand along the stallion's flank.

"Sirius."

Lucian's hand froze, remembering what his grandmother had said about Sirius featuring in his destiny. He was wrenched from his musings by a sudden coded rapping at the door.

Lanum handed the shovel to Lucian, then hurried across to the door and lifted the bar.

It was Varos with Kia.

****

"Perfect timing again." Varos grinned, scooping some ham from the shovel while Lanum led Kia over to the remaining empty stall. "You were right," he called after the blacksmith, "Avicus is being held in the dungeons beneath the Regius Tower."

"Is that a problem?" Lucian asked him.

"It makes things trickier," Varos replied, spitting out a piece of chewed-up ham and giving it to Lykka.

A hurried knock sounded at the door.

Varos tossed the shovel aside and went across to

the window. "It's Lox," he said, motioning for Lanum to open the door. "Lox is one of the jailers at the Regius Tower," he explained to Lucian. "From the look of him, something's amiss…even more amiss," he added sourly.

Lox came bursting into the forge, wringing his hands. "Princess Rhiana has been snatched by the Huskenbachs!" he cried despairingly. "The city is cursed! Cursed, I say!"

"Calm yourself, Lox," Varos said, grabbing him by the arms. "Why do you say the Huskenbachs have the princess?" he asked, glancing at Lucian.

"Her escort has been found in the Thalesian Hills," Lox explained. "All dead, every one of 'em. This means war with Varnia now for sure."

"Princess Rhiana has been taken," Varos said, "but it wasn't the Husk—"

"No, it was most certainly the Huskies," Lox retorted. "Our brave lads managed to send a few of the swine through Galdoch's Cave before they were cut down."

"I can assure you that it wasn't the Huskenbachs," Lucian told Lox.

"Lucian witnessed some of Nikobar's Valessians delivering the princess to the Galyaks at a cove close to his village and came close to paying dearly for it," Varos explained. "And we know they were Crows because they came uncomfortably close to silencing him here in the city."

Lox seemed lost in thought. "Then, that would explain what happened to the Huskies we had in the dungeons," he said, tugging thoughtfully at the scrub of graying beard on his chin. He was thin and pale-faced, with close-set eyes all but hidden beneath beetling eyebrows.

"What Huskies…Huskenbachs," Varos asked, correcting himself. "Speak, man!"

"They were bein' kept in the dungeon down on the lower level," Lox explained. "I was on duty when they were brought in. Middle of the night it was, a couple of weeks back. Croatalus, he's the—"

"I know who Croatalus is," Varos interjected sourly.

"He told those of us that were on duty that night that we weren't to breathe a word about what we'd witnessed."

"Who's to say they're not still there?" Varos asked Lox.

"Me, that's who," Lox replied. "An' I knows they're not there 'cos that's where they've put poor Avicus. And Croatalus has since ordered the guard doubled. Not only at the tower, but throughout the palace," he added sullenly.

"Do you know the reason behind Nikobar imposing martial law?" Varos asked. "The true reason," he added hurriedly.

"I heard a whisper it's 'cos Nikobar has his Black Crows out scourin' the city for a lad and his pet wolf," he added, glancing from Lucian to Lykka.

"That can only mean your identity is still safe," Lucian said to Varos.

Varos appeared lost in thought. "The gods be praised for small mercies."

"What are your thoughts?" Lanum asked Varos.

"I'm thinking these Huskenbachs that were being kept hidden away have been slain and their corpses left among those bodies of the princess's escort to bring about a war between Abador and Varnia."

Lucian was looking expectantly to Varos to reveal a plan of action when Arkan Sula's voice sounded out of the shadows.

"Only by bringing the seven together to rescue Princess Rhiana can Abador be saved."

"Is it Sula?" Varos asked, seeing Lucian's incredulous gaze. "Another thread to the tale," he said, offering Lanum a rueful smile.

"He says Abador is doomed unless the seven are brought together to rescue Princess Rhiana."

"But I have no idea where my other brothers might be," Varos replied.

"Raynor and Kadian are lost within the Labyrinth."

"He says Raynor and Kadian are lost within the Labyrinth," Lucian repeated.

Varos was visibly shaken and with good reason.

Every Kracian knew of the Labyrinth of Kamar. One of the more enduring legends surrounding the Spear of Lixivior was that Valkyar had cast it into the maw of a volcano in the Valley of Kamar. The legend, of course, had brought adventurers from all parts of Kracia and the lands beyond the seas in search of the Spear. Many of the adventurers had failed to return from the Labyrinth.

"What could have possessed Raynor and Kadian into entering the Labyrinth?" Lanum gasped.

"I suspect they went in search of Arkan Sula." Varos sighed. "You'll remember me telling you how we Xaviers are soul-sworn to Sula?" he said to Lucian. "He came to me in my dreams while Abador was in the grip of the plague ordering us to ride up into the Elovian Mountains and meet him at the foot of the pass. His Majesty was beside himself that the Elkai hadn't come to the city's aid so refused us permission. But we couldn't refuse the Elkai's summons. Sula didn't say what he wanted with us, but Avicus thought we might be able to implore him to return to Abador with us.

"With the city under quarantine, we had to sneak out of the city in the dead of night like common thieves," he continued. "It's a three-day ride to the Elovian Mountains. We waited at the pass all through the next day, but Sula failed to show. We were returning to Abador when we learned His Majesty had proclaimed us traitors. Some of us, myself included, were for continuing to the city to explain our actions. Avicus, however, said we should instead separate and go in search of Sula."

"So Raynor and Kadian must have entered the Labyrinth in search of the Elkai?" said Lanum.

Varos grimaced. "It would appear so."

"Kamar is only a day's ride from here," Lucian offered.

"It might as well be on the other side of the world if we can't free Avicus." Varos sighed. "Because the power of the Xaviers lies in our being united."

"That's going to be no easy task," Lox said wistfully. "The only thing that gets out of the dungeons on the lower levels is second-hand slops, if you catch my meaning."

Lucian was glancing about the forge hoping Arkan Sula might suggest how they could free Avicus when he noticed Lykka hunched over the drain-hole set into the floor by the stalls. Remembering how Varos had cast the shovel aside, he assumed some of the ham must have slipped into the drain.

An idea suddenly came to him. "Are the sewers large enough for a man to navigate?" he asked aloud.

"One of the seven ordeals Arkan Sula set for those of us hoping to become Xaviers involved crawling through a section of the city's sewers," Varos replied. "So, the answer to your question is 'yes.'"

Chapter Six

Uniting the Xaviers

Lucian had spent a fitful night curled up with Lykka beside the kiln. Lox had also spent the night in the forge as Varos couldn't risk running into any Black Crows patrolling the streets. The jailer had hurried home at first light to let his wife know no harm had befallen him before returning to the forge. He was walking some distance ahead of Lucian and Varos, so no one would think they were acquainted. They were making for a market square located close to the royal palace. Once there, Lox would serve as a lookout while they formulated a plan how best to get into the sewer system unobserved.

Lucian was again wearing the leather apron Lanum had given him with his cheeks and brow smudged with coal smut. Varos, however, cut a ridiculous figure in one of Lanum's shirts as it was several sizes too big and was flapping about his knees. The blacksmith had thought to provide them with a length of rope which they could tie about them to ensure they wouldn't get separated in the sewers.

The sky above the city was awash with roseate hues as Lucian and Varos threaded their way through the streets. When they came upon the Regius Colosseum, Lucian was so taken aback at its splendor that he forgot about Avicus and Princess Rhiana. Momentarily, at least.

The Colosseum was built of travertine limestone, volcanic rock, and brick-faced concrete and could house some sixty-five thousand spectators. Aside from the Abadorian Games, the Colosseum staged re-enactments of legendary battles from antiquity and dramas based on Kracian mythology. As they made their way past the statue of Xavius in front of the Colosseum's porticoed entrance

Lucian hoped that by picturing a vast crowd gathered inside the Colosseum rapturously applauding a re-enactment of himself and the Xaviers rescuing Princess Rhiana in his mind's eye might help bring it to pass.

Upon arriving at the market square, Lucian and Varos sought a vantage point close to the opening leading into the sewers from which they could observe the Valessians guarding the gate leading through to the royal palace. Varos had devised a plan whereby Lox would distract the trader whose stall was situated closest to the sewer opening by pretending he was looking for a birthday present for his daughter. Unfortunately for them, this trader sold only sekanjabin, a brew made from honey and vinegar and seasoned with mint popular among Abadorians.

Lucian and Varos were wracking their brains as to what they might do when a captain of the Abadorian Guard arrived at the square.

Lox came sidling over. "His name is Giffin," the jailer whispered, making a show of fiddling with one of his boots while careful not to look in their direction. "I'd stake my life on our being able to trust him," he added before getting to his feet and continuing into the market.

"The captain is another with a taste for sekanjabin as he's coming this way," Varos said, surreptitiously monitoring the captain's movements. "Can't stand the stuff myself."

"What do we do?" Lucian mumbled to Varos as Captain Giffin came sauntering toward the sekanjabin vendor.

"I don't doubt Lox's word about the captain's trustworthiness," Varos replied. "But he's staking more than his own life here."

Captain Giffin had made his purchase. Lucian was watching him as he retraced his steps when Arkan Sula's voice sounded in his ear.

"*Trust your instincts, Lucian.*"

Without alerting Varos to what had occurred or giving him any warning, Lucian sprang to his feet, purposely bumping into the captain and causing him to spill some of his brew.

"Sorry, Captain, sir," he wailed. "Please forgive me."

"Calm yourself, lad," Giffin said, giving his tunic a cursory wipe. "I have to confess my mind was otherwise occupied," he added, glancing up toward the Valessians at the palace gate.

On following Giffin's gaze, Varos appeared at Lucian's shoulder. "Captain, how would you answer if I was to ask, 'Who brings gifts to Soliman, Prince of the Genii?'"

Giffin was caught off guard, but the moment passed. "I would answer, 'Balkis, Queen of the Morning'," he said, accepting Varos's hand while glancing about them to ensure they weren't being observed.

"We are in urgent need of your assistance, Captain," Varos continued, guiding Giffin farther away from the sekanjabin vendor until they were out of sight of the palace gate.

"I'll do all I can to help you and do it willingly," Giffin responded. "You look vaguely familiar," he said, eyeing Varos. "Have we met?"

"Not that I recall," Varos replied. "I am Varos of the Xavier knights. We need your help in freeing my brother Avicus from the tower dungeons."

"We're the Varnian spies Nikobar has his Black Crows searching for, Captain," Lucian told Giffin. "Four nights ago, I witnessed Princess Rhiana being delivered to the Galyaks at a cove close to my village by some of Nikobar's Black Crows."

"Then you're responsible for the two dead Crows found at the Dancing Bear?" Giffin smiled.

"I only wish it were three of the swine." Varos sighed. "I allowed one of the Valessians to live. He may be aware of my true identity."

"The Valessian is squat with deep-set eyes," Lucian added.

"I know who you mean," Giffin said sourly. "His name is Gareb."

"The two dead Valessians being found at the tavern is common knowledge," Giffin said. "But if Nikobar is aware you are here in Abador, then he's keeping such news to himself."

"He is also with us," Varos said, indicating to where Lox had taken up his original position and was casting occasional glances in their direction.

"I recognize him," Giffin nodded as Lox came toward them. "He's a jailer at the tower, if I'm not mistaken."

"Yes," Varos said, motioning for Lox to come across. "Our intention is to gain access to the sewers through the storm drain yonder," he continued. "We need you to somehow draw those Crows away from the gate."

"We'll also require your help once we're in the palace, Captain," Lucian added.

"Best not to go putting the chariot before the horses, lad." Lox chuckled grimly.

"I'll pick a fight with the sekanjabin vendor saying he's short-changed me," Giffin said. "That should bring them over. If only to side with the vendor."

Lucian and Varos watched on as Giffin returned to the sekanjabin stall and made an exaggerated show of remonstrating with the trader. Only one of the Black Crows guarding the palace gate had proved sufficiently inquisitive to check on the disturbance in the square. Seeing it was Giffin arguing with the sekanjabin vendor, however, he summoned the others to come and enjoy the spectacle, allowing for Varos and Lucian to slip unnoticed into the storm drain.

****

Lucian was regretting not having had the forethought to bring one of the rags from Lanum's forge to use as a makeshift face covering as the cloying stench within the sewer was far worse than he'd imagined. Varos was advancing steadily, seemingly immune to his surroundings. But he'd been down here before, of course. "Arkan Sula must have a warped sense of humor setting one of the Xavier tasks in here," he shouted between labored gasps.

"You'll get no argument from me on that one," Varos replied. "There was only fifty or so of us left by that stage. As if grubbing around up to our elbows in our fellow Abadorians' filth wasn't bad enough, the Elkai gave the order for the screw-pumps to be switched off," he continued. "The first we knew about it, of course, was when the sewers flooded with sea water. He then weaved a charm so that the screws behaved beyond their capacity to flush the sea water from the sewers."

Lucian stopped himself from asking what had happened next as it was obvious some of the initiates had successfully navigated the task. "How did you stop yourself from being washed out into the Gidean?" he asked instead.

"If you haven't already noticed them, there are iron rings cemented into sewer wall every twenty paces or so," Varos explained. "When the sewers started to flush, I was flailing around grabbing at the walls to stop myself when my fingers happened on one of the rings. Instinct told me the rings were the Elkai's doing, so I held onto that ring for all I was worth. Those less fortunate were washed out into the sea and eliminated. Once it was over, I remember pitying the unfortunate souls who were sent down here to cement the rings in place." He chuckled. "They... Wait, do you hear that?"

Lucian craned his head and heard a faint metallic scraping.

"And I see light ahead!" Varos shouted joyfully.

Quickening his pace, Lucian came around a bend and saw a wavering light. To his mind, it was as though someone was wafting a torch over a grating. He was soon kneeling beside Varos, peering up at Griffin through a latticed grating.

"If you push together as I pull, it should give," Giffin said.

"Where's Lox?" Varos asked.

"Standing guard at the stairwell."

Lucian shuffled beside Varos, wedged his feet firmly against the wall while wrapping his fingers about the grill. On Varos's command, they heaved.

Nothing happened.

Lucian feared the grill had been cemented into place when he felt it suddenly give slightly.

"Again!" Varos grunted.

"It's coming," Giffin grunted, his face flushed from his exertions.

The grate finally gave.

Varos scrambled out and paused to assist Lucian before grabbing another torch from its becket.

****

Lucian and Varos followed Giffin along the snaking corridor to the stairwell where Lox was standing guard. Together, they set off down each stairwell. Lucian couldn't shake the feeling they were walking into a trap as each level in turn was deserted.

"Why are there no Crows standing guard down here?" Varos asked Lox.

"We're well below sea-level now," Lox explained. "The smell down here is indescribable at high tide. Not all that far removed from your good self and the lad, if you don't mind me sayin'." He grinned. "You gets used to after a time, mind."

They eventually arrived at the lowest level. There was no corridor, just one rusting metal door set into the lichen-stained wall. Giffin held his torch close to the door while Lox unclipped the large ring from his belt and slipped one of the keys into the padlock.

The key didn't turn. Nor did the next.

The tension was palpable as Lox tried one key after another until finally arriving at the last. "I suppose this is what you might call the moment of truth," the jailer said, holding up the remaining key. "I suggest you join me in sayin' a prayer to Xavius," he added, nervously slipping the key into the lock.

The padlock gave, the faint click near-deafening within the stillness. Xavius had heeded their entreaty.

Lox tugged the padlock free and shuffled aside as Varos grabbed the handle.

The door slowly creaked open. Save for faint whispers of light seeping through a small grill set high in the wall, the cell was in shadowy darkness. For an agonized heartbeat, Lucian feared Croatalus had ordered Avicus to be moved elsewhere, but then a booming voice sounded out of the gloom. "What foolishness is this?"

"The kind that landed you in here, I should imagine," Varos retorted, his face breaking into a broad grin as Avicus emerged into the light and the two Xaviers embraced.

It was only while taking in the long, narrow face framed by a mass of unkempt ringlets that Lucian realized he hadn't thought to enquire as to how long Avicus had been held prisoner. However, judging by his beard growth, he estimated it could have been no longer than a fortnight

Avicus broke away from Varos, pausing to glance from Giffin to Lox in turn before fixing Lucian with a penetrating gaze.

"This is Lucian," Varos said by way of introduction. "But this is neither the time nor place to explain what he's doing here, brother."

With Lox leading the way, they hurriedly retraced their steps up each stairwell in turn until arriving at the corridor which led into the sewers.

"I'll be waiting for you at the opening in the market square," Giffin said. "Be sure to watch for my signal." He brought his heels together and gave the Xaviers a curt nod in salute before setting off along the corridor toward the stairwell.

"Abador owes you a lasting debt of gratitude, Lox," Varos told the jailer on reaching the grate. "As do we Xaviers."

"But I can still be of use to you," the jailer protested.

"Yes, you can, by helping us put the grating back in place." Varos smiled.

"But—"

"You have a wife and children to consider," Varos said somewhat more sternly.

"Then, I will pray for your safe return with the princess," Lox said before scurrying to catch up with Giffin.

****

Lucian was leading the way, desperately trying to focus his mind on anything other than the stench. Avicus had other ideas, however.

"I'd say this is as good a time as any for you to explain why Lucian is aiding us, brother." His booming voice sounded, echoing through the sewer

"It'll be easier to let Lucian explain," Varos

replied.

And so, Lucian repeated his witnessing Princess Rhiana being delivered to the Galyaks at the cove and everything that had happened since.

Avicus remained silent throughout. "How is it you're so certain Raynor and Kadian are in the Labyrinth?" he asked once Lucian had finished his tale.

Lucian wasn't sure how best to respond.

"Arkan Sula is channeling himself through Lucian, brother," Varos answered for him.

Avicus remained silent.

Lucian's heart was hammering in anticipation of Avicus scoffing at the notion Arkan Sula had chosen him to aid the Xaviers. Lucian wouldn't have blamed him, for it really was too preposterous to comprehend...And yet it was happening.

"If it is Sula, as you say, then why has he waited till now to intervene?" Avicus asked. "Why wasn't he in Abador awaiting to smite Nikobar?"

"We've served the Elkai these past five years," Varos replied, "and we are no nearer to understanding his methods, brother. And I'm no nearer to understanding what brought you back to Abador. You surely didn't expect to find Sula here..."

"When I heard about Nikobar lifting the plague, I returned to the city to find out what I could about him," Avicus explained.

"And what did you find out?"

Lucian was as anxious to hear what Avicus had learned about Nikobar, but on coming around a curve, he saw sunlight streaking into the sewer some thirty paces ahead. "I think we're coming to the opening," he told the Xaviers.

Careful not to catch his knees, Lucian stepped up the pace. He was advancing on the opening when a sword blade appeared. He knew it had to be Captain Griffin.

"I was beginning to fear you'd gotten lost in there," Giffin said on seeing Lucian's face appear within the opening. "How do you suggest we…Quick hide!" he hissed before hurriedly stepping away from the opening.

"What are you doing?" a voice growled.

Giffin had recovered his composure. "You'll kindly address me by my rank unless you want to be put up on a charge!" he snapped at the unseen interlopers.

Lucian had no idea whether it was one of the Black Crows that were manning the palace gate or whether this was even the same opening, but whoever it was had no respect for Giffin.

"I'll address you any way I please, Captain, sir," the interloper fawned mockingly. "Unless you wants me to report you to my Lord Nikobar…?" he said rather more bluntly. "Now, what's with the cloaks?"

"Not that it's any concern of yours, they're mine," Giffin retorted. "They are both in need of repair, and I was taking them to a seamstress I use for such things. I was shifting them to my other arm and dropped the coins I intended as payment, and they rolled through the opening before I could grab them."

"Coins, you say…?"

"Yes, I—"

Lucian was craning his neck to hear better when he heard a dull thud. To his mind, it sounded like a sack of grain hitting the ground. A heartbeat later, Giffin was back at the opening. "We need to hurry!" he said, reaching for Lucian's hand.

On scrambling out into daylight, Lucian saw a Black Crow slumped unconscious. He could now hear the familiar hubbub of a thriving market beyond a clump of trees.

Lucian rushed toward the trees to keep watch while Varos and Avicus used the length of rope to secure the still unconscious Crow's hands and feet. Varos cut a strip from the Crow's jupon with his dagger and stuffed it into his mouth before dumping him into the sewer.

"I grabbed these from the stores," Giffin said, handing two hooded cloaks bearing the unicorn of Abador.

"You'll lose your life if Nikobar gets wind of your involvement in any of this, Captain," Varos told Giffin.

"What's one man's life compared to the fate of Abador?" Giffin replied stoically.

Chapter Seven

The Valley of Kamar

An eerie silence hung in the night air like a
winding sheet as Lucian cautiously edged his way
through the deserted streets with Lykka at his heel.
Avicus and Varos were a short distance ahead, with
Giffin leading their mounts and Kia by the reins. The
two Xaviers were again wearing the purloined
Abadorian Guard cloaks the captain had provided.
Lanum's confidence in their returning to the forge with
Avicus was such that in their absence, he'd fitted
leather casings over the shoes of their mounts to
minimize the noise of shoed hooves clattering on
cobbles.

There was another surprise awaiting the two
Xaviers on their return to the forge, however. Laid out
atop the blacksmith's workbench were seven gleaming
single-edged curved swords, the like of which Lucian
had never seen. There were also seven highly polished
scabbards. The swords possessed a single-edged curved
blade with a circular guard and long grip to
accommodate both hands.

Lanum revealed that Arkan Sula had visited him at
the forge several months before the plague struck,
commissioning him to craft a sword so unique it would
become identifiable with the Xaviers. The usual process

with sword-making involved heating the steel in a mixture of iron sand and charcoal before being hammered over an anvil to remove all impurities. What made these swords exceptional was Lanum having heated the blades at tremendous temperatures, so the metal slowly warped as they cooled. Avicus and Varos were armed with the curved swords, while the others were hanging from Antares' saddle wrapped in oilcloth.

Avicus had a revelation of his own. Upon their return to the forge, he explained how he was convinced he'd been betrayed by someone on Abador's High Council. If this were true, then Nikobar's web of malevolence within Abador was all-encompassing.

Giffin called a halt at the approach to an ornamental garden that looked vaguely familiar to Lucian. He'd arrived in Abador the previous morning wholly ignorant of the city's layout. Although his only thought at the time had been to get to the Dancing Bear before the alarm was raised, he was sure he'd passed this way.

"The city gate lies a hundred yards beyond these gardens," Giffin said before proceeding to explain his strategy to lure the Black Crows guarding the gate away from their post.

The plan was simple enough. As Nikobar would have his Black Crows scouring the city for Lucian, Giffin would emerge from the gardens and shout out to the Crows that he'd been giving chase after a fair-haired lad and his wolf but had lost them somewhere within the gardens. He believed the Crows would be compelled to aid him in the chase—if only to avoid incurring Nikobar's wrath.

They threaded their way through the ornamental

gardens until arriving at a sweep of magnolia trees set close to the opening facing the main gate. Lucian was to remain here guarding the horses while Avicus and Varos sought vantage points from which they could assail the Crows as they came charging into the gardens.

Lucian already had the cord of his slingshot wrapped about his wrist, but to his horror, the gardens were so well-tended there was none lying about the ground that he might use as pellets. There was no means of tethering the horses, so keeping a tight grip on the reins, he dropped to a crouch. He was scrabbling about the magnolia trees running his free hand across the grass for anything that might suffice as a weapon. Lykka appeared at his shoulder and dropped something from his maw before padding off back into the shadows. Lucian saw that it was a polished disc-shaped pebble. He was loading the pebble into his slingshot when Lykka returned with another.

Lucian had promised Varos that he wouldn't stray from within the magnolia trees. However, believing the means would justify the ends, he left the horses to graze and hurried after Lykka through the gardens. He soon arrived at a sculpture dedicated to Kia set within a mosaic of patterned pebbles. He took this as a sign that Kia herself was watching over them and mouthed a prayer to the goddess. He was filling the pockets of his breeches with pebbles when Giffin's mock-harried shouts sounded on the air. He'd no sooner arrived back at the magnolia trees when Giffin came charging into the gardens, with three Black Crows in hurried pursuit.

Lucian had taken up a position behind the magnolia tree closest to the path. Giffin's plan appeared to be working, but there was no way of knowing how many Black Crows had been guarding the gate. If another of the rogues had rushed off in search of a patrol, they could end up trapped in the gardens. Lucian needed the Crows to split up if he was to be of help as he'd have no chance of releasing a second pebble before the other two Valessians were upon him. Giffin was urging the Crows to separate while conducting the search, but they were paying him no heed.

The three Crows were almost in line with the magnolia tree Lucian was hiding behind when he heard a fluttering sound. Glancing up into the trees, he saw a black bird nestled on a branch, silhouetted against the foliage. It was a raven. The creature stared at him as though fixing him in its mind before suddenly soaring off into the night. In that same eyeblink, Lucian's worst fears were realized on seeing a half dozen more Valessians come charging into the gardens.

The three Crows with Giffin relaxed their guard on seeing their confederates so were slow to react when Varos came charging out of the shadows. He was wielding two of Lanum's swords, and to Lucian's mind, his dexterity was even more fearsome than at the stable. Two of the Crows were dead before they'd hit the ground. The third managed a spear thrust, but Varos deflected the blade with ease before delivering a sweeping blow with his other sword that caught the Crow on the nape of his neck. The Valessians were brutish cutthroats and no match for elite warriors such as the Xaviers

Varos sheathed one sword while tossing the other to Giffin. The newly arrived Valessians came at the charge, fanning out as they did so. Varos hurriedly grabbed up one of the dead Crows' spears and launched it at one of the advancing Crows. The rogue adopted a defensive stance to absorb the spear's full impact, but doing so left himself exposed to Avicus's attack.

Seeing a second of their number slump silently to the ground in as many heartbeats and Varos and Giffin charging toward them sent the Crows into a panic. Lucian sprang out from his hiding place with his slingshot poised. Realizing he wasn't needed; he went to fetch the horses instead. By the time he returned, it was all over.

According to Giffin, there was just one lone Crow left at the main gate. Avicus and Varos were content to let the Valessian live as Giffin hadn't identified himself and was confident the rogue wouldn't recognize him as being the one who'd raised the alarm. They'd charged the gate and were across the drawbridge before the hapless Crow realized what was happening.

Lucian could only hope the Black Crow at the gate reporting three riders fleeing the city with a wolf in the immediate aftermath of the fight in the gardens, coupled with other Valessian's account of what occurred at the tavern stable, would lull Nikobar into believing his quarry had escaped the city and wouldn't exact reprisals.

****

Avicus was determined to arrive at the entrance to the Sardonis Pass, which snaked high above the cavernous Brethas Gorge, before sunrise and set a heavy pace. The Sardonis Pass was notoriously hazardous to negotiate even in daylight owing to low-hanging clouds. Avicus had brokered no argument, however, as going through the pass would avoid the

Volgus Floodplains and thereby save them a half day's ride. And as Arkan Sula had neglected to say when Raynor and Kadian had entered the Labyrinth, every hour counted.

Avicus was leading the way with Varos bringing up the rear, but Lucian could see neither one owing to the dense mist. Nor could he see where he was putting his feet, and he once again imagined himself within the Winter Triangle. Varos must have sensed his unease, for he suddenly shouted out to Lucian if he'd like to hear about the six remaining ordeals Arkan Sula had set for the Xavier initiates.

"There were seven ordeals because seven is the most sacred of numbers to the Elkai," the Xavier explained. "The ordeals were open to men of the Centaurian and Abadorian Guard aged between twenty-one and twenty-eight—the mystical 'seven' at play again. There must have been a thousand or more of us who put our names forward. It was as though we were on trial for our lives, which I suppose, in essence, we were.

"The first ordeal called for us to swim across the Isar Estuary. Now, the Isar's a tricky stretch of water owing to the currents," he continued. "Of the thousand who threw themselves into the water, less than a hundred reached the other side. No one drowned, mind. His Majesty wasn't about to lose a fifth of his army to the Isar if he could help it and insisted on having boats on the water to haul in the stragglers."

"Which of the Guard were you in?" Lucian asked over his shoulder.

"I was a newly-promoted captain in the Abadorian Guard but no guesses as to which of the Guards Avicus belonged," Varos shouted to ensure his voice carried along the pass. "Yanek, Torian, and Èinor were Abadorians same as I, while Avicus, Raynor, and Kadian were Centaurians."

Lucian brought Kia to a halt to await Varos. "And you were at Zylos?"

"We were all at Zylos." Varos nodded, his eyes glazing over.

"I didn't know Yanek or Èinor at the time of the battle as they were in different battalions, but Torian and I were in the same battalion and ended up standing shoulder-to-shoulder in the shield wall that day funnily enough. It was the same with Raynor and Kadian. More so, in fact. They're so close you'd think they were blood brothers."

"How did the battle begin?" Lucian asked.

"Same as any battle, I expect." Varos shrugged. "Two armies form their shield walls, they trade insults, release their arrows, and keep releasing them until one shield-wall finally advances. That's the time when the archers become killing machines. The Galyaks favor the crossbow. Now, the crossbow is more accurate than a traditional bow, but they take longer to reload. In the time it takes to load a crossbow, a good archer can release a dozen arrows. And your average Huskenbach is mighty good with a bow."

"Which army arrived at Zylos first?" Lucian asked, picturing the scene in his mind's eye.

"Thanks to our scouts, we knew the main body of Salah Khan's army was advancing toward the Zylos River, so we marched through the night, found good ground, and formed our shield wall atop a rise overlooking the Zylos and waited. I don't mind admitting when the Galyaks advanced, I could have filled one of the city sewers single-handedly," he added with a chuckle.

Varos fell silent for several heartbeats. "The second of Arkan Sula's ordeals was of fire," he said, switching back to his original tale. "We each had to walk barefoot over a sea of glowing red and white coals with any man who cried out being eliminated. The trick, of course, is to keep to the white coals. It's surprising how many fools were ignorant of this. You already know something of what it was like in the sewers, so we can skip to the next ordeal, which was…Ah, yes…For the fourth ordeal, we were wedged inside wooden casks with the lids nailed tight and left on the harbor wall from dusk till dawn. Any man that cried out for water was…Well, I'm sure you can guess. Then we had to run twenty leagues along the shore in full battledress. Now, lugging a shield and spear for miles on end isn't as bad as you might think. It was the leather liner inside your helmet pressing into your skull with the sweat streaming into your eyes that was the worst…Well, for me at least."

"My grandmother says Arkan Sula took you up into the Elovian Mountains to undergo mystical rituals," said Lucian.

"Aye, and there are those who would have you believe we were trained in the arts of war at Valkyar's own hand," Varos replied. "Those of us remaining then had to scale the Colossus of Kracia. I'm sure you remember that one, brother," he shouted ahead. "The Colossus stands at a hundred cubits, and we had nothing more than our wits to call on. A strong grip and a head for heights helped, of course. Arkan Sula says the Colossus is one of the seven wonders of the world," he continued. "The mystical 'seven' again. He's never said what the other the six wonders are, mind."

Avicus' voice sounded out of the swirling mist. "You managing to keep your mouth shut for longer than a minute would surely prove another."

Varos ignored the jibe. "There was just the seven of us that made it to the top, but Sula wasn't finished with us just yet," he continued. "He staged a special Abadorian Games which had us competing against each other with bow and arrow and javelin, as well as battling it out with sword and quarterstaff. In a sword fight, most men will slash away as though they're trying to put out a fire, but there are only nine fundamental sword strokes. 'Learn the nine, and victory is thine,' as the saying goes. Again, no rewards for guessing who came out tops in the swordplay, but Avicus won't mind admitting to his being pushed hard by Raynor. And I'll happily crow about hitting the inner ring with each javelin throw."

"The inner ring was big enough to put a man's head through," Avicus interjected. "Clearly not Varos's head."

Chapter Eight

Into the Valley

The distant horizon was tinged with a faint sliver of gray when Lucian and the two Xaviers emerged from the Sardonis Pass. It was early spring, yet the snow still clung to the hollows on higher ground. With the Valley of Kamar still shrouded in darkness, Avicus suggested they tend to the horses and get some sleep before making their descent. Lucian's every muscle was aching, but he was far too excited to even think about sleep. After feeding and watering Kia, he grabbed a handful of the cured meat Lanum had provided from his saddlebag and stepped out onto a shelf overlooking the expansive valley. Spreading his saddle blanket on the rock, he huddled next to Lykka to await the dawn.

Lucian woke with a jolt. It was only on seeing the sun was now edging over the mountains in the distance and slowly chasing the shadows across the valley that he realized he'd fallen asleep. He was so engrossed in trying to discern the volcano within the slowly-lifting gloom that he hadn't realized Avicus had joined him on the shelf. He looked expectedly beyond the Xavier but saw no sign of Varos.

"Varos could sleep on a rusting spear-point," Avicus said matter-of-factly by way of explanation, his gaze fixed on the valley floor below. "You are familiar with the legend surrounding the Spear of Lixivior?" he asked, turning to face Lucian.

"My grandmother said the legend brought adventurers from every corner of the known world to Kamar, but that the Spear was never found."

"Did your grandmother speak of the Talvek?" Avicus asked, glancing down into the valley again.

Lucian's grandmother had spoken of the Talvek, the skeletal beast that served at Gazankulu's right-hand in Orbelium, but as with the Gogolah, he'd thought the Talvek to be the creation of an overactive imagination. On seeing the look in Avicus's eyes, however, he was no longer sure. "You think the Talvek exists?"

"I neither believe nor disbelieve in anything till I see it with my own eyes," Avicus replied, "but it's worth remembering that all legends possess a kernel of truth."

"My grandmother said the Talvek fed on the bones of the men mining for rubies," Lucian said.

"One of those seeking the Spear is said to have found a ruby that was the size of lizard egg," Avicus explained. "As you can imagine, the discovery brought adventurers from all corners of the known world to excavate the base of the volcano. In turn, merchants descended on Kamar to cater to the needs of the miners, and with more and more people arriving on a daily basis, within a year or so, a city was taking shape. The miners were forced to excavate deeper and deeper inside the volcano, creating a labyrinthine network of tunnels. But the endless digging awoke the spirit living in the volcano."

"What happened?"

"The spirit was enraged at having its slumber

disturbed and called upon the volcano to send forth a torrent of molten lava seal the entrance to the tunnels, trapping hundreds of miners within, and destroy the city. Those miners and merchants who were lucky enough to survive the carnage fled the valley, never to return."

Lucian was confused. "But if the entrance was sealed, how could Raynor and Kadian be lost within the Labyrinth?"

"The news of what happened here served to convince people that the spirit within the volcano was protecting the Spear of Lixivior," Avicus explained. "King Belos, who ruled what is now Kavashar came with his army and a horde of slaves to dig through the lava to gain access to the tunnels. Before sending his soldiers into the tunnels, Belos is said to have put a hundred slaves to the sword and had their decapitated heads cast into the volcano's maw to appease the spirit. For a time, it seemed the sacrifice had worked, but the eruption broke through into Orbelium allowing the Talvek to come into this realm. Belos's soldiers began disappearing within the tunnels. When one of those that had been missing for days spoke of seeing the Talvek, the other soldiers refused to enter the tunnels. Belos foolishly ordered a hundred of his soldiers to be sacrificed to appease the Talvek. His generals staged a coup, Belos was pitched into the volcano, and the valley abandoned."

****

Lucian fished another chunk of cured meat from inside his jerkin and tossed it to Lykka. "Why do you think Arkan Sula is channeling his energies through me instead of coming to you in person?" he asked Avicus.

Avicus sat staring at the brightening sky for several heartbeats. "Your time would be wiser spent trying to will back the incoming tide with your thoughts than to try and fathom Sula's reasoning," he said at last. "I believe the Elkai knew Nikobar was coming to Abador."

"You do?" Lucian gasped.

"Not by name, you understand," Avicus said, shaking his head. "He would speak of an approaching sinister force that was weaving its evil from within the shadows. He said this dark force would one day be allowed to take root because the gods were bored! Can you believe that? Because they were bored! It is right that we honor the gods, but the gods only live through man. And nothing brings the gods to life more than war, I find," he added bitterly.

"Are you saying the gods allowed Nikobar to come to Abador to incite a war between Abador and Varnia?"

"It would make sense of Arkan Sula not returned to Abador to challenge Nikobar," Avicus retorted.

"I believe the impending sinister force Arkan Sula spoke of was the Draconis Constellation," Lucian offered. "It is now almost directly above Abador."

"I've seen the constellation you speak of," Avicus said.

"Perhaps that is why he seeks the Spear of Lixivior," said Lucian. "To help him fight Nikobar's sorcery…?"

"Sula gave up seeking the Spear some years back to focus his energies on searching for Rhödos' youngest son, Prince Ærin."

After everything that had happened in the last few days, Lucian didn't think anything could ever surprise him again, and yet Avicus's revelation had his mind reeling.

"Did Varos tell you Sula appeared to him in a dream at the time of the plague summoning us to meet with him?" Avicus asked.

"And of how Sula didn't appear."

"I can't help thinking the Elkai lured us away from the city so that Nikobar would be free to impose his will on His Majesty," Avicus continued with his train of thought. "We Xaviers are oath-sworn to Abador, and on hearing Nikobar offering to lift the plague in return for his being given sanctuary, we would have pitched him and his Valessians back out into the Gidean."

"But His Majesty was surely torn—"

"There are those in Abador who feel His Majesty and the Senate should be held accountable for not acting sooner than they did," Avicus interjected tersely. "Because it was the migrants living in the alavi quarter that were the first to fall ill, their plight was largely ignored. It was only when the nobles started dying that the Senate took action. By then, of course, it was too late as the plague was rampant throughout the whole city, and there was nothing anyone could do other than dig burial pits."

"Does His Majesty blame Arkan Sula for Prince Tarvel's death?" Lucian asked.

"That I can't say." Avicus shrugged. "But…"

"Go on."

"There was something about Tarvel's death that didn't endure…still doesn't," Avicus said. "You see, those who fell ill lasted several days before succumbing. Yet the prince died within hours of his first showing symptoms. I can't shake the feeling

Tarvel was allowed to die; that it was the will of the gods."

"But the gods favor Abador, and Prince Tarvel was heir to the throne," said Lucian.

"May the gods forgive me, but Tarvel was never going to live up to his father," Avicus replied. "Nor did he show any desire in becoming king. None that I could see anyway."

"And what of Princess Rhiana?" Lucian asked. "Do you think she will make a great Queen?"

"We can only hope she gets the chance to be Queen," said Avicus. "What I can't yet fathom is why Nikobar has handed the princess to the Galyaks? If his intention was to incite a war between Abador and Varnia, he could have had his thugs slay the princess along with her escort."

"All I know is that Arkan Sula is channeling his energies through me to unite you Xaviers so you can rescue Princess Rhiana and save Abador," said Lucian. "My grandmother says she believes helping save the princess is my destiny. She saw it in the embers."

****

With the entire valley now awash with sunlight, Lucian saw that the volcano consisted of a funnel-shaped peak, partially encircled by the steep rim of a large cauldron-like hollow. Avicus said this had most likely been caused by the earlier collapse of a much higher structure. Lucian couldn't help picturing King Belos's mutinous soldiers hurling him into the maw. The volcano's sweeping slopes, though scarred by lava flows, were pitted with swaths of dense scrub and vegetation. Though the volcano wasn't as colossal as he'd imagined in his mind's eye, it nonetheless dominated the landscape.

The incline on this side of the valley was less severe yet still too steep for Lucian and the two Xaviers to risk making their descent on horseback. This not only slowed their progress but meant having to hack through stubborn thornbush tangles. They were advancing along the valley floor toward the volcano's blackened base when Varos called Lucian and Avicus's attention to what appeared to be a ship's sail tangled within a clump of trees. They set off at a gallop. As they drew nearer, Lucian saw the sail was a makeshift canopy. Within the shade afforded by the canopy were two piebald stallions tethered to one of the trees.

The ground beneath the canopy was covered in fresh straw, while a hollowed-out tree trunk served as a water trough. Judging by scraps of apple and carrot stumps scattered about the ground, it was obvious the horses were being well-tended. Seeing three baskets of untouched bread and fruit was rather less comforting.

"Well, there's no doubting our brothers are here," Varos called out, leaping from his saddle. "This one is Altair, Kadian's mount," he said, nuzzling the nearest piebald's ear. "The other is Adhara. I see Avicus's impatience has got the better of him again," he chided, hurriedly guided Antares toward the water trough, and wrapped the reins about a branch before rushing toward the jagged opening Belos's slaves had gouged out of the lava.

Lucian guided Sirius over to the canopy before rushing across to the opening. On arriving at the entrance, his eyes were drawn to a wooden post wedged within a cleft carved out of the lava. Tied about the post was a length of rope trailing off into an opening which he supposed Raynor and Kadian were using as a guide into the Labyrinth. Varos was standing within the opening, and Lucian was starting toward him when Lykka's sudden yowl stopped him in his tracks. Scurrying out into daylight and shielding his eyes against the sun's glare, Lucian saw a herder and his goats ambling toward them. As the herder drew nearer, Lucian saw he was a fresh-faced youth of roughly his own age.

"Hello, my friend. My name is Akeel." The young herder beamed, offering a lopsided grin. He waded through his herd, pausing to lift a bulging waterskin from the back of one goat before pushing onto another to retrieve two sacks and dumping them on the ground, his exertions causing the ragged hole under one arm of his threadbare shirt to widen. The shirt, like his britches, was all but blanched of color.

"My goats are hoping your friend has eaten well today." Akeel grinned, indicating to Lykka before lifting his arm and giving the tear a cursory glance.

The young herder's carefree mood was infectious. "I can assure you Lykka won't trouble your goats," Lucian said, returning Akeel's grin.

Varos appeared in the opening.

"As you can see, I have brought extra water and forage so I can tend to your horses while you go into the earth," Akeel said, indicating to the water skin and sacks.

"You are the one who's been helping my brothers?" Varos asked, coming around Lucian.

"Yes." Akeel beamed.

"When did you last see them?" Varos asked.

"These three days past," Akeel replied solemnly,

glancing across to the canopy.

"And yet you have returned each day…" Lucian said.

"Because I am paid to come every day."

Varos glanced at Lucian. "Who paid you?"

Akeel hesitated as though unsure how to respond. "I do not know because the man did not tell me his name."

"Then describe him."

Again, Akeel hesitated. "I have not seen him. He spoke to me while I was sleeping."

"Then how could he pay you?" Lucian asked, suspecting he already knew the answer.

"Each morning when I wake, I find a gold coin tucked into my blanket," Akeel explained. "I have very good ears, and my goats are easily panicked at night because of wild animals, and yet I never sensed a thing."

Lucian could see from the look in Varos's eyes that he was thinking the same name: Arkan Sula. "What did this voice say to you?" he asked.

"I was told I should bring fresh water, straw, and food for horses and people to this place," Akeel said. "And then fresh water and food each morning after. And today—"

"What about today?" Varos snapped.

"Today, I was told to bring extra food and water as three more people would be going into the earth."

Avicus suddenly reappeared within the opening. "And who might this be?" he asked, eyeing Akeel.

"My name is Akeel, and I have been assisting your comrades."

"Raynor and Kadian were obviously using the rope

so they could find their way out of the Labyrinth," Avicus said. "Someone has gone in there and severed the rope."

Avicus grabbed hold of Akeel's shoulders. "Who else have you seen in this place?" he demanded.

"Please!" Akeel pleaded. "I have seen no one. And I know nothing of cut ropes. I swear it!"

"It's all right, lad," Varos said, fishing some coins from his jupon and handing them to Akeel. "If the horses are still here when you return in the morning," he added, glancing across to the canopy, "then they are yours to do with as you please. For we will have no further need of them."

****

The two Xaviers had gone to explore the antechamber that Avicus said lay beyond the Labyrinth's original entrance. There was no way of knowing how long they might be inside the Labyrinth, or indeed, whether they'd ever return to the sunlit world. Lucian took care to ensure Kia and the four Xavier mounts had a plentiful supply of water and oats before going to join up with the two knights. Just as he was stepping into the opening, however, he was distracted by something circling high above the volcano.

The bird was but a dark pinprick against the sun-tinged blue vastness, yet Lucian knew that it was the same raven that he'd seen in the ornamental gardens. He also knew this was no ordinary raven.

Lucian was still watching the raven when the creature swooped through the air, streaking toward him. He instinctively brought up his hands to protect his face and felt the raven's wing brush the back of his hands as it streaked past him into the Labyrinth. Before Lucian could even think to react, Lykka let out a yowl and gave chase to the raven.

Anxious of Avicus and Varos' reaction should he lose Lykka within the Labyrinth before they'd even started their search for Raynor and Kadian, Lucian charged through the opening into what he assumed to be the antechamber Avicus had spoken of. There was no sign of the two Xaviers. As Lucian's eyes slowly grew accustomed to the murk, he saw what appeared to be openings hewn out of the rock. There were five openings in all. He approached the first opening and called after the two Xaviers.

Thinking he heard a faint howling echoing up from the Labyrinth, Lucian stepped into the opening only to be wrenched back by a vice-like grip on his shoulder.

Varos was incensed at what he saw as Lucian's foolish behavior. Nor did he hold back in venting his displeasure. He was looping the rope he'd retrieved from the antechamber about Lucian's waist when the antechamber was suddenly awash with light.

"Lucky for us young Akeel had a piece of flint," Avicus said, handing the torch to Lucian so that he could loop the rope through his sword belt.

With Lucian secured between the two Xaviers and with Avicus leading the way, the three set forth into the tunnel from which Lucian believed he'd heard Lykka's echoing howls.

As they advanced farther along the snaking tunnel, Lucian sensed the incline becoming more pronounced. After a hundred feet or so, he and the two Xaviers were forced to amble along at a crouch, their backs brushing the tunnel ceiling. The tunnel was also getting steadily narrower, but just as their exertions were becoming extremely uncomfortable, they arrived at an opening into a small antechamber with two openings cut into the rock.

Varos mooted the idea of their splitting up so they might follow the tunnel in both directions. Avicus, however, argued against this as they had only one torch. He elected they take the opening to their left, for no other reason, or so Lucian assumed, than he happened to be holding the torch in his left hand.

This tunnel was larger but was soon reeking of sulfur. It seemed to Lucian the stench was becoming ever more overpowering the farther they advanced into the unknown. The air was so fetid he feared he might faint away. His jerkin and britches were already wringing wet, and wiping the stinging sweat from his eyes was doing more harm than good. It was clear from their labored breathing that Avicus and Varos were also struggling, but neither Xavier showed any reticence in continuing into the abyss. The cloying heat was so oppressive that Lucian blindly stumbled on with his head resting on his chin. He only realized Avicus had come to a halt by blundering into him.

They'd arrived at another opening, leading into another tunnel leading in both directions. Avicus now proposed turning right. His rationale being their heading left again might see them arrive at their starting point. They hadn't gone far, however, when Avicus called them to a halt.

Ignoring the stinging sweat seeping into his eyes, Lucian saw they were standing before a large jagged cleft within the tunnel wall. He was shaking the sweat from his eyes when an eruption sounded somewhere within the bowels of the Labyrinth.

The eruption was sufficient to force Lucian and the two Xaviers to drop to a crouch to steady themselves. Lucian was getting to his feet when his left arm exploded in searing agony. Globules of lava were seeping through the rock into the tunnel. Mercifully, the quick-thinking Varos grabbed Lucian's arm and used the tip of his dagger to prize free the globule of lava eating into his flesh.

With Varos helping Lucian, the three scrambled into the cleft.

****

The cleft had allowed them to drop through into one of the lower tunnels. Lucian was plodding along in a near-daze, his mind focused only on the ragged blood-encrusted wound in his left forearm. He was suddenly wrenched from his self-pity when Avicus started flailing about with the torch as though he was warding off some unseen foe. Then Lucian caught a glimpse of something silhouetted against the tunnel wall in the dancing torchlight and knew it was the raven. Avicus was still warding off the raven when the tunnel was suddenly plunged into near-darkness.

The loss of the torch meant they now had to edge along the tunnel, feeling their way with their hands. This not only hampered their progress but left them blind to whatever dangers lay ahead. A multitude of disquieting thoughts plagued Lucian's mind, the most disturbing being that the raven was an otherworldly creature conjured by Nikobar to observe their movements.

Lucian was pondering how they might rid themselves of the raven when another, more violent, eruption tore through the Labyrinth, throwing him to the floor, the rope about his midriff tightening in a vicelike grip. It was as though unseen forces were squeezing the life from him. The pain was excruciating, and Lucian was struggling to make sense of what Varos was telling him. It was only with the pressure about his middle instantaneously easing from Varos severing the rope that Lucian realized the muffled cries echoing through the tunnel weren't his own.

Something had happened to Avicus.

As Lucian's mind came back into focus, he saw Varos was now wedged against the tunnel wall, desperately pulling on the rope. Now that the tunnel was awash with a lush golden glow, he was able to take in the situation: the latest eruption had caused a section of the tunnel floor to collapse, and Avicus had fallen into the opening. He threw himself down beside Varos and grabbed hold of the rope. Try as he might, Lucian couldn't get sufficient purchase, and the sweat-soaked rope was slipping from his grasp. Avicus was still conscious and bellowing for Varos to cut the rope so they might save themselves.

"We're not leaving you, brother!" Varos hissed through gritted teeth as he strained against the inevitable.

Lucian was beseeching Valkyar to come to their aid but suddenly fell silent. "Arkan Sula!" he shouted. "If it's truly you who speaks to me, I call upon you now!"

At first, nothing happened. But then Lucian became aware of a strange pulsating in his chest that quickly spread through his whole body, coursing through his muscles. He sensed whatever was happening inside him was also happening to Varos. As soon as Avicus was level with the tunnel floor, Lucian hurriedly looped an arm through the rope to steady himself as he edged over the opening and grabbed hold of Avicus's outstretched hand to pull him clear.

"We'll have to retrace our steps in the hope of finding another tunnel," Varos said, helping Avicus to his feet.

Lucian was following after the Xaviers when Arkan Sula's voice sounded in his mind.

"Your only hope of finding Raynor and Kadian is in following this tunnel to its conclusion."

Peering beyond the breach, Lucian saw the tunnel arced into a sweeping curve. "Arkan Sula says we must continue along this tunnel if we are to find Raynor and Kadian," he called out, bringing the Xaviers to a halt. Without waiting for their response, he turned on his heel and charged toward the steadily widening chasm and hurled himself across. Stepping to the edge, he saw the rising lava was now only a few feet from the tunnel floor.

Varos had needed no second bidding and was soon standing beside Lucian. Avicus, however, slowly approached the chasm. In a show of defiance, he spat into the lava before retreating along the tunnel and launching himself across.

Keeping ahead of the lava spilling into the tunnel, they rounded the curve only to be met with a solid mass of rock some thirty feet ahead. Lucian knew Arkan Sula wouldn't have them vault the chasm unless there was a means of escape. There had to be an opening hidden within the rock. And then he saw it—a ragged fracture between the tunnel wall and floor that appeared to be widening with every heartbeat. Mouthing thanks to Arkan Sula, Lucian threw himself into the fissure.

The fissure was so narrow they had to shuffle along on all fours, the coarse rock shredding their already bruised knees. Mercifully, the fissure widened into a tunnel, the walls of which were illuminated with a pulsating glow. They continued along the tunnel, quickening their pace toward an opening leading out onto a shelf overlooking a cavernous chamber.

Chapter Nine

The Heart of the Labyrinth

On entering the Labyrinth, Lucian's only concern had been to locate Raynor and Kadian. Once they were navigating the tunnels, his apprehension had seesawed between the lost Xaviers and finding Lykka. Then, of course, the farther they'd descended into the bowels of the Labyrinth, the more his thoughts were taken up with keeping ahead of the lava. At no point had he given any consideration to Avicus's musings on the Talvek. The evidence that the Talvek existed beyond the realm of nightmares, however, lay within a sunken pit in the center of the chamber. Amid a scattered assortment of rusted weapons, buckled shields, and flensed human bones was a mound of human skulls. Each of the skulls appeared to have a jagged hole at the crown. Despite the oppressive heat, Lucian's blood ran cold as he pictured the Talvek feasting upon a warrior's brains before adding another skull to the grisly monument.

Lucian scrambled from the shelf onto a narrow ridge that ran the entire length of the chamber and hurried after Avicus and Varos to the largest of several openings within the rock face. Instead of following the two Xaviers into the opening, he stood gazing up at the ceiling, marveling at the massed stalactites.

Peering into the tunnel, he saw Avicus and Varos

retreating toward him. Varos was carrying what appeared to be a crushed helmet. It was only when the Xaviers arrived at the opening that Lucian saw it was a bronze Xavier helmet. Avicus took the helmet from Varos, absentmindedly running a finger over the helmet's scorched horsehair comb while glancing about the chamber before angrily flinging it into the pit.

Lucian was watching the flattened helmet arcing through the air when he was aware of movement farther within the tunnel. He instinctively shrank away, thinking that it was the Talvek but stopped himself on realizing it was a man. A man in a russet tunic.

"By Xavius' beard! It's Raynor!" Varos gasped.

The wild-eyed Raynor staggered to halt, gaping disbelievingly at Avicus and Varos as though they were figments of his imagination. For a heartbeat, Lucian feared Raynor's mind had descended into madness.

"Raynor!" Avicus said forcibly. "Where's Kadian?"

"Is, is it really you, brothers?" Raynor spluttered, glancing from Avicus to Varos.

Varos stepped toward Raynor, grasping him by the shoulders. "Yes, brother. Now, where is Kadian?"

"Kadian followed the wolf," Raynor said, glancing back into the tunnel. "He believes Xavius sent the wolf to deliver us into daylight."

Lucian was elated. "You've seen Lykka?" he said, peering beyond Raynor into the tunnel.

"It's unlikely Raynor knows Lykka by name, lad," Avicus said irritably. "We'll leave Raynor here with you while we go in search of Kadian. Hopefully he'll still be with Lykka, so no need for you to go wandering off into any of the other openings."

Lucian was desperate to ask Raynor about Lykka but held his tongue while watching Avicus and Varos advancing into the tunnel. The two Xaviers had no sooner faded from view when a thunderous explosion rocked the chamber, sending Lucian and Raynor tumbling from the ridge. The chamber was still reverberating with aftershocks when a torrent of lava came cascading over the shelf into the chamber. Lucian was still scrambling to his feet when Avicus came charging back through the tunnel and threw himself into the pit a mere heartbeat before a loud crack sounded as a lattice-boned tail came scything through the air.

****

Lucian stood mesmerized, taking in the Talvek's cauterized flesh jutting from its charred skeletal frame in serrated barbs as the beast slowly emerged from the tunnel and raised itself on its powerful haunches, partially extending its ragged wings. The creature had no eyes, so flicked its bulbous head from side to side, scenting the air for Avicus. He was still taking in the nightmarish spectacle when the raven came streaking out of the opening on the shelf. The creature circled about the chamber before swooping down and coming to rest on the Talvek's shoulder. It seemed to Lucian the raven was communicating with the Talvek, for the beast slowly fixed its sightless gaze on Avicus.

The lava was pooling within the sunken pit, hungrily inching its way to where Avicus lay sprawled, his eyes riveted on the Talvek.

"Stay where you are!" Lucian shouted to Avicus. "It detects its prey only by movement."

"I'm well aware of that, lad," Avicus retorted, eyeing the advancing lava, "but time is against us."

Imagining himself within the Winter Triangle's embrace, and with his eyes fixed on the raven, Lucian eased the slingshot from his jerkin. Regretting the folly of discarding the pebbles he'd amassed in the ornamental gardens soon after fleeing the city, he glanced about him for a projectile, grimacing inwardly on espying a human knucklebone wedged in a cranny away to his right. He was readying himself to grab the knucklebone when the Talvek fixed its sightless gaze on Avicus while slowly arcing its tail.

Seeing the Talvek readying itself to strike at Avicus, Lucian hurriedly grabbed up the knucklebone and pressed it into his slingshot. There wasn't time to take proper aim, and the raven had sensed his intentions, for it soared into the air the moment he released.

Seizing his chance, Avicus grabbed up a discarded spear, vaulted back onto the ledge, and scurried into another of the tunnel openings before the Talvek could react.

"We need to follow Avicus's lead and find something to distract the Talvek," Raynor shouted to Lucian.

I haven't got anything to hand," Lucian replied.

"Then it's all in Xavius' hands now, lad." Raynor smiled.

Or Arkan Sula's Lucian said to himself as much in prayer as anything else.

It was as though the Elkai was listening, for a loud crack sounded as a massive stalactite broke away from the ceiling and crashed into the sunken pit, sending shards of rock and lava spewing into the air.

Seeing the Talvek launch itself from the ledge to

snatch at one of the shards of rock with its outstretched maw, Lucian threw himself into the nearest opening, followed a heartbeat later by Raynor.

The Talvek had spat out the shard and was scenting the air amid the chamber, which now resembled a molten lake.

"I have an inkling the gods are with us this day, lad," Raynor whispered while reaching for Lucian's hand as they slowly retreated farther into the tunnel. As soon as they were far enough into the tunnel where their movements wouldn't arouse the Talvek, they set off at a run.

Lucian, Avicus, and Varos had acted on little more than blind instinct after losing the torch. Lucian couldn't decipher anything in the blackness this time around, but Raynor seemed to have an idea of where he was heading. They hurriedly traversed one tunnel after another until arriving at an opening into a tunnel stretching in both directions.

Lucian immediately sensed Raynor's hesitation, but it was only fleeting. "It's this way," the Xavier announced, grabbing hold of Lucian's arm and pulling him to the left.

"You're sure?" Lucian asked as they set off along the tunnel.

"Kadian and I were careful to leave markers here and there," Raynor replied. "It was only when some mischievous sprite decided to play tricks on us by removing them that we got lost. This one's Kadian's helmet," he said, giving the helmet a quick rap against the tunnel wall before tossing it aside. "We can't be all that far from the surface now."

"Why do you say it was a sprite that played tricks

on you?" Lucian asked, remembering the severed guide rope.

"It's deathly quiet down here...or was at least," Raynor replied, pausing as another eruption sounded. "So quiet we would hear something scurrying about either in front or behind us. We thought it was Arkan Sula testing us."

"Did you by chance ever see a raven in here?" Lucian asked, following Raynor through into another tunnel. He couldn't see how they could be nearing the surface, but there was no denying the air was more breathable.

"Not that I recall. Why do you ask?"

Lucian was about to explain about the raven when Raynor grabbed his arm. "What is it?" he hissed.

"We're not alone in here," Raynor replied.

It was then Lucian heard a sound he feared he might never hear again. He caught a flash of gray-white before Lykka was upon him. He was mouthing a prayer to Kia for watching over the wolf when Varos's voice sounded out of the darkness to say Avicus and Kadian were with him.

With Lykka leading the way, Lucian and the Xaviers raced through the tunnels as one thunderous explosion after another ripped through the Labyrinth. It was now simply a race against time as the Labyrinth was collapsing in on itself. On emerging from the tunnels into the antechamber, Lucian wept tears of joy on feeling whispy sunlight on his dirt-streaked face.

The whole valley floor was trembling violently as Lucian chased after the Xaviers to the canopy. He hurriedly untethered Kia, threw himself up into the saddle, and clung onto Kia's reins.

They were almost clear of the valley when a thunderous explosion sounded, and the volcano finally erupted to send a towering plume of molten fire and black ash into the air to blot out the sun.

Chapter Ten

The Sister Witches

Leaving the desolation of the Valley of Kamar far behind them, Lucian and the Xaviers headed south through the Caucol Hills and onto the picturesque plains of Kevala.

Lucian pulled on Kia's reins bringing the filly to a halt. Reaching for his water flask, he sat staring out across the undulating grasslands pitted with clusters of cypress trees and olive groves and stretching in all directions as far as the eye could see. The skies were clear and after the Labyrinth's cloying confinement, riding into the wind proved wholly reinvigorating.

Lucian nonetheless felt uneasy because Arkan Sula had last spoken to him inside the Labyrinth. He sensed the Xaviers' were becoming equally perturbed at the Elkai's silence. He was splashing some water onto his face when Sula's voice sounded on the wind.

"Torian can be found in Evora's shadow."

Lucian tugged on Kia's reins to bring her alongside Varos. "Arkan Sula has just spoken. He says we'll find Torian in Evora's shadow. Does that mean anything to you?"

"By Xavius' beard!" Varos spluttered. "Are you sure those were Sula's words?"

"I heard him as plain as I hear you," Lucian

replied.

"So, Torian is in Helgos." Varos nodded.

"Where is Helgos?" Lucian asked.

Varos paused, glancing up at the sun and then the surrounding landscape as though getting his bearings. "The quickest route to Helgos from here would be to head southwest and traverse the Carpasian Mountains. "Come on, we'd best give the others the news," he said, spurring Antares on.

On hearing Varos's shout Avicus, Raynor, and Kadian came to a halt.

"The Elkai has spoken with Lucian again, brothers," Varos announced, reining in alongside Avicus. "He says we'll find Torian in Helgos."

"Helgos!" Raynor gasped.

"This can mean but one thing, brother," Varos said to Avicus.

Avicus nodded. "The Sister Witches are abroad again," he said bitterly

"I thought never to hear of those three again," Kadian said.

Lucian couldn't help feeling slightly foolish. He was the one delivering Arkan Sula's missives yet understood little of what he was relaying. "Who are the Sister Witches?" he asked.

And so, between them, the Xaviers explained all about Crepicella and her sisters, Gastrula and Grockle.

The Land of Helgos lay within a lush basin within central Kracia. It had once been a prosperous and happy land. Its lakes, rivers, and streams had teemed with fish, while the surrounding forest was filled with an abundance of game. It was said that the Helgoans were the envy of every other Kracian. But then, one summer, the Helgoans' harvest failed. The lakes and rivers fouled, the streams dried up, and the forest decayed into a desiccated wasteland.

The Helgoans feared they had somehow angered Xavius and sent emissaries to Abador to petition King Ocwan's help. The Helgoans had sworn fealty to King Ocwan, so His Majesty was honor-bound to heed their pleas. His Majesty had charged the seven Xaviers with delivering Arkan Sula from the Elovian Mountains to Abador. King Ocwan had wanted the Xaviers to accompany Arkan Sula into Helgos, but the Elkai had expressly forbidden it.

Arkan Sula had first encountered the Sister Witches when they were but children after happening upon a gypsy encampment while passing through the Land of Helgos. In keeping with tradition, the gypsies' leader had welcomed the Elkai into their camp. The leader had boasted about Crepicella, the eldest of the three girls, being possessed of the power to heal and that she had used her gift to save the life of the Helgoan Burgher's son. The Burgher, as indeed were all the Helgoans, was so overjoyed that he'd invited the gypsies to make their winter camp in the forest.

Crepicella was barely into her teens at the time, yet Arkan Sula had immediately sensed she was special-born and possessed the potential to be much more than a mere healer. The Elkai had pressing business to attend to elsewhere in Kracia and so offered to return in the spring and take Crepicella with him into the Elovian Mountains to see whether she was worthy of becoming an adept.

The winter had proved particularly harsh, however, with the ice stubbornly clinging to the passes leading up into the Elovian Mountains. When Arkan Sula arrived back in Helgos in the spring to collect Crepicella, the Helgoan Burgher explained how Crepicella and her sisters had gone for a walk in the forest and had failed to return. He and the other Helgoan men had helped the gypsies search for the girls. After three weeks of frantic searching, the grief-stricken gypsies had packed up their belongings and left the valley.

By the time Arkan Sula arrived in Helgos to deliver the Helgoans from their despair, however, several of their children had been snatched from their beds. As they had with the missing sisters, the Helgoans had left no blade of grass unturned but had found no trace of any of their children.

Many Helgoans were dying of starvation, so Arkan Sula weaved a charm to revitalize the forests, re-fertilize the soil, as well as replenish the lakes, rivers, and streams. The Elkai then weaved a revelation charm to try and locate the missing children. The charm had led the Elkai to a fissure in the earth deep within the forest. The fissure led down to a vast warren of caves. Arkan Sula found the grisly remains of those missing Helgoan children strewn before a crude effigy carved into the rock. It was an effigy of Evora, the Serpent Queen.

"And it was the work of the Sister Witches?" Lucian asked once the Xaviers had finished their grim tale.

"Crepicella and her sisters had discovered the opening leading down into the caves," Varos said. "Rather than learn at Sula's hand, Crepicella chose instead to channel her powers in homage to Evora, the Serpent Queen. She also trained her sisters in the Dark

Arts. But Crepicella's powers were no match for those of the Elkai, Xavius be praised."

"What charm did the Elkai conjure?" Lucian asked.

"Sula has never spoken about what happened in Helgos, not even to us," Varos replied. "But I should imagine his fury was unbridled that day."

****

Lucian and the Xaviers had made camp beside a fast-flowing stream on a rise overlooking a sweeping valley. At first light, they would follow the stream to where it met the River Misal on the Belanese border before then riding to Helgos.

Lucian's whole body was aching like never before. The Xaviers, however, were showing little sign of fatigue. Avicus had again pressed riding through the night, but Varos's reasoning that they rest the horses had thankfully prevailed. The five were sat huddled about a campfire, each seemingly lost in their own thoughts while the dripping fat from the spitted wild hare hissed and spat within the dancing flames.

Although utterly exhausted, the thought of the Sister Witches possessing powers sufficient to lift Arkan Sula's charms nagged at Lucian like a cracked tooth. "Do you think it possible Crepicella could have reversed whatever charm Arkan Sula placed on her and her sisters?" he asked Varos.

Varos sat staring into the fire for several heartbeats. "I don't mind admitting I'm struggling to comprehend how the sisters could have done so. But ever since you relayed Sula's message about Torian being in Helgos, I have struggled to conjure up any other reason why he would think to venture into Helgos."

"I don't know about you, brother—" Kadian

paused to give the spitted hare a turn, "—but I for one would rather face a dozen Talveks than fight sorcery." As with Raynor, Kadian had trimmed his hair and scraped the beard from his face.

"Speaking of the Talvek, you and Raynor still haven't told us how you came to in the Labyrinth...?" Avicus said, arching an eyebrow at Kadian.

"We were passing through the Valley of Kamer when we happened upon a caravan of merchants making for Belanos," Kadian explained. "It was they who alerted us to plague having broken out in Abador. They also told us of the people's anger at Arkan Sula's prolonged absence from the city."

"The merchants invited us into their camp for the night," Raynor said, picking up the tale. "At some point, the conversation turned to the legend surrounding the Spear of Lixivior, so we began to wonder if the Elkai might have entered the Labyrinth in search of the Spear."

"But you know as well as I, brother, that Sula seeks Prince Ærin," Varos said. "And he'd have hardly expected to find Rhödos' edling wandering around the Labyrinth."

"Nor was he likely to find the boy sheltering in Helgos, either," Avicus added.

Lucian was desperate to ask the Xaviers all they knew about Prince Ærin. Much to his chagrin, the conversation came back to the Sister Witches. He'd barely been able to wrench his gaze from the spitted hare, and yet all this talk of the Sister Witches being able to counter Arkan Sula's charms was playing havoc with his appetite.

"The only reason Torian could have for venturing

into Helgos was because he learned Crepicella and her sisters were once more abroad and thought he might locate the Elkai in Helgos," Varos offered.

"I mean no disrespect," Kadian said, glancing to Lucian as he spoke, "but why is Sula choosing to channel his energies through a mere youth instead of visiting with us in person?"

"It may be he's choosing our successors." Varos chuckled, reached for his water flask. He took a long draft and cuffed his lips with the back of his hand before handing the flask to Lucian. "We're not immortal—despite tales to the contrary."

"Speak for yourself, brother," Kadian said, grinning.

"One might as well try counting the stars in the night sky as try understanding the Elkai's motives," Avicus said. "All that matters is that he is with us. If only in spirit," he added, glancing to Lucian.

Lucian was suddenly struck by how Avicus's eyes changed color, depending on his mood. He'd thought them hard cobalt, but in the firelight, they now appeared a soft bluish-gray.

"If Sula were here now, I should imagine he'd explain how your being at the cove that day was preordained," Raynor said to Lucian. "The Elkai insists all our destinies are as inevitable as night following day. He believes the attack on Rhödos' stronghold to be the will of the gods; that it was predetermined that Prince Ærin should one day rule Varnia."

"Lucian's being at the cove was preordained," said Varos. "I was making for Abador when Sula spoke to me in a dream. He told me to watch out for a lad of sixteen or seventeen summers with hair as fair as the sun."

Lucian allowed his mind drifted back to that fateful day at the cove. "Do you think Arkan Sula was the hare that led Lykka into the Sucking-sands?" he asked, running a hand over the wolf's pelt.

"I wouldn't argue against it," Varos said. "I remember Sula telling me how he weaved a shape-shifting charm so that he could be on hand to ensure Prince Ærin escaped the slaughter."

"By my reckoning, Prince Ærin will be approaching the age of maturity and could challenge Agnar for the Wulvranship," Raynor offered.

Varos leaned forward and poked the spitted hare with the tip of his dagger. Satisfied the meat was ready, he slipped the hare from the spit and hurriedly set about carving the meat into five portions before casually tossing the carcass to Lykka. "But satisfying the Varnian chieftains that the lad truly is Ærin, son of Rhödos won't be easy," he said.

Silence reigned while the hare was consumed. Lucian was fishing a piece of gristle from between his teeth when Sula's voice sounded.

"To reach Helgos, you must cross the Eramian."

"What is it, lad?" Kadian asked on seeing Lucian's eyes glaze over.

"I'd say Sula is with us," Varos said.

"It was Arkan Sula," Lucian replied. "We must cross the Eramian Wasteland to reach Helgos."

"But that makes no sense!" Kadian said. "If every hour counts, why would the Elkai have us cross the Eramian? It would add at least another day's ride to our journey."

"Don't spear the messenger, brother," Varos said,

mock-throwing up his hands. "The Elkai has spoken, and we dare not heed his words. What are you thinking?" he asked Avicus.

Avicus got to his feet before responding. "I think we should get some sleep. It would appear we have an even more arduous day's ride ahead of us."

Chapter Eleven

The Riddle of the Sands

Lucian sat up in the saddle and shielded his eyes against the sun's reflected glare on the undulating sands. Avicus was some distance ahead of Raynor and Kadian, with Varos bringing up the rear. Lucian had only traversed the Eramian's outer fringes while traveling from his village to Abador. That had been arduous enough, but this heat was infinitely more oppressive. Even the buzzards that had tracked them for most of the morning had disappeared from the skies.

He'd filled the flask before setting out that morning, and yet it was now less than a third full. For a heartbeat, he considered holding off, but the temptation proved too much. He plucked the flask from his saddlebag and felt a slight shudder as the cool water splashed his parched throat. After rinsing his mouth, he spat the water into his hand and wiped the sand caking the corners of his eyes. Slipping from his saddle, he tipped water into his cupped hand for Lykka before splashing more onto a rag for Kia.

Lucian was clambering back up onto Kia's back when Raynor shouted out that Avicus was signaling.

"Let's hope for your sake Avicus has happened upon a watering hole," Varos mock-chided Lucian.

The urge to spur Kia on in the hope of Avicus

having come upon a watering hole was momentarily all-consuming. Seeing Varos and the other Xaviers maintaining the same lumbering pace checked the impulse, however. Lucian could only suppose persevering on limited water was a prerequisite of a Xavier knight.

Lucian wasn't sure whether Varos was being serious when he'd suggested Arkan Sula was channeling his energies through him because he was looking for potential future Xaviers, yet the more he thought about it, the more he thought it plausible. After all, the Xaviers were mortal, and their capabilities would diminish over time. The question he'd repeatedly asked himself ever since Varos's comment, of course, was whether he considered himself capable of becoming a Xavier. He'd certainly fantasized about becoming a Xavier often enough, and the courage he'd displayed of late would surely stand him in good stead. He was pondering which of the seven ordeals Arkan Sula had set for the Xavier inductees when Kadian's excited cry wrenched him back to reality.

Cresting the dune where the Xaviers were gathered, Lucian felt his stomach spasm as he gazed upon the tree-lined spring nestled within the shade of a rocky outcrop some two hundred yards ahead. He could hardly contain his giddiness. His only thought was to race to the inviting hole and throw himself headlong into the cool water.

"It looks deserted if you'll excuse the jest," Varos said.

"Only one way to find out, brothers," Kadian added. He gave an exhilarating whoop before charging down the rise at a gallop. "Last one there's a disease-ridden Black Crow!" he shouted over his shoulder.

Lucian needed no further bidding and spurred Kia toward the spring, laughing on seeing Lykka giving chase after Kadian in the race to the watering hole. Without bothering to bring Kia to a halt, he leaped from the saddle some thirty feet from the spring. He was puzzled why Kadian was making his way around the watering hole instead of throwing himself into the inviting water. It was only as he drew nearer to the hole that he understood why. Suspended within the trees were three large dome-shaped cages, two of which, he realized to his horror, were occupied despite the doors hanging open.

The ragged figures appeared lifeless, and Lucian feared them dead.

Kadian was almost at the cages when he suddenly became animated. "It's Yanek, brothers!" he shouted.

Avicus, Varos, and Raynor came galloping past Lucian, leaping from their saddles in their haste to reach Yanek. Lucian now understood why Arkan Sula had said they should cross the Eramian. The Elkai had known Yanek was here at the watering hole yet had said nothing as to his plight. How long had he and the other poor soul been out here? Why were they in the cages? Although the cages offered some protection from the sun, they were made of iron.

Yanek had to be suffering from some malady of the mind, for he was feebly fending off Kadian's attempts to pass him his water flask.

Raynor had noticed the other wretch was stirring. "By Xavius's beard!" he yelled. "It's Jarl Laurik!"

Lucian had never heard of Jarl Laurik, but he could see he was suffering from whatever malady was affecting Yanek for on seeing Raynor he'd scrabbled to the rear of the cage, gripping the rusted bars while muttering incoherently.

Snatching his water flask from the saddle, Lucian rushed to join Varos at the water's edge. "What ails them?" he asked the Xavier. "Have their minds been addled by the sun?"

Varos plucked the flasks from the water and got to his feet. "Your guess is as good as mine," he said, dashing back to the cages.

Varos was having no more luck in getting Yanek and Jarl Laurik to take the flasks, however. Now that he was at the cages, Lucian could see the haunted look in both men's eyes.

Varos's frustrations were mounting. Casting the flask aside, he reached into the cage and grabbed Yanek by the ankle. To Lucian's astonishment, Yanek, summoning what strength he had, lashed out at Varos with his other foot. "Leave here, brother!" he shrieked. "Leave before it's too late!"

Raynor took Lucian's water flask. "This malady is unlike anything I've seen," he said, pulling the stopper free and raising the flask to his lips.

Seeing Raynor taking a drink, Jarl Laurik scrabbled across his cage. "Noooo!"

Raynor was still slaking his thirst when Lucian espied a squat, gaudily dressed dark-skinned fellow mounted on a camel emerged from behind the outcrop. As he drew nearer, Lucian saw his parasol was made up of badly woven tree fronds.

"Who in the name of Valkyar is this?" Avicus asked no one in particular.

The interloper reined in his camel and counted

each of them off with his fingers. "You four may leave," he said matter-of-factly, pointing to Avicus, Varos, Kadian, and Lucian in turn. "But you"—he jabbed a finger at Raynor— "must go into the remaining cage, for you have drunk from my master's spring."

"We're leaving all right," Avicus retorted, striding toward the interloper. "All of us."

"Those men will remain where they reside," the interloper announced while making an exaggerated show of adjusting his colored silk robe about his grotesque belly. "I say again, all of you are free to leave here except for you," he said, looking at Raynor. "If you wish to leave with your companions, then you must first solve the riddle of the sands."

Varos came to join Avicus. "Who is to stop us?" he said, his tone brimming with menace. "You?"

The interloper remained unflustered. "You would be wise not to incur the master's wrath, my friend."

Varos came around Avicus. "Why you—"

Lucian thought he saw the sands surrounding the watering hole ripple as though something was lurking just beneath the surface.

Lucian hurriedly stepped in front of Varos. "Who are you?" he interjected. "And where is your master so we might reason with him?"

The interloper studied Lucian through one of the gaps in his parasol. "My name is Sulam, child," he said dismissively. "And I guard this spring on behalf of the master. I say again," he told Raynor, "if you wish to leave with your companions, then you must solve the riddle of the sands."

"We care nothing for your riddle, fat man," Kadian

retorted. "And I assure you we are all leaving here together."

Lucian saw that the sands surrounding the watering hole were rippling again. Something was moving about under the surface.

Sulam peered up at the sky through the fronds of his parasol before responding. "The courage of the Xavier knights is legendary throughout the whole of Kracia," he said, "but you—"

Avicus glanced to Varos. "How do you know we are Xaviers?" he asked

Sulam glanced up at the sky again. "Because the master was told of your coming."

Following Sulam's gaze, Lucian saw the raven circling high overhead. He was distracted by a sudden splash. Lykka was splashing about the watering hole.

"The master doesn't distinguish between those with two legs or four." Sulam chuckled, eyeing Lykka. "And he is fully conversant in wolf."

In that same instant, Arkan Sula's voice sounded.

"*It's the Gogolah!*"

Lucian saw the sands surrounding the watering hole were rippling again, only this time more forcibly. The Xaviers were also aware of what was occurring.

Sulam was almost thrown from the camel's back as a swirling vortex of sand shot up into the air encircling the watering hole. "You have your wish, Xaviers," he shrieked. "For the master is here."

Lucian instinctively jumped into the water to grab hold of Lykka as an eerie whooshing sounded. The sands surrounding the watering hole receded, revealing two dozen or so sun-blanched human skulls.

Two watchful eyes formed within the iridescent

sands.

****

All was silent again. Seeing the Xaviers had retreated toward the cages, Lucian scrambled out of the water to join them. Lykka, however, remained in the water, seemingly undaunted by the Gogolah.

Sulam goaded his camel toward the cages. "The master says none of you may leave unless you solve the riddle of the sands. Would you care to hear the riddle?"

"We have no time for riddles, for we are engaged on a quest," Varos said defiantly. "That is why we are crossing the Eramian."

Sulam theatrically cocked an ear toward the Gogolah. "The master cares nothing of your quest, Xavier," he sneered. "Shall I recite the riddle?"

Avicus took a step toward Sulam but kept his gaze on the Gogolah. "We are soul-sworn to Arkan Sula. It is the Elkai who has charged us with our quest. He speaks to us through the lad here," he added, indicating to Lucian. "We are making for the Land of Helgos in search of our brother, Torian. Sula knew that Yanek was being held here."

Sulam cocked his head to one side, occasionally nodding as though taking instruction from the |Gogolah. "The master knows of Arkan Sula," he said at last. "He will therefore strike an accord with you, Xaviers. If you solve the riddle of the sands, you will be free to continue on your way. But for your comrades to go free, you must set me a riddle. Should I solve your riddle, however, the boy and his wolf must remain."

"Agreed," Lucian said before any of the Xaviers had the chance to respond. "Without Torian the 'Circle of Seven' can never be whole," he said to Avicus. He then turned to Sulam. "Let's hear your infernal riddle."

Sulam closed his eyes and steepled his fingers. "I have seas with no waters and coasts with no sand. I have cities without people and mountains without land." He opened his eyes again. "So, what am I?"

"A sea of desert has no water," Kadian offered. "They have watering holes obviously," he added, his voice trailing off.

"I know of coastlines that have shingle instead of sand," said Raynor.

"You're thinking too logically," Lucian said irritably. "Riddle-solving calls for imagination."

"Arkan Sula didn't think to set riddle-solving as one of the seven ordeals," Varos said sullenly.

Lucian closed his eyes to focus his concentration. "The seas, coasts, cities, and mountains within the riddle don't exist in a real sense," he said, more to himself than anyone else.

"You must give your answer," Sulam shouted. "The master is growing impatient."

Lucian shut Sulam, the Gogolah, and everything else from his mind. "If the seas, coasts, cities, and mountains within the riddle don't exist in a real sense, we must…" he suddenly fell silent. "The answer is 'chart,' " he said. "For a chart details seas, coasts, cities, and mountains and yet has no need of water, sand, people or land."

Sulam looked most put out. "You are to be congratulated, child," he said haughtily. "But now you must set me a riddle." He smiled coldly. "And I warn you, child, I am as skilled in solving riddles as I am in setting them."

Arkan Sula's voice sounded.

"*Not as skilled as I, my friend!*"

Varos saw a smile spreading across Lucian's face. "You have one, don't you?" he grinned.

"*I am possessed of a halo of water and walls of stone.*"

"I am possessed of a halo of water and walls of stone," Lucian repeated.

"*I have a tongue of wood, and long I have stood.*"

Lucian's smile grew ever-wider, for he knew the answer. "I have a tongue of wood, and long have I stood.... What am I?"

"Is that the best you can do, child?" Sulam scoffed.

"If the answer is so easy, then why do you delay in answering?" Varos snapped.

"Get used to your new home, child," Sulam crowed. "The answer to your pathetic riddle is 'castle.' Castles are possessed of a halo of water, walls of stone, and a tongue of wood."

Lucian glanced from one Xavier to the other, savoring the moment. "You are correct in what you say, Sulam," he said at last. "A castle does indeed possess a halo of water, walls of stone, and a tongue of wood. But the answer I required"—he turned his gaze to the Gogolah—"is 'Abador.' For not all castles are built of stone..."

"Of course, all castles are built of stone," Sulam said indignantly.

"Abador's coastline is pitted with abandoned moat and bailey castles made of earthworks and wood," Lucian continued as though Sulam hadn't spoken.

The eyes within the sand narrowed as though the Gogolah was deep in thought. The eyes suddenly widened again and fixed on Sulam.

"No, master!" Sulam shrieked as a spume of sand shot out, toppling him from the camel. He was still pleading as a widening maw appeared within the sand and swallowed him up before collapsing to leave an eerie silence about the watering hole.

****

On leaving the Eramian Wasteland, Lucian and the Xaviers continued through the night until arriving at a defile bordering the land of Helgos. On making camp by a wellspring, Avicus, Kadian, and Raynor had ventured out in search of their supper. Lucian was sitting by the fire with Lykka. Yanek and Jarl Laurik were sound asleep while Varos was resting against a tree lazily scraping at his throat with his dagger.

With Varnia lying far beyond the Carpasian Mountains, Jarl Laurik was the first Huskenbach Lucian had knowingly met. He'd been surprised to learn the Jarl was Rhödos' brother-in-law.

Though Abador and Varnia had a checkered history in recent times, Lucian could see the Huskenbachs weren't all that different in appearance to Abadorians. Jarl Laurik's skin was ruddier, but Lucian supposed this was due to Varnia's bracing mountain air. He was also fair of hair. Many of the people in his village, including himself, were also fair-haired. But this was perhaps to be expected with Kalimar lying close to Varnia's southeastern border.

The Huskenbachs worshipped the same gods. They also believed a warrior had to die sword in hand so he could pass through Galdoch's Cave and take their place in the Great Feasting Hall on Mount Herros. Should a warrior meet his end without a sword in his hand, his soul would be cursed to wander Geshena, an otherworldly purgatory, never to be given another body and return to the sunlit world.

Lucian imagined the souls of Huskenbach women, children, and all those who lived their lives without ever wielding a sword in anger, also went to the place known as the Asphodel Meadows. He was suddenly struck with an image of Prince Tarvel standing within a flower-filled glade. Remembering Avicus's assessment of the prince's dynastic failings, he felt compelled to ask Varos whether he was of a similar opinion.

Varos paused to wipe the blade against his trews. "It's impossible to say whether he would have made a good king," he said. "But I don't think I would be doing Tarvel's memory disservice in saying he showed more zeal for poetry than he ever did politics."

Lucian saw that Yanek and Jarl Laurik were stirring. "What about Princess Rhiana?" he asked, turning to face Varos again. "Do you think she'll make a good Queen?"

"There's no arguing her stubbornness is matched only by her beauty," Varos said. "And she has a quickness of tongue that would bring trouble raining down upon her pretty little head were it not for who she is."

Lucian was taken aback at such forthrightness. "You shouldn't speak of Her Royal Highness like that," he spluttered.

"Hear that, brother?" Varos called across to Yanek. "Sounds like Lucian's fallen for our future Queen."

Lucian felt his cheeks flush but thought better of responding on seeing Avicus, Kadian, and Raynor returning with their arms laden with horse mushrooms.

Varos got to his feet and came around Lucian. "Is

this all you could find, brothers?"

Raynor dumped his mushrooms by the fire. "If you find so much as a tree frog in there," he retorted, gesturing toward the trees, "I'll go in search of Torian single-handedly."

Kadian added his mushrooms to the pile. "I, for one, would prefer an evening free from talk of what awaits us come tomorrow," he said with a wistful smile.

Lucian offered to gather more kindling for the fire.

He knew Varos had only been speaking in jest, but for reasons he couldn't explain, his feeling for Princess Rhiana went beyond simply snatching her from the Galyaks. He'd even allowed himself to believe King Ocwan would be so overjoyed in his daughter's safe return he'd offer him her hand in marriage. He knew it was absurd, of course, and that's why Varos's words had stung him so.

Suddenly sensing he wasn't alone, Lucian glanced up, expecting it to be Varos. To his astonishment, it was Jarl Laurik. He knew the Huskenbachs revered the wolf above all other creatures, so wasn't overly surprised when Jarl Laurik appeared more interested in Lykka than helping collect firewood. The jarl's words certainly took him unawares, however.

"Would you consider selling Lykka?" Laurik asked.

"I—I couldn't possibly sell Lykka," Lucian spluttered.

"A trade then…?" Laurik pressed. "I have many fine horses."

Another Huskenbach trait Lucian had come to recognize through witnessing Jarl Laurik's interaction with the Xaviers was their straightforwardness.

Whereas Abadorians tended to couch their words, always skirting for maneuver, the Huskenbachs just cut right to the heart of the matter.

Lucian gathered up the few twigs he'd amassed. "I'm sorry, Jarl Laurik," he said, setting off through the trees at a brisk pace, "but parting with Lykka is unthinkable."

Jarl Laurik remained undeterred, however. "I do not wish Lykka for myself," he said, keeping pace with Lucian. "I would make a gift of him to my nephew, Varnia's rightful Wulvran, upon his return to his people."

This, unsurprisingly, brought all activity within the camp to a standstill.

"You have proof that your nephew lives, my prince?" Avicus asked.

Yanek got to his feet. "It might be best if I explain, my prince," he said.

All eyes turned to Yanek.

Yanek was olive-skinned. He had a lean, angular face and watchful eyes. What struck Lucian most about Yanek was the gap between his front teeth. He remembered his grandmother saying those born with such a gap were favored by the gods.

"I was in the port of Alezzi looking to book passage on any merchant ship bound for Brogia," Yanek explained.

"What in Xavius's beard were you doing in Alezzi?" Raynor asked. "You're lucky you still have a throat in need of scraping."

"My skin goes unnoticed there." Yanek smiled wanly. "I heard a whisper Arkan Sula had been seen in Brogia and thought I should at least look into it.

Anyway, while in Alezzi I got into conversation with the landlord at one of the taverns. He was as drunk as his customers and loose with his tongue. He spoke of overhearing two Brogian merchants discussing Jarl Thordol Forkbeard having delivered Prince Ærin to Agnar."

"Agnar made a pact with Thordol Forkbeard to down an uprising among the northern clans," Jarl Laurik revealed. "Those northern clans are still loyal to Rhödos' memory."

Lucian shuddered at the mention of Thordol Forkbeard, for he was Wulvran of Ardassia, and his father, of course, had died defending their village during an Ardassian raid.

The Ardassians were a feral seafaring race from the Iscatian Ice Lands beyond the Polaric Sea. They had once occupied much of modern-day Varnia. Indeed, with Varnia's Outer Islands being located closer to the Ice Lands than the Varnian mainland, those clans spoke in a tongue that was an amalgam of Ardassian and Huskenbach.

It was Agnar's being the supreme chieftain of the Outer Island clans that had allowed him to seize the Wulvranship.

"It might have been nothing more than a drunken landlord's tale, brother," Yanek conceded. "But I thought it worthy of pursuing. I managed to book passage on a ship bound for Varnia. It was Jarl Laurik who told me that we'd been proclaimed traitors by our Lord King."

"But even if the story is true, Prince Ærin is surely dead," Varos said.

"There is a rumor on the wind that Agnar is having

to keep my nephew alive on the orders of Lord Nikobar," Jarl Laurik said.

"What I wouldn't give to know his schemes," Avicus growled.

"If I can find my nephew and return him to his people, the mainland clans will rise against Agnar," Jarl Laurik continued. "Yanek and I were traveling to speak with the chieftains of the northern clans when we were ambushed by a band of brigands while traversing in the Lutniga Pass."

"That's how we ended up in the Eramian," Yanek said.

"The swine murdered my men," Jarl Laurik said somberly. "I swear on all I hold sacred that I will have my revenge on them. If not in this world, then the next."

"Was one of the brigands missing an eye?" Lucian asked.

Yanek paused. "Yes, I remember him vividly. And I hope to meet him again."

"Then you'll need to enter Orbelium, brother," Varos said.

"He was one of Nikobar's Valessian mercenaries," Lucian added.

"May Xavius guide your hand, my prince," Avicus said. "If we weren't otherwise engaged, we would help you in your quest."

Yanek got to his feet. "I'm not otherwise engaged."

"What are you saying?" Avicus challenged.

"I'm saying that with Ocwan having proclaimed us traitors, I have released myself from all obligations to Abador," Janek replied coldly.

"But you are soul-sworn to Arkan Sula," Varos

said. "And you are sworn to us and our brothers Torian and Èinor."

"And where is Sula?" Yanek retorted. "We are nothing but throw-pieces in the Elkai's games."

"The Elkai is with us, Yanek," Varos said. "He speaks to us through Lucian. It was he who guided us to the watering hole."

"We know not yet what has become of Èinor," Raynor said, "but our brother, Torian, is here in Helgos."

"We fear the Sister Witches have returned to the sunlit world," Varos added.

"What does that say of the mighty Elkai's powers," Yanek sneered.

"You would be wise to curb your tongue," Avicus said sharply. "For Sula is truly with us."

"It was Sula who told Lucian that Raynor and I were lost within the Labyrinth at Kamar," Torian said.

This caught Yanek off-guard. "What in the name of Valkyar possessed you to enter the Labyrinth?"

"We went in search of Sula," Raynor said sheepishly.

"And I suspect it was learning the Sister Witches were abroad again that lured Torian here in the hope of finding the Elkai," Kadian offered.

Yanek turned to Lucian. "If Sula is here, then have him give us a sign."

"That's not the Elkai's way as you well know, brother," Varos said wearily.

"Or is it that you're afraid to face Nikobar?" Avicus cut in.

"Your mind games are wasted on me, Avicus," Yanek said coldly. "I'd enter Orbelium itself if I thought Sula was in there. As I would for any of you."

"I don't know why the Elkai is choosing to operate from within the shadows," Avicus said. "But how will you feel when the time comes for you to pass through Galdoch's Cave, knowing you left your brothers in their most trying hour of need?"

Chapter Twelve

Evil in Helgos

Jarl Laurik had bid farewell to Lucian and the Xaviers on their breaking camp soon after first light. The Huskenbach chieftain understood the Xaviers' quest to rescue Princess Rhiana was as important as his own and had assured them he'd do all he could to avert a war between Varnia and Abador. Raynor had gifted Jarl Laurik Adhara to speed him on his journey.

Lucian had suffered a restless night as he'd been unable to rid his mind of the Sister Witches being abroad again in Helgos. It had been a cloudless night, and it seemed the Draconis Constellation was silently mocking his agitation. He hadn't been alone in his unease, however. On waking and seeing Kadian sat staring into the flames, seemingly lost in his own tormented thoughts, Lucian had joined him by the fire. Remembering Varos saying how Kadian had served in the Centaurian Guard before becoming a Xavier knight, they'd talked about the battle of Zylos, the Xavier ordeals.

Lucian had naturally been curious about Yanek. He'd suspected Yanek was of mixed race, of course, but had been astounded to learn he had Galyak blood owing to his mother having been snatched during a raid on his people's village and taken into slavery. Kadian had gone on to explain that while Yanek's hot-headedness drove him and the other Xaviers to distraction, there was no one he'd rather have at his side in a do-or-die situation. Although Avicus was the most skilled of the Xaviers, Yanek was the absolute warrior.

Having eaten his fair share of horse mushrooms, Lucian hadn't given much thought to the forests being devoid of life. It wasn't until he and the Xaviers had crested a rise and caught sight of the crumbling steeples and collapsed roofs of the abandoned township of Helgos that he'd grasped the enormity of the evil they faced. Everything he had seen since entering the forest was evidence enough that Crepicella and her sisters had indeed found a way to break free of Arkan Sula's charm.

They'd continued through the forest in silence. The wizened trees were denuded, and yet the woodland was so dense in places they had to advance in single file.

Lucian was exhausted. So much so he found himself dozing in the saddle. He almost paid for his lethargy in being unsaddled by a low-hanging branch. He'd been jolted awake by a familiar fluttering sound. In that same instant, he realized to his horror that he was utterly alone. Lykka and the five Xaviers were nowhere to be seen.

Lucian was scanning the surrounding forest, calling out each Xavier's name in turn, when a frenzied yowling erupted somewhere behind him. Lykka was in pain. He was wheeling Kia about when the filly reared up, throwing him from his saddle. He was scrambling to his feet when he saw snaking tendrils of mist drifting through the trees enveloping the forest. He could hear nothing but the sound of his heart hammering inside his chest but immediately sensed he wasn't alone. Someone or something was moving within the mist-shrouded trees.

He was slipping the slingshot from his jerkin when a sharp snap sounded. He was trying to source from which direction the snapping came when the mist suddenly evaporated, and he caught sight of a shadowy shape moving within the trees. He dropped to a crouch, frantically scanning the blackened ground for something he might use as a pellet. A sickening stench suddenly filled the air. Wheeling round, he caught sight of a hooded robe before his world dimmed, and he slumped silently to the ground.

****

Lucian woke to find himself lying spread-eagled within a crudely etched pentagram with candles mounted at each of its five points. He instinctively knew that he was in the Sister Witches' lair. As his eyes became accustomed to the gloom, he saw a stone altar beyond which an effigy of Evora loomed in the shadows. Craning his neck, he could make out the Serpent Queen seated upon a throne in the shape of a coiled serpent, the serpent's head rearing up behind Evora to form the throne's backrest.

There were no restraints about Lucian's wrists or ankles, and yet he found he couldn't move either his arms or legs. He was struggling against these otherworldly bonds when the rancid stench he remembered from the forest returned. He was suddenly aware he wasn't alone. Craning his neck again, he saw a figure cloaked in a heavy robe shuffling toward him. Was this Crepicella or one of her sisters? The robed figure continued past the altar and genuflected before the effigy, muttering an incantation. On finishing the indecipherable liturgy, the robed figure got to its feet again and turned toward Lucian.

Lucian lay still, pretending to be unconscious, as the robed figure got down on its knees beside the pentagram and slowly drew back its hood. "I know you are awake, Man-child," Crepicella cooed, tenderly brushing a strand of hair from Lucian's face.

Arkan Sula had weaved a decaying charm that had slowly eaten away at the witches' flesh. Although Crepicella had conjured a charm to stem the decay, reversing the Elkai's charm was as yet beyond her powers. Her parchment-like skin was split, revealing putrid flesh. One of her eyes was missing, the blackened socket a running sore. Her remaining eye was as sharp as a winter's frost, however.

"Open your eyes, Man-Child." Crepicella grabbed a lock of Lucian's hair and yanked it tight, causing him to cry out.

"Ahh, such beautiful eyes," Crepicella croaked while tracing a finger around Lucian's right eye. "Perhaps I should take one for myself and feed the other to our black-feathered friend...?"

Managing to tear his gaze from the nightmare of Crepicella's ravaged face, Lucian saw the raven sat perched on Evora's shoulder. A searing pain erupted behind his eyes, and he cried out in agony. He thought his eyeballs would explode, but the pain suddenly melted away again.

"If you wish to keep those pretty eyes, you will tell me of the Xaviers' intentions, Man-child," Crepicella said.

"I know nothing of any Xaviers," Lucian

responded. "I was making for—"

"You think me an imbecile, Man-child!" Crepicella shrieked. She pointed a putrefied finger to the cave wall where an image was slowly forming within the rock. Lucian saw himself and the Xaviers advancing through the forest.

"Why have the Xaviers come to Helgos, Man-child?" Crepicella asked as the image faded. "Do they come in search of their comrade?" she cackled as a second image began forming within the rock to show a rider Lucian assumed to be Torian making his way across a dried-out riverbed. "But why have the Xaviers come for him…To become seven again?"

Lucian was aware of two hunched figures wrapped in robes identical to Crepicella's. "My sisters and I do so enjoy company, Man-child. We look forward to entertaining the Xaviers should they be foolish enough to enter the Serpent Queen's domain."

"And if you wish to save yourselves from Arkan Sula's wrath, you and your sisters should release Torian and—"

"So you can save Abador, Man-child?" Crepicella asked, glancing over to the raven again. "Is that why the Xaviers need to be seven?"

"The Xaviers will never be seven, Man-child." Gastrula cackled, revealing a blackened mouth. "For one of their number is here and shall remain here as our plaything."

"And what do you intend for me?" Lucian asked, mustering as much defiance he could.

"You, Man-child?" Crepicella smiled. "You are a most unexpected boon."

"Allow me the honor of draining the Man-child,

sister dear," Grockle rasped.

"No!" Gastrula whined. "Our sister promised me the honor."

"Silence!" Crepicella shrieked, causing Gastrula and Grockle to shy away.

Crepicella got to her feet and shuffled toward the altar, where she raised her arms aloft while uttering another incantation. As the witch droned on with her invocation, Lucian slowly lifted from the floor until he was suspended in mid-air as though held by invisible hands.

Grockle joined Crepicella at the altar and added her rasping tone to the enchantment. Gastrula grabbed up a rusting chalice and placed it at the pentagram's center directly below Lucian before shuffling to the altar and joining in with the diabolic incantation.

Crepicella picked up a ceremonial dagger from the altar and shuffled toward the pentagram flanked by Gastrula and Grockle. She held the tip of the dagger to Lucian's forehead and slowly traced it down between his eyes and across the bridge of his upturned nose. "Our mistress has decreed the Xavier in our possession shall have the honor of performing the ceremony, Man-child," she said, bringing the tip of the dagger to rest on Lucian's exposed throat. "Step forward from the shadows, Xavier knight," she shouted.

Lucian watched a lengthening shadow moving slowly across the cave floor until Torian came into view. "Your fellow Xaviers are here in Helgos, Torian," he shouted.

"Hush, Man-child." Crepicella chuckled as Torian came trance-like toward the pentagram. "The Xavier cannot hear you." She held out the ceremonial dagger.

"Come, sir knight, take the dagger," she commanded.

Torian stepped toward Crepicella. He was reaching for the dagger when Avicus' booming voice reverberated about the chamber.

****

Lucian twisted round and saw Avicus and the other Xaviers striding into the cave. Gastrula and Grockle shrank away hissing and spitting curses at the Xaviers, but Crepicella paid them little heed. "Take the dagger, Xavier," she repeated to Torian.

"Torian, it's us, your brothers," Varos shouted.

"Torian is under the witches' sorcery," Lucian warned the knights.

"Hush now, Man-child," Crepicella said before turning her attention to the Xaviers. "Welcome, sir knights."

"We have no quarrel with you, crone," Avicus said, motioning for his fellow Xaviers to halt while continuing toward the pentagram. "Release our brother and the lad, and we shall be on our way."

"You are servants of the Elkai, Xavier," Crepicella screeched. "And that is quarrel enough."

"Arkan Sula has not been seen these many months," Avicus replied, taking another couple of steps toward the pentagram. "We have been proclaimed traitors by His Majesty King Ocwan, so we are outcasts like yourselves."

"You say you are outcasts, sir knight, and yet you ride to save Princess Rhiana," Crepicella countered. She paused to pluck a maggot from her festering cheek and held it to the light before popping it into her lipless maw. "They say the royal princess' beauty matches my own?" she chuckled to herself.

136

"Whoever told you we ride to save Princess Rhiana lies," Avicus said.

"You would be wise to not try my patience, Xavier," Crepicella sneered. "Your comrade here," she cocked her head to Torian, "came to Helgos in search of the Elkai, did he not?"

"That is true," Avicus acknowledged. "But we no longer care what happens to Abador, so give us—"

"I care, sir knight!" Crepicella snapped. "And it pleases us that Abador is set to fall...as will all Kracia. For Asima Na approaches. When the Dragon Lord returns to the sunlit world, He will take Evora as His Queen. And when that happens, sir knight, my sisters and I will scour the earth in search of the Elkai. His soul will be our plaything. And when we tire of tormenting his soul, the Elkai's blood will flow. Do you hear me, Elkai!" she screeched. She fell silent, glancing about the cave's shadowy recesses as though Arkan Sula might materialize. "Now be on your way, Xaviers," she said dismissively. "You are to be commended for finding your way out of the Labyrinth, but you would be wise not to incur my wrath."

"But what if I were to offer you a covenant in return for our brother and the lad, Crepicella?" Avicus said.

Crepicella scrunched her remaining eye at Avicus. "What could you possibly have that is of interest to me, sir knight?"

Avicus took another couple of steps until he was within a few feet of the pentagram. "I know where Arkan Sula might be found," he said, taking yet another step toward the pentagram. "While searching the Elkai's cave within the Elovian Mountains, I happened upon a parchment."

Crepicella turned to the effigy of Evora for several heartbeats before returning her attention to Avicus. "You have my attention, Xavier."

Avicus reached inside his jupon, producing a folded sheet of parchment. "I don't profess to know the meaning of what is written on here," he said, holding the parchment out to Crepicella. "But I recognize the Elkai's hand when I see it."

"Take the parchment from the Xavier, sister," Crepicella told Gastrula. "If the parchment is of use to us, sir knight, we will release your comrade," she said to Avicus.

"The lad also comes with us, Crepicella," Avicus said as Gastrula shuffled toward him.

"The Man-child stays, sir knight," Crepicella said. "Now give the parchment to my sister."

Avicus held the parchment out for Gastrula. As she reached for it, he grabbed her robe and pulled her toward him, wrapped an arm about her throat, and yanked back the cowl.

Gastrula's face was more ravaged than Crepicella's. Her skin was all eaten away, while her nose was nothing but a ragged hole.

"Release them both, Crepicella," Avicus shouted, catching the leather water flask Varos tossed him. Gastrula struggled to wriggle free, so the Xavier tightened his grip and held the flask above her ghastly upturned face. "This is Chaste water from Mount Herros, sanctified by the Goddess Tanitha."

"The Xavier lies, sister," Grockle rasped. "He lies."

"Let's see if I lie," Avicus retorted, tipping the flask closer to Gastrula's face.

"No!" Crepicella shrieked. "I will release them both."

Crepicella's remaining eye burned with hatred as she began intoning another incantation.

Avicus was so focused on Crepicella he didn't spot the raven as it came streaking out of the shadows until the creature was upon him. He involuntarily threw up his arm to beat off the raven. In doing so, he caused some of the water to spill from the flask onto Gastrula's face.

Gastrula let out an ear-splitting screech then fell silent again.

Avicus's bluff had failed.

****

Avicus still had hold of Gastrula. Tossing the flask aside, he forced the witch to her knees, drew his sword, and rested the burnished blade against her neck. "Release our comrade and the lad, Crepicella, or I take your sister's head."

Crepicella stepped toward Torian and held the ceremonial dagger to his throat. "We are at something of a stalemate, sir knight," she said. "You can take our sister's head, just as I could slit your comrade's throat. Time is of no import to us, but every heartbeat is of great magnitude to you Xaviers, for you are on a quest to rescue your precious princess in the hope of saving Abador. And the Man-child is also of great significance," she added, glancing at Lucian. "So, what say I offer you a covenant?"

"What do you propose?"

"If you wish to leave here with your comrade and the Man-child, then one of you must fight your comrade...and it will be a fight to the death," Crepicella said. "What do you say, sir knight?"

"Agreed," Avicus said. "I will fight Torian."

"What are you doing, brother?" Varos gasped, coming across. "You can't fight Torian."

"What choice do we have?" Avicus snapped. "Stand guard over this one," he said, letting go of Gastrula, who hurriedly pulled the cowl over her head.

Crepicella had her head turned to the effigy of Evora. "How do we know you will honor your side of the bargain?" Varos shouted to her.

Crepicella slowly turned to face the Xaviers. "And how do I know you will honor yours?"

"Because we are Xavier knights," Varos retorted

Crepicella fell silent for a few moments. "Then what do you suggest, sir knight?"

"Release the lad from whatever sorcery you are holding him under," Varos said, "and I will release your sister."

Crepicella returned her gaze to Evora's effigy, intoning another incantation. In that same eyeblink, Lucian slowly descended to the floor.

Finding himself free of his ethereal bonds, Lucian sprang to his feet and almost collapsed again as the blood emptied from his head. He waited within the pentagram, watching as Gastrula shuffled over to join Crepicella and Grockle at the altar before sprinting across to the Xaviers. "What's Avicus doing?" he asked Varos. "Is he really going to fight Torian?"

"Avicus only agreed to the fight so as to give us time to think our next move," Varos replied. "Although what that move might be, I have no idea."

Crepicella looked over to where Lucian and the Xaviers were gathered. "Whatever move you make is doomed to failure, sir knight." She cackled as the raven swooped down and came to rest on her shoulder. "Isn't that right, my feathered friend?" she cooed.

"You are forgetting the Elkai watches over us, crone," Avicus said. "Arkan Sula has already proved his powers are greater than yours. When all this is over, he will hunt you and your sisters down and smite you once and for all."

"And we were getting along so nicely." Crepicella cackled. "You would be wise to stay your tongue, sir knight. There are powers at play beyond your comprehension, and the Elkai shall soon know the horrors of Orbelium. And should you prove victorious in your fight today, the powers the Elkai invested in you Xaviers will be forever broken, and your deaths will be bloody. Now, kindly draw your sword, sir knight," she said to Torian.

The trance-like Torian drew his sword and held the blade out for Crepicella.

Crepicella slowly ran a gnarled finger along the blade while muttering an incantation. "These men, your one-time comrades, mean to do me and my sisters harm," she said. "You must kill them all...starting with the one you know as Avicus."

"Kill him!" Gastrula shrieked. "Kill them all!"

Torian saluted the three witches with his sword before slowly turning to face Avicus.

Crepicella and her sisters began chanting in unison, their voices ringing about the chamber: "Kill Avicus! Kill the Xaviers! Kill Avicus! Kill them all!"

Seeing Torian advancing toward him, Avicus adopted a defensive stance.

Torian was being held in a dream state, but there

was nothing sluggish about his movement as he suddenly sprang at Avicus, lunging, cutting, and slashing with his sword.

Avicus expertly parried and sidestepped each blow in turn but was hesitant about going on the attack.

"We must do something." Kadian hissed between his teeth. "Avicus is unsurpassable at swordplay, but he is fighting sorcery here."

"Whatever you suggest, brother," Varos retorted, flinching on seeing Avicus stumble under the force of Torian's latest assault.

Gastrula and Grockle were huddled together within the pentagram now, one crouched behind the other, rocking in unison while continuing their mantra: "Kill Avicus! Kill the Xaviers! Kill them all!"

"We need to distract Crepicella," Raynor offered.

"And how do we do that?" Varos asked, his exasperation mounting.

Sensing the raven was distracted by the fight, Lucian scanned the temple floor. Keeping his eyes on the raven, he surreptitiously set about prizing loose a stone from a crevice with the heel of his boot.

"Avicus can't keep this up for much longer," Varos said as Torian launched another flurry of attacks.

Moving behind Raynor, Lucian sank to one knee, grabbed the stone, and loaded his slingshot. The raven had sensed what Lucian was doing, however, for it launched itself from Crepicella's shoulder. Its agitated caw at least served to distract Crepicella.

Seeing Torian suddenly hesitate as though free of Crepicella's sorcery, Raynor dashed out and hurled his sword at Gastrula, the curved blade slicing through the witch, pinning her to her sister.

Crepicella's tormented shriek reverberated about the temple as Gastrula and Grockle slumped to the floor as one, their blood slowly pooling within the pentagram. Turning to Evora's effigy, the witch began mouthing another incantation.

An eerie grinding noise sounded about the chamber, faint at first but slowly getting ever louder. As Evora's effigy slowly came to life, the serpents serving as her crown dropped to the floor.

Lucian stood transfixed on seeing Evora open her slit-yellow eyes and fix him with her gaze.

Kadian charged toward Lucian. "Don't look into her eyes!"

The Xavier's warning came too late, however. For Lucian was engrossed by the Serpent Queen's reptilian gaze.

The serpents were almost upon Lucian when Arkan Sula's voice sounded.

"The water is now Chaste, Lucian!"

Hearing the Elkai wrenched Lucian from his torpor.

Keeping his eyes riveted to the floor, Lucian was reaching for the water flask when one of the serpents lunged at Kadian, sinking its fangs into his calf.

Seeing the other serpents closing in Kadian, Lucian flung the flask at Evora.

A blinding flash illuminated the cave as the Serpent Queen and her children were returned to stone.

Chapter Thirteen

The Rock of Galtar

On emerging from what Lucian fervently prayed would remain the Sister Witches' subterranean sepulcher for all eternity, he and the Xaviers had ridden into the setting sun until the Land of Helgos was far behind them.

Torian appeared none the worse from his ordeal at the hands of the Sister Witches. Indeed, the Xavier had been more concerned about the whereabouts of his horse. Thankfully, his fellow knights had happened upon Mirach grazing with Kia while Lykka guided them to the opening leading into the cave network. Lucian could only suppose Lykka had picked up his scent.

The same could not be said for Kadian, however. The Xaviers had done what they could for him at the temple, but the flesh surrounding the ragged puncture wounds was still swollen and had now turned an ugly black. Avicus had since applied a tourniquet, but Lucian was fearful all the same. Even if they could get Kadian to an apothecary, what possible use would earthly medicines and potions be against the serpents' otherworldly poison?

Everyone was utterly exhausted, but with Kadian's condition steadily worsening, they'd ridden through the night until arriving on Kracia's western coast. They had then headed south, keeping to the coastal road. They'd made camp within a cave overlooking the estuary of a river just as dawn was breaking. The estuary was teeming with fish. Although food had been the last thing on Lucian's mind, he'd soon found his appetite and eaten his fill.

They were now making for the Rock of Galtar, a monolithic promontory on the Volarian Peninsula, which lay within what was known to all as the lost lands.

The Volarian Peninsula had been under Salah Khan's dominion. Following their victory at Zylos, King Ocwan and Rhödos of Varnia had announced they were conferring the peninsula to King Jarod of Belanos for his holding out against Salah Khan. Rhödos was assassinated before the proclamation could come into effect, however. With Agnar having refused to meet with King Ocwan since becoming Wulvran, the Galyak settlements and fortifications along the peninsula were left to the cormorants, guillemots, and the other wild birds that nested on this stretch of coastline.

They were heading for Galtar because Arkan Sula had told Lucian they should do so. The Elkai had made no mention of Èinor or why they should make for Galtar, however. The Elkai's latest communiqué had resulted in a heated debate among the Xaviers. Raynor insisted they should seek a healer for Kadian because they were unlikely to find one anywhere on the Volarian Peninsula

The Rock of Galtar was one of the legendary twin Pillars of Kholar. The other pillar being Hadi Phorus, which was said to have stood on the Kavashan side of the Zylos Estuary.

Lucian had felt such a thrill upon their arrival at the Zylos Estuary, for these waters led to the sloping plains where the armies of Abador and Varnia had given battle to the Galyaks.

It was written that Krotos, father to Xavius, had stood atop the two promontories and cradled the newborn moon in his arms until she came of age. The sole means of reaching the promontory was by crossing Belan's Causeway, a stretch of interlocking basalt columns that were only accessible on the outgoing tide.

Thanks to his grandmother's teachings Lucian knew the Rock of Galtar had once been home to a highly advanced yet secretive sect known as the Ermitians. At the Tor's summit, the Ermitians had erected two horseshoe-shaped series of pillared arches to form the heel and sole of a human footprint to represent where Horus had stood atop the promontory. As to where the Ermitians had located the chalk-white stone from which they'd fashioned the pillars was a mystery in itself, for none was to be found anywhere on Kracia.

Of course, by far the most perplexing question that had intrigued Abador's scholars throughout the ages was by which means the Ermitians had hauled the pillars up the towering, abrupt slope; their industry had also extended to carving a stairwell into the rock.

Lucian's grandmother said the Cyrene Sandal, as the temple was known, was one of the wonders of the ancient world. He'd promised himself that he would one day visit Galtar but had never imagined he'd be doing so under such fantastical circumstances.

The promontory was as yet hidden within the fog

rolling in off the Gidean, but before this day was out, he would see for himself whether the temple lived up to the old woman's narrative.

They had passed the ruins of several Galyak settlements while threading their way along the coastal road. These were the lost lands, yet Lucian had still expected to encounter people along the way. They had yet to see a solitary soul.

The fog was thinning with every mile they covered. While scouting ahead, Torian had espied a stream. Having cleansed Kadian's wounds and reapplied the tourniquet, they'd let their mounts have their fill from the stream.

Lucian was replenishing the water flasks when something caught his eye. Shielding his eyes against the sun's glare, he saw two figures, both cloaked in dark robes, advancing along the coastal road some five hundred yards to their rear. Seeing them reminded him of the day he'd encountered Varos while en route to Abador.

The robed figures were still some distance off, but Lucian could see one was much older than the other, for he was near doubled over and reliant on both staff and the arm of his companion.

A grandfather and grandson, perhaps?

****

By the time Lucian and the Xaviers were ready to resume their journey, the robed figures had more or less caught up with them. Lucian had anticipated the two veering off to the stream to refresh themselves, for the heat was already oppressive. Yet to his surprise, they were showing no indication of doing so.

"Where do you suppose those two are making

for?" Varos said, appearing at his shoulder. "I know there's no law against traversing the lost lands, but it's arduous enough on horseback. Good day to you, friends," he called to them.

The robed figures came to a halt

"Good day to you, kind sir," the younger one said, throwing back his hood.

Lucian saw the lad was of fair complexion and around the same age as himself. "My name is Rojan, and this is Brother Lodigar. Brother Lodigar is a Lunarian, and I am his ward."

It was hard to determine Brother Lodigar's age, for his face remained hidden within the cowl of his robe. But going off his hunched frame and measured gait, Lucian estimated him to be some years older than his grandfather.

Avicus and Yanek came across. "Do you mind me asking what brings you and Brother Lodigar into the lost lands?" Avicus asked Rojan.

"We are Lunarians returning to the Rock of Galtar."

"Forgive me, but I've never heard of the Lunarian Order," Varos said.

"We are a peaceful order who pay homage to the moon goddess, Alunia," Rojan explained.

"You say you're returning to Galtar?" Avicus asked.

"Yes." Rojan nodded. "Our order has taken possession of the old Galyak settlement on the promontory," he explained. "I am still a novice but will become a Lunarian once I have completed my training."

"But the ownership of these lands has yet to be

decided," Avicus said.

Brother Lodigar let his staff rest against his shoulder and started gesticulating.

"Brother Lodigar says no one man can decide the ownership of the land upon which other men walk," Rojan said.

"All men must obey the laws of the land," Varos said testily. "Even Lunarians."

Brother Lodigar gesticulated again.

Rojan appeared hesitant about interpreting the old man's gestures. "Brother Lodigar wishes to know why outlaws such as yourselves would care for such laws?" he said at last.

The three Xaviers looked at each other.

"It would appear Brother Lodigar knows our identity," Avicus responded warily.

"Brother Lodigar knows many things." Rojan smiled without offering anything more. "May we accompany you the rest of the way to Galtar?" he asked instead. "Brigands are known to hide out in those foothills," he added, glancing to a heavily wooded range of hills in the distance.

"And how is it you know we are making for Galtar?" Varos asked.

Rojan glanced along the coastal road in both directions before responding. "What other reason could you possibly have for traversing the peninsula?" he asked with a knowing smile.

"Are there any within your order who are skilled in medicine?" Yanek asked Rojan. "Our comrade has...he's suffered a serpent bite."

Brother Lodigar pushed his way past Lucian and the Xaviers attention and, with Rojan's help, shuffled over to where Raynor and Torian were tending to Kadian. He peered at the puncture holes in Kadian's calf for several heartbeats, gesticulating as he did so.

"He says Brother Elco possesses certain healing skills," Rojan explained. "Brother Elco is new to the order, but…"

"But what?" Raynor snapped. "We have coin."

"It's not a question of payment," Rojan said patiently. "It's just that men of the sword are not permitted on Galtar."

Varos turned to Avicus. "I suggest we worry about crossing that bridge when we arrive at Galtar."

"Oh, there is no bridge." Rojan shook his head. "The Rock can only be accessed by crossing Belan's Causeway when the—"

"It's a metaphor, lad." Varos smiled.

"Perhaps Brother Lodigar would care to ride the remainder of the way?" Lucian asked Rojan, indicating to Kia.

Brother Lodigar cocked his head to Lucian and made a quick gesture with one hand.

"Brother Lodigar asks for your name," Rojan said.

"My name is Lucian."

"Brother Lodigar thanks you, Lucian." Rojan smiled again. "I will need help getting him into the saddle, please."

With Torian's help, Lucian and Rojan managed to hoist Brother Lodigar into the saddle.

"Brother Lodigar is a man of few words," Torian said, handing Rojan the old man's staff.

"That's because he has taken a vow of silence," Rojan said.

****

On resuming their journey to the promontory with Brother Lodigar and Rojan, Lucian had anticipated further debate as to whether the Xaviers would be permitted to cross over the causeway, but the knights were seemingly content to let the matter rest.

Though wary of incurring Brother Lodigar's displeasure, Lucian had been curious to know more about the Lunarians. He'd therefore thought it best to broach the subject by asking Rojan why he had chosen to devote his life to the Lunarian order. To his astonishment, Rojan had offered nothing more than to say he was simply following Brother Lodigar's bidding.

The Rock of Galtar dominated the landscape and more than lived up to everything Lucian's grandmother had told him. Upon arriving at Belan's Causeway, he'd mouthed a prayer of thanks to Valkyar. For although the incoming tide was in full flow, it was still possible to cross the swirling torrent.

But, of course, men of the sword weren't permitted on Galtar.

"What's to stop us crossing?" Raynor snapped, echoing Lucian's thoughts.

Brother Lodigar started gesticulating wildly, clearly agitated by Raynor's manner. Rojan whispered something to the old man to calm him down.

"Because we come in peace, brother," Varos said forcibly. "Can't an exception be made?" he asked, turning to Rojan. "You have seen for yourselves that our brother Kadian is in great need of medical help."

Brother Lodigar gesticulated again.

"He says he will need to confer with Abbot Gwilym, the leader of our order," Rojan explained. "But you will have to remain here."

"But the tide is coming in," Raynor retorted. "By the time you've sought out this Abbot Gwilym, it will be too late for us to make the crossing."

Rojan leaned into the old man again and muttered something to which the old man nodded curtly. "Brother Lodigar has consented to your comrade crossing with us," he said, turning to Lucian and the Xaviers.

The old man gesticulated again.

"And Brother Lodigar will accept responsibility for your comrade," Rojan continued. "He must leave his sword and any other weapons behind. He also says you and your wolf may also cross," he told Lucian.

"Why me? Lucian frowned.

"Because you are pure of heart."

"Expecting Lucian to get Kadian across the causeway unaided is madness," Raynor retorted. "All it will take is for Altair to lose his footing. I know Altair better than any man, so I beseech you to let me help him across," he said, turning to Rojan. "I'll swim back across if I have to."

Brother Lodigar suddenly jerked a hand into the air, gesticulating wildly.

"What is it?" Varos asked Rojan.

Lucian knew without looking that it was the raven.

Sure enough, on glancing to the skies, he saw a dark speck circling high overhead.

"I sense impending mischief." Torian sighed.

"Whatever mischief awaits us, I would rather face it with Kadian on the other side of the causeway," Avicus said firmly. "You'll have to forgive us our trespass, Rojan, but we're all coming across."

Chapter Fourteen

The Hellion

Lucian kept a tight grip on Lykka's pelt with one hand and held onto Kia's tail with the other as Rojan guided Brother Lodigar through the eddying current. Yanek and Torian were flanking Kadian, with Raynor mounted behind to prevent him tumbling from his saddle, while Avicus and Varos brought up the rear. On reaching the jutting shelf upon which the Galyaks had built the settlement the Lunarians were now calling home, Varos and Lucian assisted Rojan with getting Kia and Lodigar free of the water.

Aside from the Eramian Wasteland, the windswept promontory was the most inhospitable place Lucian had seen. He could only assume, judging from the ramshackle assortment of huts, that the Galyaks had been in the process of erecting the settlement at the time of Zylos. Some of the buildings were of such flimsy construction he was amazed they hadn't been blown off the shelf into the sea.

Aside from the various livestock skittering about in their pens, the settlement appeared deserted. Lucian assumed the Lunarians must be at prayer. Just then, however, a slender youth with buck teeth and fiery-red hair emerged from the nearest hut carrying a broom. He stumbled to a halt, glancing beyond Lucian to the

Xaviers before suddenly starting with his broom as though he might sweep the interlopers from the shelf into the causeway.

"It's all right, Yora," Rojan shouted. "Brother Lodigar has permitted these men across. I assure you they mean us no harm."

The youth continued his advance, sweeping furiously as he came. "M-m-men of the s-s-sword are not permitted here," he stammered. "M-m-men of the s-s-sword m-m-must leave."

Ignoring the youth's ranting, Lucian helped Rojan assist Brother Lodigar from Kia's back.

"Where is Abbot Gwilym, Yora?" Rojan asked, returning his attention to the youth.

"M-m-men of the s-s-sword are not permitted here," the youth repeated without letting up from his sweeping.

Rojan went across and took the broom from the youth. "It was a necessity, Yora," he said soothingly. "Brother Lodigar has taken responsibility for these men. Make your comrade comfortable while I go in search of Abbot Gwilym," he told the Xaviers before setting off across the settlement, still clutching the broom.

Lucian offered Yora a reassuring smile while watching Raynor and Torian lift Kadian from the saddle, carry him over to another of the huts, and set him down against a section of the wall that was still out of the sun. Kadian was becoming agitated again, however, and Raynor was mopping his fevered brow to try and ease his torment.

Lucian went across to see what assistance he could lend to making Kadian comfortable until Rojan returned with Abbot Gwilym but halted on seeing Avicus and Varos set off toward the causeway. Following their gaze, his eyes were drawn to a band of horsemen making their way down from the foothills.

Were these the brigands Rojan had mentioned?

****

The approaching horsemen were more distinct now. From their ambling gait, however, the riders were in no apparent haste to reach the causeway. Lucian assumed this was because they were familiar with the tides.

Yora came idling across, pausing to pick at his nose while gazing across the causeway. He gave the tip of his finger a cursory inspection before wiping it against his shirt. Lucian felt compelled to pass comment but stayed his tongue on seeing Rojan hurriedly approaching in the company of two men dressed in robes similar to that of Brother Lodigar.

"The-the-these m-m-men are—"

"Thank you, Yora," the Lunarian Lucian assumed to be Abbot Gwilym cut in. "I will deal with our guests. You may return to your duties. We have learned to forgive Yora his trespasses," he said, turning to face Lucian and the two Xaviers, "for he suffers from an ailment of the mind."

"Yora is nonetheless correct in what he says, Abbot," the second Lunarian said haughtily. "Men of the sword are not permitted on Galtar."

Whereas the Abbot was tall and lean with a gentle face, the other Lunarian was as short as he was stout, with cold, deep-set eyes.

"I assure you we mean you no harm," Avicus said. "And you might have need of our swords," he added, glancing over the causeway to the approaching horsemen.

"You expect us to put our faith in one band of outlaws against another?" Brother Paulus sneered. "You're probably in league with those rogues across the causeway."

All eyes turned to Rojan.

"I thought it only right to mention what Brother Lodigar said of you," Rojan offered.

"Then allow me to reveal all that you need to know about us," Avicus said to Abbot Gwilym. "We are Xavier knights, and we have been unjustly proclaimed traitors by His Majesty King Ocwan," Avicus said. "Whether the approaching column are here for us, I cannot say. We are engaged on a quest to rid Abador of the ills that plague our beloved Abador and restore our honor. And I assure you we have only come to Galtar because one of our brothers is in grave need of medical expertise."

"You can expect no help from us," Brother Paulus retorted haughtily.

"Brother Paulus, please," the Abbot said with a sternness Lucian hadn't suspected. "I understand your comrade has been bitten by a serpent," he said, glancing across to Kadian and the other Xaviers?"

"More lies," Paulus interjected brusquely. "You know as well as I, Abbot, that there are no poisonous serpents to be found anywhere on Kracia."

Avicus hesitated before responding. "This was no ordinary serpent," he said warily. "For we have come from the Land of Helgos."

Brother Paulus suddenly became hysterical. "May the gods protect us!" he shrieked. "These rogues have brought sorcery to Galtar! Oh Alunia, Goddess of the Night," he yelled, pressing his clasped hands to his breast, "we beseech you to cast these heathens into Orbelium!"

Avicus ignored his histrionics. "We have come here because Brother Lodigar said one among your order has knowledge of healing," he said to Abbot Gwilym.

"That would be Brother Elco." Abbot Gwilym nodded. "He is new to our order."

"He is in the temple, Abbot," Rojan offered.

"Brother Elco is new to our order and spends much of his time up there in meditation," Abbot Gwilym told Avicus.

"Those in meditation cannot be disturbed." Brother Paulus huffed indignantly before striding away.

"Brother Paulus's impetuosity tests us all," Abbot Gwilym said with a rueful smile, "but he is quite correct in what he says. Those in meditation cannot be disturbed."

Torian came tearing across. "We have no quarrel with you, Abbot, but I will ascend the Tor and drag this Brother Elco down here if I have to."

"I will not be bullied, my friend," Abbot Gwilym countered, meeting Torian's gaze. "Not even by a Xavier knight."

"Brother Paulus isn't the only one whose impetuosity drives to distraction on occasion." Avicus sighed. "But if you know of us, you must surely know we are oath-sworn to Arkan Sula."

"May we anticipate the Elkai's arrival?" Abbot Gwilym asked, his eyes widening.

"Sula has not been seen for many months," Avicus

replied.

"I saw him once," Abbot Gwilym said. "You see, I am Helgoan by birth. My brother was the Burgher at the time of…the time of the Sisters."

"You can rest assured Helgos is again free of Crepicella and her sisters," Avicus said.

"Then the gods be praised." Abbot Gwilym smiled. "Our rule regarding meditation cannot be challenged, but should you wish to ascend the tor to meditate…"

****

Abbot Gwilym had consented to Kadian being taken into one of the huts. Raynor, Torian, and Yanek chose to remain in the settlement. Having cajoled Yanek to keep an eye on Lykka, Lucian accompanied Avicus and Varos up the promontory.

The Ermitians had carved a series of steps into the rock face, yet the climb proved arduous enough owing to the wind whipping across the promontory. The sun had chased away the last vestiges of the lingering mist, revealing a panoramic view of the Volarian Peninsula and beyond.

While taking in the splendid vista, Lucian paused to observe the brigands, who were now settling themselves on the opposite side of the causeway awaiting the tide. They numbered around thirty or so. Abbot Gwilym had said how the brigands seldom bothered them upon discovering the Lunarians had taken a vow of poverty. It was likely, therefore, that the rogues had espied strangers—himself and the Xaviers—from their lair and had come to see if there were any pickings to be had. There was no need to worry about the brigands until the tide turned at least. But what then…?

Hopefully, Arkan Sula would provide the answer.

****

The Cyrene Sandal stood within a hollow basin. The temple truly was a wonder to behold. Even Avicus and Varos were taken aback by its awe-inspiring majesty. The chalk-white pillars were not as tall as Lucian had imagined in his mind's eye, but he now understood the conundrum that had plagued Abador's most learned minds through the centuries: how had the Ermitians hauled the pillars up the rock? Nor was it known from where the Ermitians had brought the chalk-white stone from which the pillars were hewn as none was to be found anywhere on Kracia. He was still marveling over the Ermitians' ingenuity when Avicus called attention to a robed figure standing before the temple's altar.

Lucian hurried to catch up with the two Xaviers as they made their way down the slope and advanced toward the temple. If Brother Elco was aware of their presence, he gave no indication.

"Brother Elco," Avicus called out as they entered the main temple, "forgive our intrusion, but we must speak with you."

Brother Elco didn't turn to face them. Lucian, however, was sure he'd seen the Lunarian flinch slightly on hearing his name called. He only hoped it wasn't because he was affronted at having had his deliberations interrupted.

"Our comrade is stricken with fever," Avicus continued without breaking stride. "He was bitten by a serpent, and we fear his blood is poisoned."

This was enough to stir Brother Elco. Turning to face them, he slowly drew back his cowl.

"I have no healing powers, brothers, but it is good to see you again."

"Èinor!" Avicus spluttered. "What in the name of Valkyar are you doing here?"

"Arkan Sula visited me in my dreams," Èinor explained as they embraced. "He told me I should make for Galtar and boast of my supposed powers of healing. I've come up here every day since arriving on the Rock. In fact, you interrupted my latest pleadings to Valkyar beseeching Him for another sign from the Elkai."

Varos came past Avicus and heartily embraced Èinor. "He has heeded your prayers, brother. Arkan Sula is watching over us. He communicates to us through Lucian here."

"What's this about Kadian being bitten by a serpent?" Èinor asked, glancing beyond his fellow Xaviers to acknowledge Lucian. He had a narrow face with chiseled features and intelligent eyes.

And so, Avicus and Varos, with Lucian's help, explained all that had happened since the Xaviers had gone their separate ways in search of Arkan Sula.

"I'm surprised you made it here to the peninsula," Èinor said when they'd finished recounting their tale. "I hear King Jarod is offering our bodyweight in gold. He thinks delivering one or more Xaviers to Abador in chains will bolster his chances of King Ocwan allotting the peninsula to Belanos."

****

Lucian, Avicus, and Varos descended the promontory with Èinor to find Kadian's fever had mercifully broken. Indeed, he might well have fallen over had he not been lying down. The puncture wounds in his calf were still an angry red, but he was more or less back to his usual self.

Raynor and Yanek had also near tripped over themselves on seeing Èinor. Of course, had either of them thought to enquire whether the Lunarians had a stable so they might tend to the horses, they would have discovered Èinor's mount, Bellatrix, in one of the storehouses.

The Xaviers were united at long last. All that was required now was to formulate a plan on how to best the brigands. The Lunarians possessed a couple of small fishing boats, but they were of no use as they would be obliged to leave the horses behind. With time of the utmost essence, this simply wasn't an option.

Leaving the Xaviers to their council of war, Lucian went to check on Kia and the other horses. He was making his way to the storehouse that was now serving as a makeshift stable when he sensed he was being observed. Glancing about the settlement, a sudden movement high up the promontory caught his eye.

The raven had returned.

With Lykka at his heel, Lucian retreated across the settlement to alert the Xaviers to the raven's presence.

When Lucian and the Xaviers emerged into the settlement, they found Abbot Gwilym, Brother Paulus, and a dozen or so other Lunarians gathered at the shelf, watching the raven lazily circling high above the causeway.

"The creature's taunting us," Raynor said as they advanced as one across the settlement.

"It thinks we're stranded here," Yanek said, the despondency evident in his tone.

"Until we think of some means of ridding ourselves of those brigands, we are stranded," Torian said.

"I don't know about the rest of you, but dealing with brigands will prove light relief after the Talvek and Sister Witches," Varos offered, attempting to lift the mood.

"And I'd feel a whole lot easier if we could rid ourselves of this infernal bird," Kadian said

Yora suddenly appeared clutching a pail filled with rusting crossbow quarrels, offering them to Avicus.

"A grim reminder as to Galtar's previous occupants," Abbot Gwilym explained.

"Then more's the pity the Galyaks didn't think to leave any crossbows behind," Varos said with a wistful sigh.

"We don't need a crossbow," Lucian said, eyeing the pail. Taking one of the quarrels, he placed it at an angle against a rock and brought his heel down hard on the shaft close to the head. Picking up the bolthead, he slipped the slingshot from his jerkin. Without taking his eyes off the raven, he slowly slipped the bolthead into the sling, drew back his arm, and released.

From the ground, it appeared the bolthead narrowly missed its target. The raven, however, gave no indication of even being aware it was under attack and continued circling high above the water.

Leaving Varos to snap the quarrels, Lucian rapidly shot one bolthead after another with similarly frustrating results. He was taking aim again when Èinor drew their attention to the swirling waters within the center of the causeway.

"Is this a regular occurrence at high tide?" Avicus asked Abbot Gwilym.

"Not that I'm aware," the Abbot replied.

"I warned you not to let him stay, Abbot." Brother Paulus jerked a finger at Èinor. "Didn't I say he was lying about his possessing healing powers?"

"Calm yourself, Brother Paulus," Abbot Gwilym said absently, his eyes focused on the churning waters.

"But none of this would be happening if you'd have only listened to—"

"Enough!" the Abbot snapped. "There will be time enough for reproach when..." his voice suddenly trailing away on seeing a partially denuded arm rise from the churning cauldron clutching a rusting spear.

Lucian felt his knees give slightly as a dozen or so nightmarish creatures in varying states of putrefaction broke the surface in unison and advanced toward the shelf. Each was clad in disintegrating leather breastplates and rusted armor.

"What are they?" Abbot Gwilym gasped, his voice little more than a whisper.

"They are Hellion," Avicus said gravely as he and the other Xaviers fanned out to await the Hellion. "The undead."

Seeing the Hellion emerge from the water had proved too much for the brigands. Many of them forgot about their horses in their urgency to flee the causeway.

Panic had also set in among the Lunarians, of course. "My brothers and I will ascend to the temple and call upon Alunia," Abbot Gwilym shouted over his shoulder.

"I suggest you call upon every god and goddess that comes to mind, Abbot," Varos called after him. "The fools can't think they'll be safe up there," he said to Avicus

"Being in the Sandal will hopefully provide them

with comfort," Avicus replied.

Lucian released a bolthead, catching one of the Hellion with force enough to shatter the skull yet failed to halt its steady advance. The realization dawned on seeing another Hellion break the surface roughly where the bolthead had landed in the foaming waters.

"This is the raven's doing." Lucian could feel his frustrations spilling over. He grabbed another quarrel, snapped off the head, and loaded it into the sling. "It's channeling the boltheads to summon the Hellion."

"Then I suggest you improve your aim," Varos said with a wry smile as Lucian snapped off another bolthead and loaded it into his sling.

"I assure you I won't miss this time," Lucian retorted, releasing the bolthead just as the raven made another swooping arc above the settlement. The bolt flew true, clipping one of the raven's wings, dislodging a feather.

The feather lazily floated on the breeze. As for the raven, there was no sign.

Lucian hurriedly plucked the feather out of the air before it drifted out over the causeway.

The Xaviers had fanned out to await the Hellion. Instead of advancing onto the shelf, however, the Hellion halted at the water's edge. And there they remained.

"What are they waiting for?" Torian asked out loud. He took a step toward the shelf. "Come on then," he shouted defiantly.

"The Hellion can't come onto the shelf, Torian, because I have consecrated the ground."

Lucian readily recognized Arkan Sulu's voice but never had his words sounded so clear. It was as though the Elkai was at his shoulder.

Turning on his heel, Lucian saw Brother Lodigar with Rojan at his side.

There was something different about the elderly Lunarian, however. He appeared more robust than before. And certainly taller.

In the eyeblink, the idea formed in Lucian's mind, Brother Lodigar slipped back his cowl.

The Xaviers dropped to bended knee as one with their heads bowed.

Chapter Fifteen

The Return of The Elkai

Arkan Sula shrugged off the robe and made a show of brushing at his garment, which Lucian saw was overlain with mystical symbols long-faded by the sun. "No need to stand on ceremony," he said, impatiently summoning the Xaviers to their feet.

It wasn't until that moment that Lucian realized he'd never thought to ask the Xaviers how they might describe Arkan Sula. He'd imagined how the Elkai might look many times over in his mind's eye, of course, and was secretly pleased the angular face and hawklike nose were exactly as he'd imagined. He'd also imagined a shock of unkempt white hair, yet the Elkai's head was shaved except for a tonsure at the crown, while his plaited beard near reached down to his waist. The sorcerer's staff had also transformed as Lucian observed a tiny bird's skull mounted at the tip.

"Yes, Lucian, the plaits of my beard are secured with the whiskers of a black cat," the Elkai said with a knowing smile. "To use the whiskers of any other cat would be most unwise. Oh, don't look so surprised, dear boy," he mock-scolded, jerking Lucian from his musings. "If I can enter your thoughts, I can certainly read them."

"You...you were here when I arrived on Galtar,

lord," Èinor stammered.

"Impatiently awaiting your arrival, I might add, Èinor," Arkan Sula replied. "Though I must admit the Lunarians are far more agreeable than some religious sects I could mention. Christians, for example," he continued. "Whereas the Lunarians worship the Ermitian moon goddess, Alunia, Christians pay homage to a son-God who was put to death by being nailed to a wooden cross, as far as I can ascertain. Christians traverse the land gaining converts through torture and burnings, and yet they preach of turning the other cheek on being provoked. They also mark themselves with the symbol of a fish and insist on dousing each new convert in the nearest stream."

"Where have you been all these months, lord?" Kadian asked.

Arkan Sula frowned. "Carrying out Xavius's will, of course. You do ask the most absurd questions, Kadian."

"So, this is all Xavius's will?" Avicus asked caustically.

"What else could it be?"

"You didn't think to forewarn us?" Avicus pressed.

"Forewarn you?" Arkan Sula gasped as though the word was unfamiliar to him. "Does the king take his pawns into his confidence?"

"This isn't a game of chatrang." Irritation laced Avicus' voice.

"Ah, but that's where you're wrong, Avicus," Arkan Sula retorted, bringing the butt of his staff down hard. "This is very much a game...One in which the stakes couldn't be any higher, I might add. And to use the chatrang analogy," he continued, "Nikobar had to believe he was free to make his opening move."

"But thousands of Abadorians died of plague," Avicus countered. "Was that merely another of Xavius' moves across the board, lord?"

Arkan Sula's eyes flashed fire. "You dare to question the will of Xavius?"

Avicus, however, was determined to stand his ground. "His will, no…Only His motive."

"Careful you don't go too far, Avicus," Arkan Sula said, his voice taking on an ominous tone.

"So long as Nikobar finishes on the losing side when the last dice are rolled," Varos interjected, hoping to alleviate the tension.

"Who is Nikobar, lord?" Lucian asked, voicing the thought that had plagued him since setting off for Abador what now seemed like a lifetime ago. "And what does he intend to do with Princess Rhiana?"

The Elkai kept his eyes on Avicus for several uncomfortable heartbeats. "Nikobar is passing himself off as a Cygian enchanter," he said at last. "The Cygians were a highly-advanced race that lived on an island that rested on the very edge of the world," he continued. "They were favored by the gods above all others. For reasons beyond comprehension, the Cygians chose to believe Gazankulu to be of equal deity to Xavius. They sent out emissaries to spread the word of their infernal Dragon Lord! Those Cygians foolish enough to come to Kracia to spout their heresy were cast back into the sea, but they found favor in Ursia Minor—notably among the Galyaks. Xavius, therefore, called upon Merwin, God of the Seas, to send a mighty tidal wave to wash the Cygians into the void. None survived."

"Then who is he, lord?" Lucian asked again.

Again Arkan Sula hesitated. "I suppose the simplest explanation I can give you is that whereas I am the light, Nikobar is the darkness. A darkness that has taken human form and will sacrifice Princess Rhiana on Asima Na to return its master Gazankulu to the sunlit world."

"I remember Crepicella speaking of Asima Na, lord," Lucian said, reluctantly casting his mind back to recent events.

"According to the ancient prophecy, Asima Na occurs every thousand years," Arkan Sula explained. "It is the time when the portal twixt the sunlit world and Orbelium can be manipulated." He then recited the prophecy Lucian remembered from the Sister Witches' lair: "When the Dragon lights up the sky, from the Netherworld shall Gazankulu return. With fiery breath and wings unfurled, He will bring death and desolation to the world. The Draconis Constellation rises in conjunction with Asima Na. The Draconis Constellation consists of five double stars representing the harbingers of the apocalypse: war, famine, drought, pestilence, and death. If my calculations are correct, Asima Na is five days hence."

"On the day I witnessed Princess Rhiana being handed to the Galyaks, I suffered a nightmare in which I was in a temple with an effigy of a winged dragon at its center, lord," Lucian said.

"Of course, you did, my boy," Arkan Sula said. "It was I who transported you to the temple in your dream state."

Lucian was agog. "So, the temple I saw is the one where the Galyaks are keeping Princess Rhiana?"

"It is the Temple of Hadeas," Arkan Sula replied. "The temple is on Necros, a remote island roughly halfway between Kracia and—"

"I know of Necros, lord," Èinor interjected.

"Good, Èinor." Arkan Sula nodded. "A knowledge of Necros will prove most useful in the days ahead. Now, where was I... Oh, yes, that's right. Nikobar has made it appear as though Agnar is behind Princess Rhiana's kidnapping. He cares little about the outcome of a war between Abador and Varnia, of course. His sole interest in involving Varnia was to ensure the main body of Abador's army is anywhere other than Abador."

"So that Abador will be left defenseless against a Galyak attack, lord?" Kadian asked.

"Has Evora's poison totally addled that brain of yours, Kadian?" the Elkai chided him. "My apologies for underestimating Crepicella's powers," he said in a soothing tone, his eyes moving from one Xavier to another. "Nikobar is simply exploiting the Galyaks for his own ends. He has come to Abador because he needs the Amulet of Meshtar. The amulet that houses the blood-encrusted scale Valkyar tore from Gazankulu's hide before casting Him into Orbelium. You see, the Dragon Lord cannot return to the sunlit world unless he is whole. And without the Amulet of Meshtar, Nikobar cannot perform the ritual."

"And you know where this amulet is to be found?" Kadian asked.

"There you go again, Kadian," Arkan Sula said with a quick shake of his head. "Of course I know where the amulet lies. I'm the one who hid it."

"Then surely all you need do, lord, is return to

Abador and retrieve the amulet from its hiding place before Nikobar finds it," Avicus offered.

"Nothing would be easier, Avicus. But Xavius has determined Nikobar should find the amulet."

"But why, lord?" Raynor gasped.

"Because He wills it so, Raynor," the Elkai replied solemnly. "Did you and Kadian leave what little common sense you have behind in the Labyrinth?"

"And how are we to reach Necros, lord?" Lucian asked, hoping to spare Kadian's torment.

"Thank you, Lucian, just as I was beginning to fear no one was ever going to ask an intelligent question." Arkan Sula smiled, turning to look out into the Gidean. "Ahh, here she comes now."

Shielding his eyes, Lucian could make out a single-masted craft on the horizon.

"While we await your ship, I might as well deal with the Hellion," Arkan Sula said.

The Hellion were still poised at the shelf, weapons in hand, and with their empty eye sockets fixed upon the Xaviers.

"May I trouble you for the feather?" The Elkai asked Lucian.

"Are you saying you can defeat the Hellion with a feather, lord?" Torian gasped.

"This is no ordinary feather, Torian." Arkan Sula smiled, taking the feather from Lucian. "The raven served as Nikobar's eyes, plaguing your every move. But thanks to Lucian's ingenuity in thinking to retrieve the feather before it was lost to us, I can cast the Hellion back to Orbelium. I would have preferred to put this feather to better use, but that can't be helped now. And I suppose it's only fair that I restore Galtar to some sort of normality. Though I doubt the Lunarians' lives will ever be the same again."

With Lucian and the Xaviers watching on, Arkan Sula knelt at the edge of the shelf with the raven's feather nestled in his outstretched palm and weaved his charm. Whispy curlicues of smoke slowly exuded from the feather. At the same instant, the waters within the center of the causeway started to churn, the churning increasing in intensity to form a raging whirlpool. One by one, the Hellion were sucked into the vortex.

And all was again calm on Galtar

****

The tide was finally beginning to ebb, and the single-masted vessel Lucian had seen approaching Galtar now lay at anchor in the causeway. As with the Drakkar, Lucian had seen at the cove, the ship was possessed of a shallow-draft hull for speed. She was also double-ended, the symmetrical bow and stern allowing for reverse direction.

"She looks a splendid craft, lord," Varos said.

"She is indeed, Varos," Arkan Sula said. "As you will observe, she's identical in design to the Galyak Drakkar. I couldn't bring myself to utilize carved effigies of Gazankulu, but Karna—an obscure God from the lands far to the north—will pass for the Dragon Lord. From a distance, at least. I named her Cassiope because we are going to need all the good fortune that we can muster in the days ahead."

"What happened to her crew, lord?" Kadian asked.

The Elkai stepped toward Kadian, gently rapping him on the forehead with the tip of his staff. "I do wonder what goes in there at times, Kadian," he scolded. "It is common knowledge that I always call upon sea wraiths when I have need of a crew."

Lucian had heard of sea wraiths but had thought them to be malevolent creatures that lurked within the depths of the Zargrado Sea awaiting unsuspecting ships.

"Just as it's common knowledge, I abhor sea wraiths, lord," Kadian replied meekly.

"Though I always make sure to rid the wraiths of their malevolence," Arkan Sula continued as though Kadian hadn't spoken.

"If you could provide us with a good wind, I think we should manage without wraiths, lord," Avicus said.

"As if controlling the tide isn't taxing enough." Arkan Sula mock-harrumphed. "She is fitted with horse stalls," he said, jabbing his staff toward the Cassiope's steering oar. "Though I see Yanek and Raynor have been careless with their mounts."

"Forgive me, lord, but I didn't exactly lose Castor," Yanek replied. "He was taken from me by Nikobar's Black Crows while I was helping Jarl Laurik search for Prince Ærin."

"And I only loaned Jarl Laurik Adhara, lord," Raynor added.

"See to it that you get them back," Arkan Sula chided him. He suddenly turned to Lucian. "Might I have a word?"

"Of course, lord," Lucian said, still struggling to contain the giddiness at being in the Elkai's presence.

Arkan Sula walked a few paces towards the Cassiope. "Were you aware that some ancient civilizations associate the wolf with war?" he asked, studying Lykka. "The Huskenbachs, of course, believe Varnia's founder, Vargulus, was suckled by a she-wolf. I, myself, believe the wolf to be aligned with light and order."

"I know of the Huskenbachs' veneration of the wolf, lord," Lucian said, glancing at Lykka. "Jarl Laurik wanted to purchase Lykka as a gift for Prince Ærin."

"Did he now…" Arkan Sula said somewhat distractedly. "Do you remember seeing Lykka on Necros while in your dream state?" he asked suddenly, startling Lucian.

"I didn't, lord," Lucian answered. "But my grandmother said Lykka features in my destiny. She saw as much in the embers."

"Ah yes, pyromancy." Arkan Sula fell silent for a moment. "Pyromancy is one of the ancient methods of divination, though rudimentary. "Nonetheless, your grandmother's understanding of pyromancy is the reason we are here this day."

"Is there any significance in Lykka not featuring in my nightmare, lord?" Lucian asked.

"Ahh, Brother Gwilym," the Elkai said suddenly, wheeling round to face the Lunarian

Like the handful of other Lunarians that had ventured down from the Tor, Abbot Gwilym's eyes had a vacant stare.

"Many thanks, Abbot, for allowing young Rojan and I to live among you these past few weeks," the Elkai said. "And you may rest assured Galtar will remain your home for as long as you care to stay here."

"Thank…thank you, lord…" Brother Gwilym managed to stammer before falling silent.

"Will you be accompanying us to Necros, lord?" Torian asked.

"I have a more pressing task," Arkan Sula replied.

Lucian wondered what could be more pressing than securing the rescue of Princess Rhiana but held his tongue. He was also curious about Rojan. It was clear Arkan Sula had taken Rojan into his confidence as to his true identity. He couldn't help now but wonder about Rojan's own identity. Could Rojan be Prince Ærin…?

"I dare not risk speaking through you, Lucian, once you set foot on Necros as this is where Nikobar's energies will be focused," the Elkai said somberly. "It isn't only Abador's fate you have in your hands now, but that of mankind as a whole." He suddenly jabbed his staff at the Cassiope again. "It's time you were getting aboard. Summoning Vulturna while holding the tide at bay will take all my concentration. And there's no guarantee Vulturna will assist us, of course, for She is most temperamental."

Once Lucian and the Xaviers were aboard and the horses safely tethered in their stalls, Arkan Sula thrust his staff into the air and began mouthing an invocation to Vulturna, Goddess of the East Wind.

As he did so, the empty eye sockets within the bird's skull mounted at the staff's tip began emitting a pulsating crimson glow.

****

Vulturna had mercifully heeded Arkan Sula's summons, and the Cassiope was slicing through the waves at a brisk pace with her sail at full stretch.

The Xaviers were understandably wary of approaching Necros during daylight hours, however, as the Galyaks would surely have lookouts. Keeping sight of Barrati's eastern coastline, they were pushing farther out into the Gidean in a sweeping arc that would take them far beyond Necros. The Cassiope, being of identical design to the Galyak longship, had satisfied any Galyaks observing from the shore. All being well, they would approach Necros as the sun was setting.

While making an inspection of the ship, Èinor had found food supplies, a churn of milk, and two barrels of fresh water. Arkan Sula had thought to provide the Xaviers with new uniforms: russet-colored tunics, bronze breastplates embossed with the rampant unicorn of Abador, leg greaves, and full-faced helmets plumed with dyed horsehair cut into a stiff russet comb. It was the Xaviers' circular shields that Lucian found the most fascinating. The shields were comprised of three layers. The inner layer was made of leather, the center layer was of dense wood, and the outer layer was of beaten bronze. Unlike other shields, the Xavier shield's grip was at the edge and supported by a leather fastening for the forearm at its center to provide a much firmer hold.

Arkan Sula had also thought to provide several bows and quivers of arrows, three dozen short stabbing spears, several javelin-esque throwing spears with eyeholes in the butts that reminded Lucian of giant sewing needles, scaling hooks, and ropes.

Lucian sat against the gunwale, watching the Xaviers changing into the new uniforms and inspecting the weaponry. Torian hadn't seen the point of donning the uniforms until Avicus thought to point out that one or more of them—perhaps even all of them—might find themselves crossing through Crucian's Cave before much longer. And if that was what the gods decreed, then the Xaviers would enter the Great Feasting Hall dressed as though they were going into battle.

Varos had found an oilskin-wrapped object among

the spears. He cut the twine and partially opened the oilskin. "This must be for you," he called across to Lucian.

Lucian got to his feet and made his way across the deck. He could see that it was a sword but was taken aback on catching sight of the ornate handle. With the Xaviers watching on, he eased the sword from its leather scabbard, marveling at the burnished blade inlaid with chased whorls and mythical symbols. While strapping on the sword, Lucian dared to hope this was all part of his grandmother's prophecy: that he would one day wear the fabled Xavier russet.

Seeing the many Galyak settlements pitted along Barrati's coast, some of which appeared very large and formidable, had unnerved Lucian. If the Galyaks continued strengthening, it was only a matter of time before Kirgus Khan set his sights on the Kracian mainland. He was so engrossed with his thoughts he'd failed to notice Torian was now standing a few feet farther along the gunwale.

"Fear not, Lucian, we beat the Galyaks once," Torian said, as though reading Lucian's thoughts.

"You were in the Centaurian Guard at Zylos," said Lucian, returning his gaze to the retreating Barrati coast.

"To listen to the balladeers, you could be forgiven for thinking Zylos was an easy victory." Torian smiled. "But it was a mighty close affair. And I assure you our shield-wall breaking was no feint."

"Were Salah Khan's Bloodshields as ferocious as the balladeers make out?" Lucian asked.

"That's the one thing about Zylos the balladeers haven't exaggerated," Torian acknowledged. "The

Bloodshields were the fiercest of Salah Khan's warriors. If he'd have had several more cohorts of his Bloodshields that day, Khan might still have claimed victory."

"Did you see Salah Khan die?"

"Well, there was quite a lot going on at the time." Torian grinned. "But you could ask Avicus. It was he who killed Khan."

This certainly was a revelation. "Varos spoke a little of the battle while we were making our way through the Sardonis Pass but said nothing about it being Avicus who put Salah Khan to the sword."

"Avicus is the finest man I have ever known," Torian replied. "He's also the least-conceited man I've ever met. If Avicus had heard Varos singing his praises, he might well have pitched him into the Brethas Gorge…Or threatened it at least."

Avicus suddenly arrived at their side. "What's that about being threatened?"

"I was just saying to Lucian it's always the low-hanging clouds that threaten rain," Torian said, sharing a conspiratorial wink with Lucian. "We were discussing the likelihood of young Rojan being Prince Ærin," he added, subtly changing the subject. "It would explain Arkan Sula's absence at least."

"I suspected the lad was Prince Ærin the moment Arkan Sula revealed himself in the temple," Avicus replied. "And I have been praying that he is the prince ever since, for Jarl Laurik will be able to unite the northern clans and rise up against Agnar."

Chapter Sixteen

A Sacrifice at Sea

Lucian was tending to Kia and the Xaviers' horses, making sure they each had sufficient oats and water. With the Cassiope resuming her original course, there was little for Xaviers to do other than give their breastplates, greaves, and helmets an extra polish. Finishing with the horses, Lucian wandered across and grabbed up one of the stabbing spears, testing its weight before replacing it and picking up one of the bows.

"Why don't you try stringing it," Varos offered. "You'll need to put your back into it, mind. Stringing a new bow is hard business. And if the wood hasn't been spliced in accordance with the grain, you'll have no more luck trying to string the mast."

Lucian knew about the splicing needing to go with rather than against the grain, but try as he might, he couldn't get the string anywhere near the nock cut into the bow's tip.

Varos took the bow from Lucian, the muscles in his neck and shoulders straining as he bent the bow and slipped the string into place. "Have you ever fired a bow?" he asked, handing the bow back to Lucian.

"Best find yourself another teacher, Lucian," Yanek shouted over. "Varos struggles to hit a drawbridge at fifty paces."

"Care to put your money alongside that big mouth of yours, brother?" Varos riposted.

Yanek came across and snatched the bow from Varos' hand. "I'll be putting your coin with mine soon enough, brother. Nearest to the center of the mast, is it?"

Yanek took an arrow from Kadian, retreated toward the bow, and slowly drew back the cord, the muscles in his forearms rippling as he took aim.

The other Xaviers burst out laughing as the arrow shot past the mast and disappeared into the Gidean. "The wood's defective," Yanek grumbled, tossing the bow to Varos.

Varos went to stand where Yanek had stood, drew back the string, and released. The arrow slammed into the mast with a resounding thud. "Something's surely defective, brother," he shouted to Yanek. "Grab a quarrel, and we'll see how good you are," he said, summoning Lucian across.

Lucian took the bow, feeling very self-conscious about being the center of attention. "If you hit the mast, first go, lad, I'll give you whatever Yanek cares to owe me."

Lucian sighted the arrow, slowly drawing back the cord until his right hand was at his cheek. His arm flinched as he released, however, and the arrow sailed off into the waves. His cheeks flushed an angry red.

"Happens to the best of us." Varos smiled, handing Lucian another arrow.

Lucian drew back the cord a second time, but his nerves were such that he released too early, and the arrow skittered harmlessly across the deck before coming to rest by Avicus' foot. He angrily snatched a third arrow from the quiver and was drawing back the cord when a familiar voice sounded in his ear.

"An archer doesn't aim with his eye. He aims with his mind."

Lucian drew back the cord a third time. Closing his eyes, he pictured the arrow striking the mast and released. The arrow thudded into the mast, dead center.

Before Varos or anyone else had time to react or pass a comment, Lucian grabbed another arrow from the quarrel, drew back the cord, and released. The arrow struck the mast within a hair's breadth of the first, splintering the wood.

Varos set off along the deck. "Now," he shouted over his shoulder, "let's see what you're like with a moving target. Hand me the water flask, brother," he called to Raynor. Taking the flask, he suddenly hurled it into the air without warning.

Remembering what the voice had said about aiming with his mind, Lucian drew back the bow and focused his mind. He glanced at the flask arcing through the air, then closed his eyes and released.

The arrow struck the flask flush, the force momentarily lifting it back into the air before it plummeted silently into the sea.

"The lad's a natural." Varos beamed.

****

Lucian was at the rail absentmindedly watching the ship's prow slicing through the water when Èinor came across. "I should have mentioned it earlier, but I was born in Thengos, so I know Kalimar well," he said. "I also know the cove where all this began for you. I'm guessing that night wasn't the first occasion you dared cross the Sucking-sands?"

"It was, actually," Lucian replied. "You see, my grandparents forbade me from entering the sands."

"Their worry wasn't without reason, lad. The cove was a known hideout for slave traders and pirates. What about your parents?"

"My mother died giving birth to me," Lucian replied. "And my father was killed defending our village during an Ardassian raid while I was still in swaddling."

"That must have been hard on your grandparents," Èinor said.

"Yes, I suppose it was," Lucian said. "They seldom talk about it."

"We have more in common than I thought, for my father was killed during an Ardassian raid," Èinor revealed. "I was fifteen when the raid occurred. I was taken captive, along with my mother and two older brothers, and many others. The Ardassians torched the village, and the sound of the livestock being slaughtered as the flames illuminated the waves as their longship stole off into the night haunts me still."

Lucian was intrigued. "How did you get away?"

"When we arrived at the Ardassians' Iscatian stronghold, they began separating the women from the children. One of my brothers made a run into the trees, and I instinctively followed him.

"It was a moonless night, so we could hardly see where we were running. My brother caught his foot and twisted his ankle. I helped him as best I could, but with the Ardassians giving chase and gaining ground, he purposely sacrificed himself so that I might still get away."

Èinor stared out onto the water for several

heartbeats before continuing. "I hid inside a rotted tree trunk, expecting to be discovered any moment. But the gods were watching over me that night, Lucian, for the Ardassians had their hunting dogs, and yet I escaped recapture. It was so cold, and I was in shirt and trews. I didn't have my boots as one of the Ardassian swine had taken them for his own. I stayed shivering inside that trunk until I was sure the Ardassians had given up. It was only then that I discovered what the Ardassians had done with my brother. They had staked him to the ground, slit his stomach open, and left him for the beasts of the forest. I had no means of burying him, so I had to leave him there."

"But how did you get away from Iscatian Ice Lands?" Lucian asked him.

"As I say, the gods were watching over me," Èinor continued. "I was wandering aimlessly along the shore when I came upon a coracle. You know what a coracle is? It's a small, lightweight craft made from interwoven willow rods and bark and covered in animal hide and waterproofed with tar. The Ardassians use them for fishing, I suppose. The coracle was damaged yet still seaworthy. I waited until nightfall before casting off. Those were the longest hours of my life, at least up until then. I had no oar, so I used my hands. The water was freezing, so I soon gave up for fear of losing my fingers. I don't know how long I drifted, but I was picked up by a merchant ship bound for Alezzi. The merchant was kind enough to pull into Abador. I saw little point in returning to Thengos, so I enlisted in the Abadorian Guard."

"Thengos is again a thriving village," Lucian said. "I often accompany my grandfather there to trade our surplus catch for supplies."

"And I visited Kalimar often with my grandfather," Èinor said. "But this was long before you were born. I should very much like to visit the place again, for the captain of my cohort hailed from there. He was a good man and an excellent captain. Yet, for reasons none of us could understand, he resigned his commission. He'd already left Abador by the time I found out, and I never saw him again."

Lucian frowned. "I know every family in the village," he said. "Yet none has ever boasted of having a former captain of the Abadorian Guard. What was your captain's name?"

"Lansing, Captain Willam Lansing…What is it?" Èinor asked, seeing the look of incredulity in Lucian's eyes.

"Will…William Lansing is my grandfather?" Lucian spluttered, his mind whirring. "But why would he keep quiet about such a thing?"

"Perhaps he doesn't want to relive the memories," Èinor replied. "He wouldn't be the first man to do so, believe me."

A disturbing thought crept into Lucian's mind. "It must have been because he did something shameful," he said.

"I cannot believe that, Lucian," Èinor said, shaking his head. "Your grandfather received his captaincy for holding the line at Humran, the decisive battle of the third Threjan War. And Torian, Yanek, Varos, and I served under him at Zylos."

Lucian was reeling. At that moment, if one of the sea beasts that trawled the murky depths had risen up to swallow the ship whole, he wouldn't have been more astounded.

His grandfather had saved the day at Humran and had also fought at Zylos. Yet neither he nor his grandmother had ever said a word about it. Lucian was still trying to make sense of everything Èinor had told him when a warning sounded.

They had company.

****

Lucian looked into the sun and saw three dark rectangles in stark contrast against the surrounding hazy blue skyline. The Cassiope had been running on a north by northeast setting, but on seeing the three ships turning to follow them, Varos had taken over the rudder and was now steering the Cassiope dead north.

Shielding his eyes, Lucian saw the rectangles shift slightly as the ships changed direction accordingly. The ships were as yet too far off to make out any markings on the sail.

Avicus came up beside Lucian. "We have to assume they're Drakkars," he said.

"Then why are they pursuing us?" Varos asked. "The Cassiope is near-identical to a Galyak longship."

"It could be because we are displaying no markings," Èinor offered.

Lucian kept his gaze focused on the ragged rectangles. While it could have been a trick of the light, he was sure the sails were more prominent than when they'd first sighted the longships.

"Fear not," Varos said, clasping Lucian's shoulder. "There's no crew this side of Orbelium that can compete with Vulturna," Varos said.

"True enough," Avicus replied, his gaze focused on the three Drakkars. "But Sula didn't stop to consider

Vulturna would aid any ship in these waters. What do we do if the Galyaks don't abandon the chase?"

"We could let them catch up with us," Èinor offered.

"I admire your optimism, brother," Avicus mock-chided him.

"I'm serious," Èinor said. "As yet, they have no idea as to who or how many we are. If we make it look as though we're having trouble with the rudder, we might only have to deal with just the one ship."

"That still leaves odds of eight or nine to one," Varos said.

"I didn't say anything about letting them board us," Èinor continued. "When they get in range, we can launch fire arrows and set their sail alight."

"It's as good a strategy as I can think of," Varos said to Avicus.

"Then we'd best lower our sail, should they have the same idea," Avicus said.

****

Èinor's deception appeared to be working. Two of the Drakkars had given up the chase. Lucian could only assume Arkan Sula had called upon Vulturna to desist as the winds had dropped the moment that they'd lowered the sail.

The Xaviers had brought the Cassiope about so that the covered stall housing the horses was facing the longship. Aside from giving the horses and Lykka protection from stray quarrels, Kadian could make a fire out of sight of the Galyaks once the Drakkar came in range. Raynor and Èinor were huddled by the rail on either side of the ship, gripping an oar, but with the sail lowered, they were drifting aimlessly.

The Drakkar was easily closing the gap, its dirt-gray sail becoming ever more distinct.

Lucian could already distinguish a dozen or so Galyaks gathered at the prow, several of whom were preparing grappling hooks.

"They can see how few we are and think we are easy pickings," Varos said.

"They're in for a rude awakening," Yanek said, glancing at the bow and quivers of arrows by his feet.

The Galyaks waited until they were within thirty feet or so of the Cassiope before throwing the first grappling hook. The distance was still too great, however, and the hook fell some feet short from the gunwale.

Avicus, Varos, Yanek, Torian, and Lucian were huddled in a crouch at the prow. The Galyaks that Lucian had seen at the cove had looked fierce enough from a distance, but seeing them close up was truly terrifying.

Another hook came sailing over the gunwale and scrabbled along the deck. Avicus drew his sword and waited until the hook found purchase before slashing at the rope, the scaling hook clattering to the deck like a severed fish head. He grabbed up the hook, tossing it overboard as a flurry of quarrels thudded into the prow or zipped over the gunwale.

Lucian was watching the quarrels skittering harmlessly along the deck when he felt splatters of rain on his face. He'd no sooner glanced over to Kadian when the heavens opened.

Kadian angrily swiped at his flint and tinder before grabbing up a spear and hurling at the Drakkar, catching one of the Galyaks full in the chest. He hurriedly threw himself to the deck again and scrabbled to the gunwale as the Galyaks launched another flurry of bolts.

A grappling hook wrapped itself about the prow, quickly followed by two other hooks snagging the port gunwale. A number of the quarrels were lodged in the mast, so he knew they couldn't hope to raise the sail without being struck down.

Arkan Sula's voice suddenly sounded on the wind.

"Vulturna is your only hope now. But calling upon Her again will require a sacrifice in return."

An idea began to form in Lucian's mind. Shutting the cacophony of thudding quarrels and the Galyaks' scornful taunts from his mind, Lucian focused his thoughts on summoning Vulturna…while offering himself as the sacrifice.

Arkan Sula's voice sounded again.

"No! I forbid you!"

The Elkai's admonition came too late, however, for Vulturna was heeding his summons.

The Galyaks' euphoric cries quickly turned to anguished screams as the waters surrounding the Drakkar became a swirling maelstrom.

With the Xaviers watching on as the Drakkar was sucked beneath the waves, Lucian was climbing when Lykka sprang out of the stalls and over the gunwale.

Lucian's anguished cries melded with Galyaks' agonized shrieks as Lykka disappeared within the vortex.

The sea was again calm.

With a heavy heart, Avicus gave the order for the sail to be raised.

Chapter Seventeen

Necros

Lucian sat hunkered beside Kia in the stalls. Each of the Xaviers had offered words of comfort, but he was beyond consolation. He had lost his best friend and constant companion. He'd willingly offered himself as a sacrifice to Vulturna and would do it again a hundredfold if it meant defeating Nikobar. He'd faced the fire and sand demons, as well as the Sister Witches' sorcery, yet seeing Lykka leap into the water was seared into his brain and would haunt him till the end of his days. He now understood why Arkan Sula had enquired if Lykka had featured in his nightmare. He also understood why the Elkai hadn't explained his reason for doing so. Because he knew Lykka's sacrifice was preordained.

Lucian knew it wasn't man's place to dare question the will of the gods, but why hadn't Xavius called upon Vulturna to whip up a tempest to send Nikobar's ship to the bottom of the Gidean long before it ever reached Abador? Gazankulu would have been consigned to spend another thousand years trapped within his Netherworld realm. If the gods had decreed Princess Rhiana should ascend to Abador's throne, they could surely have arranged an accident to befall Prince Tarvel instead of delivering a pestilence where thousands of

Abadorians suffered an agonizing death.

He could only assume it was just as Arkan Sula had said: the gods viewed all earthly creatures as throw pieces on a chatrang board. All he could do now was honor Lykka's sacrifice by rescuing Princess Rhiana and defeating Nikobar.

Darkness was descending when they first caught sight of Necros' ragged outline, the island's stark malevolence becoming ever more tangible as Vulturna carried the Cassiope closer to the island.

Èinor had scratched a crude map of Necros into the deck. To Lucian's thinking, the island resembled an elongated boar tusk, with the southern extreme being the tusk's root. As his grandmother had foreseen within the embers, the Temple of Hadeas was situated atop a plateau at the north-easternmost tip of the island.

To be assured of their approach to Necros going undetected should the Galyaks have lookouts posted across the plateau, they would circumnavigate a cluster of treacherous reefs known to all sailors as Merwyn's Daughters before making for the island's southeast shore. The reefs were easy enough to spot during the day, but with the new moon still in its infancy, they were steering a course farther out to sea so they might make a sweeping bend about the reefs and approach the temple from the northwest.

It wasn't time against them now, but rather the tide.

The sole means of arriving at the plateau unobserved lay in navigating the River Styron to its headwaters. However, according to Èinor, the Styron's estuary had a treacherous undercurrent. Unless they arrived at the Styron's mouth while the current was in abeyance, they would have no option but to head back out to sea until out of sight of the island and wait until the following night before making another attempt.

Losing a whole day was an eventuality no one on board was willing to contemplate, and yet despite Vulturna's help, they'd arrived at the Styron's estuary to find the waves breaking white against the granite rocks rising sentinel-like on either side of the Styron's churning mouth.

They'd lowered the sail, but keeping the Cassiope steady with wave after wave pounding the prow was all but impossible. It was as though Merwyn was mocking them, for, beyond the estuary, the Styron's waters were perfectly calm; a snaking silver-black tongue beneath a mist-shrouded moon.

Lucian was in charge of ensuring the horses remained secure. Kadian and Raynor were manning the steering oar as best they could. Avicus and the other Xaviers were gathered at the prow trying in vain to find purchase within the granite rocks with the scaling hooks and ropes.

The Cassiope was taking a pummeling, and Lucian could see more and more gaps appearing within the gunwale where the tarred wool caulking had washed away. If they didn't get beyond the estuary soon, they risked the ship breaking apart. Lucian was weighting down the loose fodder with the Xavier shields Arkan Sula had provided when his eyes fell on the javelin-esque throwing spears. He suddenly knew why he'd thought them giant sewing needles.

Satisfied the horses were as secure as possible, Lucian grabbed up two throwing spears. Keeping a tight grip on the gunwale, he edged his way along the deck toward the prow.

"Unless Merwyn takes pity on us, we'll be dashed against the rocks for sure," Varos shouted above the foaming roar. "What do you intend doing with those?" he asked, eyeing the spears.

"We thread the rope through the eyelets with the scaling hooks attached," Lucian shouted, spitting the sea spray from his mouth. Without waiting for a response, he grabbed the scaling hook from Varos and hurriedly threaded the other end of the rope through the eyelet before handing it back to Varos. Avicus had grasped Lucian's intentions and was busy securing the other rope and scaling hook to the other spear.

Lucian made his way along the rail to collect the remaining throwing spears from the stalls. Returning to the prow with the remaining spears proved difficult, however. He couldn't hold onto spears and the rail. He might well have been washed overboard by a wave had he not stabbed the spears into the deck.

With all the scaling hooks and ropes attached, Lucian went to take over from Kadian at the steering oar.

Lucian and Raynor watched on as the other Xaviers retreated toward the mast, throwing spears in hand. Maintaining their balance was no easy task, with the Cassiope bobbing about like a cork, and Varos and Èinor both took a tumble. Avicus and Varos charged toward the prow and flung their spears, remembering to duck their heads to avoid getting caught with the flailing hooks. Watching the spears streaking into the blackness, Lucian mouthed a prayer to Valkyar, calling upon His help. His heart was in his mouth as he watched Avicus and Varos pull on the ropes. But Valkyar was with them as the hooks had found purchase.

While Avicus and Varos set about securing their ropes to one of the bulwarks, Kadian and Yanek sprinted along the deck and launched their spears. Lucian mouthed a prayer of thanks to Valkyar as their hooks found purchase in the rock. With all six ropes secured to bulwarks, the Xaviers engaged in a tug-of-war with the elements, slowly hauling the Cassiope through the churning waters.

The Styron's estuary had one last sting in its tail, however. Just as they were pulling clear of the estuary, a wave crashed over the rail to send Yanek sprawling along the deck, badly wrenching his shoulder.

****

Upon arriving at the Styron's headwaters, Avicus fashioned a makeshift sling for Yanek from a discarded jerkin. With the Xaviers having only five horses between them, Raynor doubled up Kadian while Yanek rode with Torian.

While making their way upriver, the Xaviers formulated a battle plan based on the Galyaks being camped somewhere on the plateau, most likely on the rise leading to the temple. The surest means of reaching the plateau without being spotted by the Galyak sentries were to scale their way up the rock face. Remembering how scaling the Colossus of Abador had been one of the ordeals Arkan Sula had set for the Xavier inductees, Lucian couldn't help but wonder whether the Elkai had foreknowledge of Nikobar's arrival in Abador.

Forging a path to the opposite side of the island, they had followed the shoreline to a butte overlooking the Strait of Horus until arriving at an abandoned watchtower atop the butte that Èinor recalled seeing when he'd visited the island many years earlier. Despite his repeated protestations that he could still wield a sword, Yanek would remain at the tower with the horses.

The circular stone tower stood some thirty feet in height, with a ditch surrounding the base, which Lucian suspected had once served as a moat. There was also a drawbridge, but the mechanism for raising the bridge was broken beyond repair. The door, though stout, was hanging off its hinges. The walls were also surprisingly devoid of arrow slits. No one had dared voice it, but the tower would serve as a redoubt should their plans go awry.

On reaching a lagoon where two Drakkars lay at anchor, the Xaviers had separated. Lucian would accompany Avicus, Varos, and Torian up the rock face to the plateau, while Raynor, Kadian, and Èinor were to overpower any sentries guarding the Drakkars and cast the longships adrift in the lagoon before setting them ablaze. This would hopefully cause sufficient distraction to bring the Galyaks running.

Avicus, Varos, and Torian's progress up the rockface was being hampered by their cumbersome shields. Varos also had to contend with a bow and quiver of arrows. Lucian had a bow and quiver, but not having to worry about a shield saw him soon speed ahead of the Xaviers. The climb was arduous, nonetheless. Avicus had made him swear that he wouldn't make for the plateau alone. Upon arriving at a narrow ledge jutting out from the cliff face some thirty feet below the plateau's ridge, he collapsed against the rock, sucking in mouthfuls of air to steady his breathing.

Seeing the three Xaviers were almost at the ledge, Lucian got to his feet and resumed his climb. Wrapping a hand about an exposed tree root, he was reaching for a cleft in the rock with his other hand when the root came away. He made a desperate lunge for the cleft. His groping fingers found nothing but air, and he would have fallen to death had Torian not saved him.

****

A mist was lazily rolling in off the Gidean by the time Lucian and the three Xaviers arrived at the plateau. To reach the spinney overlooking the temple, they'd had to crawl through a swath of blackthorn bushes. Lucian's britches had spared his knees, but his palms and forearms were covered in angry red welts.

Other than the effigy, the temple's layout was just as Lucian remembered from his nightmare. And though it wasn't moving against the wind, the mist was also steadily thickening just as it had in his nightmare. For an insane heartbeat, he expected to catch sight of Princess Rhianna skipping carefree through the temple.

The Galyaks' encampment was within a shallow basin a hundred yards or so beyond the temple. Lucian could make out indistinct shapes moving about within the eddying mist.

The Xaviers main worry was whether the Galyaks had brought their war dogs to Necros. Varos had said the Galyaks reared the dogs on human flesh and kept the beasts half-starved. When the Galyaks went into battle, they would unleash the dogs to break an enemy's shield wall. If there were dogs in the camp, the beasts would surely pick up their scent.

Keeping to a crouch, Lucian followed behind the Xaviers as they inched their way farther along the spinney to get a better view of the temple's inner ring.

It was only on their settling into position that enabled them to see what appeared to be a torch-lit opening within the ground. Was this where the Galyaks were holding Princess Rhiana? Lucian was voicing his suspicions when several Galyaks emerged from the opening and approached the altar.

"Is it my imagination, or is Khan favoring his left leg?" Varos asked no one in particular as they watched the Galyaks making their way through the temple. "Khan is the one in the horned helmet," he said for Lucian's benefit. "He must have picked up an injury of some sort since we last met under the sign of the Amarok."

Lucian was stunned. "Since you...you've met Khan?" he gasped, his eyes still focused on the Galyak Werloga.

"We are brothers under Valkyar," said Varos.

"The Galyaks have their own gods," Avicus explained, "but Khan has long been initiated into the Valkyarian mysteries. As was his father."

"But Galyaks can't worship Valkyar!" Lucian exclaimed.

"You only know Valkyar as the Kracian God of War, but He is a soldiers' god," Avicus continued. "We are oath-sworn never to reveal anything of the Valkyarian mysteries on pain of death. But I can tell you that should one Valkyarian find himself facing another on the field of battle, he is enjoined to kill him swiftly and with mercy."

"As Avicus did with Salah Khan at Zylos," Varos told Lucian.

"And as he would have done should I have found

myself under his sword," Avicus said.

Lucian's mind was reeling at the thought of men who were blood enemies belonging to a warrior fellowship. "And he bears you no ill will for slaying his father?" he asked Avicus.

"I wouldn't go that far," Avicus replied, allowing himself a brief smile.

"You know what Khan's presence here means, brothers," Torian said, looking beyond the temple to the Galyak encampment.

"These Galyaks are Bloodshields." Avicus nodded.

****

The Xaviers' strategy was wholly dependent on the Galyaks abandoning their encampment and racing down to the lagoon to try and salvage their ships. Bloodshields or no, they wouldn't stand idle while their ships burned. Lucian was eyeing the camp when he caught an acrid whiff on the breeze. It was the unmistakable smell of burning wood.

Peering down into the lagoon, he thought he saw the faint flickering of flames within the swirling mist. He was picturing Kadian, Raynor, and Èinor making their way back to the watchtower in his mind's eye when the plateau erupted in a frenzied crescendo.

Lucian cocked his head but couldn't discern any howling within the uproar. The Bloodshields had left their war dogs on Barrati.

It was impossible to know how many Galyaks remained on the plateau, but it stood to reason those guarding Princess Rhiana wouldn't have abandoned their posts. With Varos and Lucian leading the way with arrows poised, they'd edged their way down the mist-shrouded rise toward the temple.

Mick O'Shea

On reaching the inner ring, they paired off. Avicus and Varos continued their advance to stand guard at the far side of the temple to watch for any Galyaks, while Lucian and Torian cautiously approached the torch-lit opening. Sensing no sign of movement, they descended a short stairwell hewn out of the rock with Lucian leading the way.

Finding himself in a small antechamber with a large fissure in the rock serving as a tunnel instantly transported Lucian back to the Labyrinth of Kamar. Uncomfortably so.

The fissure opened out into a larger chamber.

Lying bound and gagged within a pentagram identical to that he remembered from the Sister Witches' subterranean temple in Helgos, was a girl in a crimson gown with tumbling auburn locks. Lucian was momentarily taken aback at finding Princess Rhiana looked and was dressed exactly as he remembered in his nightmare

Two Galyaks were slouched against the rock. Both were armed with crossbows but mercifully had their heads turned away from the opening. On seeing Princess Rhiana's eyes widen, however, both Galyaks sprang forward.

Lucian's arrow caught one of the Galyaks full in the chest. Torian leaped over Princess Rhiana and drove the rim of his shield up under the other Galyak's chin, snapping his neck.

Lucian rested another arrow against his bow and stood guard by the opening while Torian rushed to free Princess Rhiana from her bonds.

"Torian, is it really you?" the princess gasped, near-collapsing into his arms.

"And my brothers are with me, Your Highness," Torian replied. "This here's Lucian," he added, seeing the princess peering over his shoulder.

Lucian's eyes met Princess Rhiana's. In that same fluttering eyeblink, Lucian knew he'd forever lost his heart to the princess.

Princess Rhiana turned back to Torian. "My father was wrong in what he—"

"We can leave that for another time, Your Highness," Torian interrupted her.

With Lucian again leading the way, they retraced their steps along the fissure and through into the antechamber. Ascending the stairwell, they emerged from the opening to find the temple all but hidden within a dense mist.

There was no question of risking Princess Rhiana shinnying down the rock face to the lagoon. This meant passing through the Galyak encampment and onto the pathway the Galyaks had taken in their rush to save the longships. They were counting on the light from the Galyaks' torches revealing the path.

With the plateau blanketed in mist, there was no way of knowing whether any Galyaks remained in camp. Nor could they risk calling out to Avicus and Varos. This wasn't the time for being overly cautious, however. Should they run into any Galyaks, then Princess Rhiana being struck down by a crossbow quarrel was preferable to her being sacrificed to Gazankulu on Asima Na.

****

With Princess Rhiana holding onto Lucian's sword belt, they hurried through the temple, making for the outer ring, the pillars of which soon became discernable within the mist. Worryingly, there was no sign of either Avicus or Varos.

Lucian was turning to Princess Rhianna to offer reassurance when a bone-chilling screech shattered the silence. Sensing movement beyond the pillars, Lucian mouthed a prayer asking Valkyar to guide his aim and fired off an arrow. His entreaty was rewarded with an anguished cry, but a half dozen other Galyaks came shrieking out of the mist.

Torian emitted a howl and charged to meet the Bloodshields.

In that same heartbeat, Avicus and Varos appeared within the mist.

Lucian resisted releasing his arrow until he was sure none of the Bloodshields was armed with a crossbow. Seeing three of the Galyaks turn to meet Avicus and Varos, he felled the Galyak readying to hurl his spear at Torian.

Another Bloodshield, a huge brute with tattooed markings on his face and torso, was coming straight at him, however. Knowing he needed to keep his composure for fear of sending Princess Rhiana into a panic, Lucian plucked an arrow from his quiver, only partially drawing back the cord before releasing. The arrow caught the Galyak in the throat but failed to slow his momentum. The Galyak came barreling into Lucian, sending them both crashing to the ground.

Lucian was getting to his feet when the Bloodshield grabbed his ankle, wrenching him back down. He instinctively lashed out with his other foot, catching the Bloodshield full in the mouth. The Galyak was dying but was still possessed with strength enough to keep his grip. Leering through a mouth of broken teeth, the brute crawled on top of Lucian and brought his arm across his throat.

Lucian could feel the blackness descending as the Bloodshield applied pressure to his throat, their faces close enough for him to smell the sickly aroma of mead on his breath. Scrabbling about him with his free hand, Lucian's fingers fell upon an arrow that had spilled from his quiver. Mustering his remaining strength, he wrapped his fingers about the arrow's shaft and thrust it deep in the Galyak's side. The Galyak's eyes suddenly dimmed, his ebbing life spewing from his throat in a froth of blood.

Lucian was wriggling free from the dead Galyak when Varos offered a helping hand. His news was bleak, but Lucian had already surmised from the frenzied shrieks reverberating about the temple that the main body of Bloodshields was streaming up the hillside.

Taking hold of Princess Rhiana's hand, Lucian followed the three Xaviers into the tree line on the opposite side of the encampment. Their only hope now lay in finding an alternate route down from the plateau. If they could make it to the watchtower without the Bloodshields picking up their trail, they might yet still reach the Cassiope.

This side of the plateau was also thick with swaths of the prickly blackthorn bushes. Hacking their way through the tangled brushwood would sure bring the Bloodshields running, however. Dashing back into the Galyak encampment, Lucian grabbed up the first spear he happened upon before charging at the brushwood and vaulting into the scrub.

Ignoring the agonies of the thorns tearing at his

exposed limbs, Lucian probed the brush immediately to his front with his sword. Arriving at a less dense patch, he hurriedly scythed at the brush until forcing an opening.

With dawn still some way off, it was impossible to discern any natural pathways within the shadowy murk. Straining his eyes, Lucian saw a snaking seam that was darker than its surroundings some way down the hillside. If it was a river, all they needed to do was follow the current.

Lucian eased himself back through the brushwood. Keeping his voice to little more than a whisper, he hurriedly explained what he'd found before tossing the makeshift staff to Avicus.

Varos was the first to join Lucian on the other side of the brushwood, closely followed by Torian, Princess Rhiana, and finally Avicus. Before making her jump Princess Rhiana grabbed the hem of her gown, tearing it up to her thigh, tying the cloth about her waist.

The descent was much easier now they were finally free of the blackthorn brushwood. But the seam that Lucian had hoped might be a river was actually a meandering gorge stretching in both directions as far as the eye could see.

Chapter Eighteen

The Chasm of Death

The skies to the east were at last beginning to brighten. It could simply have been a trick of the dawning light, but to Lucian, it seemed as though the chasm narrowed significantly where a misshapen tree overhung the maw a couple of hundred feet farther on. On approaching the tree, they saw the blackened trunk was near cleaved in two and was still warm to the touch.

Lucian knew that Valkyar had cast a lightning bolt from Mount Herros. If they could split the tree to its core, the trunk looked as though it would traverse the divide. The only means of achieving their aim would be for one or more of them to climb onto the trunk and force a break. Should their calculations be wrong, of course, there would be no time to leap back onto the lip before the trunk fell away.

Avicus had arrived at the same conclusion, for he threw down his shield and clambered onto the twisted trunk. Grabbing hold of an overhanging branch that was mercifully within his reach, Avicus slowly edged his way out over the chasm, careful to test the trunk with his foot before adding his weight. The trunk creaked and splintered but showed no sign of giving.

Varos handed his bow, quiver, and shield to Torian

and climbed onto the trunk. Wedges of charred bark fell way into the shadow-filled void as Varos grabbed the branch and edged his way along the trunk to join Avicus.

The rent widened, yet stubbornly refused to yield.

Torian clambered onto the trunk. Instead of edging out to where Avicus and Varos stood perched like two exotic birds, however, Torian wedged himself against the trunk's upright base, using his back as leverage.

With the tree still refusing to yield, Torian got to his feet and tentatively edged his way along the trunk to make way for Lucian.

Lucian offered Princess Rhiana a reassuring smile and climbed onto the trunk. He'd no sooner done so, however, when a nerve-shredding crack sounded as the trunk finally gave, leaving Avicus, Varos, and Torian dangling from the branch. Lucian's heart lodged in his throat as the splintered trunk lurched suddenly before coming to rest on a jutting lip.

One by one, the three Xaviers dropped onto the trunk. Avicus and Varos went over to the opposite ledge while Torian rejoined Lucian and Princess Rhiana.

Lucian volunteered to help Princess Rhiana across. Avicus, however, insisted Lucian come across alone with the bows and quivers as he and Varos could deter any Galyaks that might arrive at the gorge while Torian helped the princess across.

Slinging the bows over one shoulder and the quivers over the other, Lucian stepped out onto the trunk. Because the trunk had rolled over before coming to rest on the lip, Lucian only had to focus on his footing while navigating an awkward knot burl midway across.

Once Lucian and Varos had each found suitable vantage points allowing a clear view along the gorge in both directions, Avicus signaled for Torian to bring Princess Rhiana onto the trunk.

Lucian's stomach lurched on catching sight of movement within the tree line a hundred feet farther along the opposite ledge.

Torian and Princess Rhiana were almost at the knot burl when the princess suddenly pushed past Torian and retreated back to the ledge. Despite the horrors she'd already undergone, were they expecting too much of the princess? The princess had only returned to the ledge to tug off her boots, however. Refusing Torian's help, Princess Rhiana stepped back out onto the trunk, boots in hand.

Lucian was willing the princess across when she suddenly halted and stood peering into the chasm. For an insane heartbeat, he thought she was contemplating throwing herself into the void rather than face recapture by the Galyaks.

Varos sprang onto the trunk just as a torrent of bats emerged from the gorge to engulf the princess. The Xavier made a desperate grab for Princess Rhiana but couldn't prevent her from slipping off the trunk. Without thinking, Lucian released his arrow, catching the princess's left forearm and pinning her to the trunk.

Lucian dashed out from his hidey-hole, but with Torian already advancing across the trunk, Avicus ordered him back for fear of their combined weight dislodging the trunk. With Varos gripping Princess Rhiana's forearm in both hands so as to ease the pressure from the arrow tearing at her flesh, Avicus unbuckled his sword belt, slid the sword free, and tossed it onto the ledge. He hurriedly looped the belt about the princess's other shoulder. He and Torian then carefully hoisted the princess onto the trunk.

The bats had all but dispersed. The screeching, however, had alerted the Galyaks Lucian had seen making a sweep of the trees farther along the gorge.

Mercifully, they were only three in number.

Torian dashed back onto the opposite ledge, grabbed up his shield, and went to meet the Bloodshield leading the charge.

Filled with an all-consuming rage, Lucian sighted his arrow on the Bloodshield that had stopped to take aim with his crossbow and released. The arrow slammed into the brute's tattooed chest, sending him tumbling into the abyss. The third Galyak had ducked into the trees. Lucian was trying to spot him when Torian shouted out a warning.

More Bloodshields were streaming along the ledge from the other direction.

****

Lucian and Varos's arrows were keeping the Bloodshields from making a charge for the trunk, but Lucian was down to his last three arrows, and he suspected Varos couldn't have many more. The Galyaks' quarrels, of course, were keeping Torian from attempting a crossing.

It was as though Avicus had read Lucian's thoughts, for he emerged from behind the rocky outcrop where he'd tended to Princess Rhiana's arm. "Get ready to let fly with your arrows," he told Lucian and Varos, grabbing up his shield. "Now!" he shouted, springing out and hurling the shield over the chasm as Lucian and

Varos released.

Quarrels zipped through the air, several of them thudding into the tree behind which Avicus had thrown himself.

Avicus's offering himself as a target had distracted the Galyaks long enough to allow Torian time to grab Varos's shield.

"It's now or never, brother," Varos shouted across to Torian.

Lucian and Varos kept their next arrows trained on the tree line where the Bloodshields were lurking while Torian readied himself for getting across. With a shield looped on each arm, he hurried onto the trunk.

It seemed to Lucian that Valkyar was deflecting the quarrels to Torian's shields. He was almost across, however, when a quarrel struck him in the calf. The force of the blow almost dislodged him from the trunk, but he mercifully made it across.

Fearing their quarry was getting away, the Bloodshields came bursting out of the trees.

Lucian felled a Galyak armed with a crossbow with his next-to-last arrow. He was drawing back his bow again, however, when the cord snapped. Casting the bow aside, he hurriedly gathered up some stones for his slingshot.

Seeing a Bloodshield wielding a double-bladed ax come charging onto the trunk, Varos grabbed up his shield and advanced to meet him. Keeping his eye on the ax, Varos waited until the Galyak lunged before throwing up his shield to deflect the ax to send him off-balance and tumbling into the abyss.

Avicus, Varos, and Torian threw themselves down beside the trunk, shoving with all their might. The irony wasn't lost on Lucian that having prayed the trunk would hold, he now wished nothing more than to see it gone.

The trunk slowly started to give, inch by torturous inch.

Realizing their quarry's intentions, the Galyaks charged. The added weight and rapid movement caused the trunk to lurch and give way, however.

Two Bloodshields managed to leap back onto the ledge, but the others tumbled into the void, their shrieks trailing in their wake.

****

With Avicus assisting Princess Rhiana and Lucian and Varos shouldering Torian between them, they set off down the hillside. Avicus had fashioned the princess a bandage and makeshift sling using the hem of her gown. She was very pale and in obvious distress, but mercifully, the arrow had only chipped the bone. There was still serious risk of the wound becoming infected, however. Lucian consoled himself with it, having come under extenuating circumstances, but there was no getting away from his having shot an arrow at the sole heir to the Abadorian throne. If his aim had been off, he might have killed her.

Circumventing the plateau to reach the watchtower was out of the question owing to Princess Rhiana and Torian's injuries. Before parting company at the watchtower, Avicus had told Yanek, Raynor, Kadian, and Èinor that if they hadn't returned with Princess Rhiana before first light, they were to assume the worst and make for Styron so they could catch the outgoing tide.

It was well past first light now, of course, but

Lucian had been with the Xaviers long enough to know the Cassiope would still be at anchor. And seeing the Bloodshields retreating in the direction of their camp instead of continuing along the ledge in one direction or the other had filled Lucian with hope because it suggested there was no means for the Galyaks to traverse the gorge.

The descent was arduous, but they eventually arrived at the base of the plateau. They were totally unfamiliar with their surroundings, of course. While making their way down the hillside, only rocky outcrops poked above dense vegetation as far as the eye could see. Avicus scrabbled atop one of the larger outcrops but saw nothing that provided a bearing. He did, however, espy a waterfall a few hundred yards away. They'd used a strip from the princess's gown as a tourniquet for Torian's calf, but their exertions getting down the hillside meant the wound hadn't congealed and was bleeding badly. The waterfall would allow them to at least clean Princess Rhiana and Torian's wounds. And it was as good a direction as any for now.

Fortunately, the undergrowth wasn't as impenetrable as it had appeared while making their way down the hillside. It was still heavy going, nonetheless. Torian's boot was saturated with blood by the time they reached the waterfall.

Princess Rhiana had regained some color to her face, at least. Seeing the ragged hole in the princess's forearm when Avicus removed the bandage reminded Lucian of the enormity of his actions. Avicus, Varos, and Torian had each praised him for his quick thinking. He knew he was being foolish, but it was the princess's forgiveness he sought.

It was only on watching Avicus wringing out the bandage that Lucian stopped to consider when Princess Rhiana had drunk last. Scooping up some water in his cupped hands, he made his way across to her. For a fluttering heartbeat, the princess's beauty took his breath away. The way her rosy-apple cheeks accentuated her wedge-shaped face.

Torian's suddenly pitching forward with a quarrel lodged in his back wrenched him from his trance readily enough, however.

Lucian grabbed Princess Rhiana's uninjured arm and was pulling her to her feet when he felt a searing pain in his left shoulder. Ignoring the blood seeping through the tear in his jerkin, he dragged the princess behind a tree. Avicus and Varos were dragging Torian to the safety of the trees when two Bloodshields burst into the clearing.

Leaving Torian to Lucian, Avicus and Varos turned to face the Bloodshields. Sidestepping one Galyak's lunge, Avicus brought his sword around and side-slashed the warrior's ribs. Varos blocked the other Galyak's sword thrust, then slammed him between the eyes with the pommel of his sword.

Lucian suddenly became aware of approaching horses. His heart soared on seeing Kadian and Èinor come thundering through the trees. Leaping down from Bellatrix, Èinor helped Lucian lift Princess Rhiana into the saddle before throwing himself up behind her and speeding off into the trees. As soon as Kadian was up behind Torian, Lucian and the other Xaviers set off for the watchtower. Kadian was careful to keep Adair at a steady canter, however, so Lucian, Avicus, and Varos could keep pace.

Their arrival at the tower coincided with Raynor shouting a grim warning from the battlements.

The Galyaks were advancing on the watchtower in force.

****

Leaving Èinor, Raynor, and Kadian to secure the door as best they could, Lucian followed Avicus, Varos, and Yanek up onto the battlements. The Galyaks were spread out within the trees some thirty feet from the base of the butte. Beyond the Galyaks, Lucian could make out the path he and the Xaviers had followed upon their arrival at the Styron's headwaters.

Instead of launching a frontal attack, the Galyaks seemed content to remain within the trees and hurl insults.

"What are they waiting for?" Varos asked, echoing Lucian's thoughts. "Why don't they attack?"

"They'll attack," Avicus said.

"How can you be so sure?" Yanek asked him.

"Because Nikobar needs Princess Rhiana if he's to perform his infernal ceremony on Asima Na," Lucian responded.

Varos unshouldered his bow and drew back the cord, fixing his imaginary arrow on a Bloodshield. "If only we had more arrows..." he said, releasing the cord.

Making his way back down the stairwell, Lucian saw that Èinor and Kadian had shored up the door with some loose timbers weighted with stones. He doubted the Galyaks would be hard-pressed, smashing their way inside once they attacked.

Kirgus Khan surely knew the Xaviers were inside the tower, but he wouldn't necessarily know it was only the seven knights he was facing. Of course, with every Galyak on Barrati set to arrive on Necros in time for Asima Na, Khan would have the numbers to pull the tower apart brick by brick.

Their only hope lay in holding out until nightfall, but that was many hours from now.

"How long is it before this ceremony the Elkai spoke of?" Kadian asked out loud.

"Asima Na is four nights from now, according to Arkan Sulu's calculations," Lucian replied, glancing to Princess Rhiana.

"Now that they have us trapped like fish in a barrel, they might choose to wait until the day of the ceremony before attacking," Raynor offered.

"Then we'll just have to think of something that will incite them to attack," Varos said. "Any suggestions...?"

Princess Rhiana came over to Lucian. "Promise me that when the Galyaks come, you will—" She fell silent, flinching as a quarrel slammed into the door. "Promise me you won't let them take me."

"It won't come to that, Your Highness," Lucian said, hoping to reassure her. "Arkan Sula won't abandon us."

Another quarrel slammed into the door.

"They're trying to set the door afire," Raynor shouted.

Lucian saw a tendril of wispy smoke coming through a split within the wood

Grabbing up his water flask, Raynor rushed across to douse the wood on this side of the door.

"That's another consideration, brother," Varos said to Avicus. "We have limited water and no means of getting any more." With that, he grabbed up a quiver of arrows and set off for the stairwell.

Lucian grabbed up one of the remaining bows and quivers and followed after Varos.

On reaching the parapet, Lucian heard the telltale sound of axes on wood echoing within the trees. The Galyaks were constructing a battering ram. He could only assume the Galyaks had been unaware of the tower's existence; otherwise, they wouldn't be wasting time with the battering ram.

Avicus had joined them with the remaining bow. Their arrival on the ramparts brought a barrage of quarrels, but the bolts either clattered against the stonework or sailed harmlessly overhead.

Taking up a position directly above the drawbridge, Lucian emptied the quiver, spreading out the arrows, so they were in easy reach. Risking a look through the crenellations, Lucian saw a Bloodshield emerge from behind a tree poised to fire another flame quarrel at the door. Springing up, he launched his arrow, catching the Galyak in the shoulder, which deflected his aim at least.

Lucian, Avicus, and Varos had no choice but to wait for a target to present itself. The Galyaks, it seemed, had a plentiful supply of quarrels, for each arrow fired from the parapet was met with a barrage.

The trundling of wheels sounded on the air.

Risking another peek over the wall, Lucian saw a dozen or so Bloodshields emerge from the trees pushing a heavy trunk secured to a wooden cart and with the end fashioned to a crude point. It would take great effort to push the battering ram up the gradient, but more Galyaks were rushing out to either join in the task or protect others with their shields. He shouted a warning to Avicus and Varos before leaping up and firing an arrow at the battering ram in the hope of hitting one of the Galyaks.

Avicus jumped up and released another arrow, ducking down again a heartbeat before a volley of quarrels flew out from the trees. "We have to stop them getting anywhere near the door," he said.

"They don't need the ram to get through the door, brother," Varos said. "A decent shoulder charge would do it," he added dourly.

"Once they get close to the door, we won't be able to get out with the horses," Avicus said. "If we're to get out of here, we have to take the fight to them."

Lucian scooped up his remaining arrows and set off after Avicus and Varos.

With the timber and stones cleared away, Raynor and Kadian were holding the door in place. Einor had taken it upon himself to look after Torian, while Princess Rhiana and Yanek were also mounted. Avicus and Varos were in discussion by the stairwell. Whatever they were debating, Lucian sensed it was serious.

Lucian was peering through a split in the door, monitoring the Galyaks' progress with the battering ram, when Avicus summoned him across.

"Once we're past the Galyaks with the ram, you're to swing to the right and make for the path that leads to the Styron," Avicus told Lucian. "If the gods are with you, you should catch the tide."

Lucian glanced from Avicus to Varos. "What about you?" he asked.

"If you're to fulfill your destiny in saving the

princess, then I fear our odyssey must end here this day," Avicus said somberly.

Varos clasped Lucian's hand. "It has been an honor riding with you, brother. We'll keep a place for you in the Great Feasting Hall for when you pass through Crucian's Cave many years from now."

Lucian made to protest, but the look in Avicus's eyes was enough to silence him. Without a word, he went and clambered up behind Princess Rhiana.

Avicus and Varos climbed into the saddle.

On Avicus's signal, Raynor and Kadian stepped away from the door.

The door suddenly falling away caused some Bloodshields to abandon the battering ram. Seeing the Xaviers come thundering out onto the drawbridge sent others into a panic.

Obeyeing Avicus's instructions, Lucian wheeled Kia away to the right on reaching the clearing. He'd no sooner entered the trees when the forest erupted in a cacophonic crescendo of noise.

****

It was all Lucian could do to hold onto Kia's reins. His grandfather had presented him with the filly on his thirteenth birthday. He'd taken her out every day since but had never suspected she possessed such stamina. It was as though they were being chased by all the nightmare creatures of Orbelium.

The bandage about the princess's forearm was soaked with blood again, which meant the wound had reopened.

They were approaching the Styron's headwaters, however, when Lucian glimpsed a Bloodshield standing at the Cassiope's prow. He leaped down and helped

215

Princess Rhiana out of the saddle before tethering Kia to a tree. Skirting through the tree line to get a clearer view of the Cassiope, he espied two more Bloodshields by the stalls rummaging through the clothing the Xaviers had discarded on changing into the new uniforms Arkan Sula had provided.

Focusing on the Bloodshields standing at the prow, Lucian loaded a stone into his slingshot and advanced toward the Cassiope until he was close enough to hear the other two Galyaks arguing over something they'd found in the stalls. The force of the stone sent the Galyak at the prow tumbling over the gunwale into the river. He loitered long enough for the other Galyaks to see him before dashing off through the trees to rejoin Princess Rhiana.

Lucian's spur-of-the-moment stratagem was wholly reliant on the two Galyaks remaining together rather than separating. On reaching the princess, he hurriedly untethered Kia and motioned for her to scramble behind a tree with his sword gripped tightly in both hands.

Coming upon the princess seemingly alone caused the Galyaks to relax their guard just as Lucian was hoping. He waited until the Galyaks reached the princess before pricking Kia's flank with the tip of his sword, causing her to rear up and career into the Galyaks, sending one of them crashing to the ground. Everything was a blur as Lucian sprang out from behind the tree and slashed his sword at the other Galyak's neck.

Without bothering to see whether either Galyak was dead, Lucian grabbed hold of Princess Rhiana with one hand and Kia's reins with the other and set off for the Cassiope. Once they were aboard, Lucian raised and secured the sail before then dashing over to the prow and slashing at the rope to release the anchor.

Stabbing the sword into the deck, he raced across and took hold of the steering oar as the Cassiope slowly began to pick up speed.

Five hundred feet ahead, Lucian recognized the twin slanting crags that loomed high above the river and reminded him of two outstretched hands destined never to touch. He also remembered how the Styron had narrowed as they were making their approach to the crags while coming upriver. The gap between the two protrusions was eight feet or more, but the left-hand crag had a more generous gradient and allowed for a running jump. Lucian was steering the Cassiope closer to the opposite bank when a quarrel came skittering across the deck while another thudded into the steering oar.

A handful of Bloodshields came charging onto the riverbank. The Styron was approaching high tide now, however, and the current was at such intensity the Cassiope easily left them in her wake.

As the Cassiope passed beneath the outstretched rocks, Lucian saw a solitary warrior come charging up the left-hand slope and launch himself into the air.

It was only when the Galyak landed on the deck that Lucian realized it was Kirgus Khan.

Abandoning the steering oar, Lucian went to grab for his sword, but Khan kicked the blade from his grasp. Emitting a reptile-like hiss, Khan then brought his fist down hard on Lucian's injured shoulder before grabbing him by the hair and dragging him over to the mast. Princess Rhiana bravely threw herself at Khan, clawing at his eyes, but he backhanded her, sending her crashing against the gunwale.

Keeping his foot against Lucian's throat, Khan hurriedly lowered the sail. He grabbed Lucian by the hair again, dragging him to his feet. Sensing Khan's intention, Lucian tried bringing his knee up, but the Galyak Werloga had positioned his thigh in anticipation.

Wrapping the rope about Lucian's neck, Khan hoisted him into the air.

Lucian grappled at the rope with his one good hand but couldn't get purchase. He could feel his world dimming when he suddenly collapsed back to the deck. As his eyes came back into focus, he saw Khan lying prone, staring into oblivion, and Princess Rhiana standing over him with a bloodied arrow gripped in her hands.

Freeing himself of the rope, Lucian pitched Khan's body over the gunwale.

Leaving Princess Rhiana at the steering oar, Lucian set about hoisting the sail again. He was rushing along the deck to take over from the princess when a dazzling flash of light came swooping out of the clouds to leave a perfect imprint of the Goddess Kia within the sail, with her golden wings outstretched, to propel the Cassiope along the Styron.

As the Cassiope headed out into the open waters of the Gidean, Lucian swore that as soon as order was restored to Abador, he would return to Necros and erect a balefire for the fallen Xaviers. He also mouthed a prayer asking Kia to keep a watchful eye over her four-legged namesake.

Chapter Nineteen

Return to Abador

Lucian woke with a start. As the shadowy surroundings of his bedchamber slowly began taking shape, he realized he'd suffered a nightmare similar to the one he'd experienced on falling asleep in the abandoned bailey the day of Princess Rhiana's abduction. In this nightmare, he and the princess were being chased through the Temple of Hadeas on Necros by a demon with baleful hooded eyes. He collapsed onto the bed and once again cursed his misfortune. The Xaviers' sacrifice now appeared to have been in vain, for by the time they'd arrived back in Abador, King Ocwan had already left the city with three cohorts of the Abadorian Guard to meet up with the cohorts of the Centaurian Guard at the Varnian border. Emissaries had also been sent out to the commander of the Abadorian Fleet, as well as the generals commanding the cohorts patrolling the Kavashan coastline, ordering them to make for the Varnian border with all haste. This, of course, left Kracia's southeastern coast open to a Galyak invasion.

His Majesty had left Nikobar to rule Abador in his stead, but Princess Rhiana had summoned the High Council to a meeting later that day to challenge the Cygian's right to rule.

Arkan Sula's warning as to Nikobar's true intentions was seared into Lucian's mind, but since arriving back in Abador, he'd managed to piece together what had occurred in the wake of Nikobar's sailing into Abador's harbor at the time of the plague.

The Cygian had petitioned King Ocwan for an audience, claiming he alone possessed the power to lift the plague and that he would do so in return for his being granted sanctuary for himself and his Black Crow mercenaries. Nikobar's ship was said to have been laden with gold, diamonds, and rare gemstones, which he'd also offered as a gift to Abador.

His Majesty had given Nikobar one hour to be away from Abadorian waters. Following Prince Tarvel's death, however, His Majesty had sent his ships out in search of Nikobar's vessel.

Nikobar had returned to Abador and had conjured a charm to lift the plague. The gold and jewels Nikobar had offered were no longer on board his ship, but King Ocwan had gold and jewels enough of his own. His Majesty was beside himself with joy that Nikobar had rid Abador of the plague and so had readily granted him sanctuary.

It was soon after Nikobar took up residency in Abador that King Ocwan issued his proclamation declaring the Xaviers to be traitors. Thinking about the Xaviers filled Lucian with an all-consuming sadness. They had given their lives to save Princess Rhiana and had died without having the chance to redeem their honor, and Lucian could have wept at the injustice of it all.

Lucian wearily threw back the covers, shuddering slightly as the crisp night air settled on his sweat-beaded skin. He'd no idea as to the hour, but going off the wispy motes of grayish light seeping in through the windows, he sensed dawn wasn't far away. He was rubbing his eyes when he saw someone standing within the open doorway. He rubbed at his eyes again, thinking they were deceiving him. "Varna?" he gasped. "Is it really you?" He clambered from his bed but halted on seeing shattered pieces of a porcelain water bowl lying amid a spreading pool of water at Varna's feet. He suddenly understood it was Varna's dropping the water bowl that had wrenched him from his nightmare. He could have kissed her.

Seeing Varna staring beyond him, Lucian turned to follow her gaze and was astonished to see a familiar figure lurking within the shadowy recess.

Nikobar.

****

Nikobar emerged from the alcove and came striding into the center of the bedchamber. To Lucian's mind, Nikobar cut a comical figure. There was no mirth in those hooded eyes, however. They reminded Lucian of a toad sunning itself on a rock.

"Forgive my intrusion, Master Lucian," Nikobar lisped, glancing to the doorway where Varna was hurriedly gathering up the broken pieces of porcelain. "But I was sure I heard you cry out in your sleep as I was making my way past your bedchamber." As he turned, the myriad of tiny encrusted jewels sewn into his silk gown shimmered as they caught the faint torchlight emanating from the outside corridor.

Lucian had no way of knowing whether he'd cried out on being wrenched from his nightmare by Varna dropping the water bowl, but that didn't explain what

Nikobar was doing lurking in the alcove, and he said as much.

"Whatever would make you think I was 'lurking' as you put it?" Nikobar asked, emphasizing the word. "As I say, I thought I heard you cry out and came to investigate. I was merely satisfying myself that all was well within when this miserable wretch"—he paused to glower at Varna—"dropping the water bowl startled us both. And you will pay for a new water bowl as punishment for your clumsiness!" he snapped at her.

"Come, my Lord Nikobar," Lucian said, glancing at Varna and offering her a smile before returning his gaze to Nikobar. "A man as powerful as yourself is surely above punishing servants. And I'd wager it was Varna finding you in here that caused her to drop the bowl?"

"But if servants were allowed to go unpunished for their infractions, the day will soon arrive when the world shall be bereft of water bowls."

"Then I'll pay for the water bowl," Lucian said.

"As you wish, Master Lucian." Nikobar stood glaring at Varna until she moved away from the doorway.

"One moment, my lord," Lucian called after Nikobar, bringing him to a halt out in the corridor. "What was it you heard me cry out?"

Nikobar stepped back into the doorframe. "Why, you called out Arkan Sula's name," he replied. "And it was most distinct. That is what caused me to enter your bedchamber. I thought perhaps the Elkai was visiting you in your dream state?" He fell silent as though expecting Lucian to reveal what he remembered of his nightmare. "And now, if you have no further need of me," he said when the information wasn't forthcoming, "I have pressing matters to attend to."

"I take it there is no word of His Majesty?" Lucian asked, stopping Nikobar in his tracks.

Nikobar returned to the doorway a second time. "Alas no, Master Lucian," he said with a quick shake of his head. "All we can do is offer prayers our emissaries locate His Majesty before he leads the army into Varnia."

And what of Jarl Laurik? Lucian thought to himself. Had he succeeded in uniting the northern clans against Agnar? Perhaps the northern clans had already risen up against Agnar and overthrown him?

"Seeing Lord Nikobar moving about in the alcove gave me such a start," Varna said, indicating to the broken pieces of porcelain.

"There are probably a hundred such bowls within the palace so one won't be missed," Lucian said. "But I'll happily pay for a replacement if needs be. I don't ever remember you saying you worked here in the palace." He arched a mock-accusatory eyebrow.

Varna's cheeks flushed. "I've been a lady-in-waiting to Princess Rhiana these past sixteen years," she confessed. "I never said anything to your grandmother because sneaking away from the palace to have my fortune told would have been frowned upon. I suspect your grandmother saw it all in the embers but was too kind to make mention of it." She surprised Lucian by taking his hands in hers. "I cannot tell you how much I rejoiced on hearing you had returned Princess Rhiana to Abador. Let's only hope His Majesty is not long behind her. Now," she said, breaking away, "I need to go find one of the other ninety-nine water bowls you mentioned."

Lucian closed the door behind Varna before going across to the window and throwing open the shutters, taking several deep breaths to clear the fug from his brain.

The sky was roseate with sun-kissed cloud, but Lucian saw it was going to be one of those ill-omened days, for the moon still shared the sky with the sun; the moon swollen somewhere between half and full.

He was returning to his bed when Varna arrived with another water bowl, which, he saw, was identical to the one that was broken. "Is there anything else I can do for you, Master Lucian?" she asked after placing the bowl on the stand in front of an ornate wood-framed mirror.

"Yes, there is," Lucian replied, scrambling back under the covers. "I'd very much like to hear one of your stories."

****

Lucian awoke from a mercifully dreamless sleep and walked across to the mirror. He'd always had to content himself with staring into a millpond or pail of water to see his appearance. The mirror, however, allowed him to see himself as others saw him. His eyes were still puffy and bloodshot, but the color had at last returned to his cheeks. He paused to inspect the angry-red three-inch gash atop his left shoulder where the Galyak crossbow quarrel had caught him. During the sail back to Abador, Princess Rhiana had bathed the wound to keep it from getting infected.

Upon arriving at the palace, His Majesty's personal physician had stitched up the wound before applying an eye-watering fungal poultice that had heralded his arrival before he entered the room. There was no denying the poultice was quickening the healing process, however. The wound was still painful to the touch, but Lucian found he could move his arm more freely than the previous day.

The water in the bowl had long since cooled, but Lucian scooped some into his cupped hands and splashed his face. He then grabbed up his blond locks and secured them with a thin strip of leather. He was turning away from the mirror when something on his shoulder blade caught his eye. It was a blemish of some kind. Dismissing it as being merely another of the injuries he'd sustained over the last few days, he was turning away again when something about the blemish stopped him.

Moving closer to the mirror while keeping his body at an angle, he saw the blemish was actually a birthmark. What's more, it resembled a bird of prey in flight. Then again, he supposed less excitable eyes might see a squashed bug.

He could understand why His Majesty's physician hadn't thought to mention the birthmark while stitching the wound as he would have assumed the mark was known to him. He was nonetheless puzzled as to why neither of his grandparents had ever thought to point out the mark to him.

Lucian was tugging on his boots when a loud crash sounded in the courtyard. Hurrying his foot into the other boot, Lucian dashed across to the window. The courtyard was a bustle of activity, but all eyes were focused on the two Black Crows standing on either side of a shattered cart with pieces of masonry scattered about them. The fools had overloaded the cart and broken the axle.

Nikobar had initially assigned his Black Crows to carry out some urgent repairs to the outer wall of the royal crypt due to supposed water damage. He'd since coerced every stonemason in Abador to help with the work. The royal crypt held the remains of Abador's Kings and Queens from Old King Megras onward. Princess Rhiana had demanded she be allowed to see the extent of the damage, but Nikobar had insisted it was as yet still unsafe. What Lucian found interesting was Nikobar only press ganging the stonemasons into service after Princess Rhiana's return to the city.

According to palace gossip, Nikobar had only ordered the repairs to be carried out following King Ocwan's departure from Abador with the Centaurian Guard.

Lucian knew the real reason why the Black Crows were in the royal crypt, and he took heart the swine had yet to unearth the Amulet of Meshtar. He was idly watching the hapless Crows loading the broken masonry onto another cart when he saw Croatalus emerge from the archway leading down to the crypt.

****

Lucian had been surprised to learn Croatalus was only twenty-five years old. It was a young age for someone charged with commanding a body of men, but what Croatalus lacked in maturity was more than compensated with vanity. He'd heard tell he spent an hour each morning oiling his jet-black hair, which he plaited into shoulder-length braids. He wore black jerkin, britches, and knee-length black leather boots, with a coiled, steel-tipped black-leather whip hung from his sword belt.

Lucian had been back in Abador less than a day, and yet stories of Croatalus's cruelty were commonplace about the palace. He had happened upon the Valessian savagely beating one of the servants while he'd been taking a stroll the previous evening. He'd stepped in, of course. Croatalus's eyes had flashed fire, and Lucian suspected they would have a reckoning before too long. Prior to his escapades with the Xaviers, he would have been sick to the pit of his stomach at the thought of a confrontation with a bullying brute such as Croatalus, but he was no longer the same naïve, fresh-faced youth that had set off for Abador.

He was filled with an overwhelming urge to let fly at Croatalus with his slingshot. He was chuckling to himself at the thought of the Black Crows' commander clasping a bloodied ear while glancing all about him when another Valessian emerged from the same archway, the same knot-headed rogue he'd last seen at the cove.

****

Lucian charged out of his bedchamber and out into the corridor. He had to alert Princess Rhiana about what he'd just witnessed.

Upon arriving at the princess' private chambers, he considered bursting straight in without knocking but stopped himself at the last moment. For all he knew, she might have been in a state of undress, and that would have been most awkward. The urgency of his knocking brought Varna to the door quick enough. She told him the princess was at her meditations in the mezzanine gardens temple. She also told him to be careful. Lucian thanked Varna before setting off back along the corridor and down the stairwell into the palace kitchens that led through to the courtyard.

Knowing Princess Rhiana was safe while she was at prayer, Lucian arrived at the archway leading down into the royal crypt in time to see the same two mutton-head Black Crows that had overloaded the cart descending the stairwell. He could hear the sound of muffled hammering and chiseling emanating from somewhere within the crypt.

Keeping close to the wall so that his descent remained hidden in shadow, Lucian set off down the stairwell.

On arriving at the foot of the stairwell, Lucian caught a whiff of decaying lavender and juniper berries. As his eyes became accustomed to the sepulchral gloom, he saw the crypt was "L"-shaped in structure, and the part he could see into consisted of a dozen or so arched catacombs. Save for the catacomb housing the sarcophagus of Queen Enid, who had died giving birth to Prince Travel, they had all been sealed with stone. Nikobar only cared for finding the Amulet of Meshtar, of course, so had cared little about the desecration to the royal crypt. Princess Rhiana's return had changed all that, however.

Lucian could only suppose Nikobar brought in the stonemasons to reseal the catacombs while his infernal Black Crows continued with their search for the amulet.

Several of the catacombs within the main section of the crypt, Lucian saw, were yet to be resealed. The main section appeared empty. The alcove beyond the far wall, however, reverberated with hammering and chiseling.

Lucian was edging his way farther inside the catacomb when he heard voices on the stairwell. He ducked into the nearest of the catacombs yet to be resealed, hurriedly side-stepping past the sarcophaguses until he was hidden in shadow. It was Croatalus and Knot-head.

Knot-head was clearly a Valessian of rank, for on his advancing into the vault and barking a command, the hammering and chiseling ceased abruptly. Moments later, a half-dozen dust-covered Black Crows came scurrying into view, making for the stairwell.

Croatalus waited until his men had ascended the stairwell before turning to Knot-head. "Where are the masons?" he snapped.

"My Lord Nikobar learned the princess had requested an audience with the stonemasons, so he's placed them in the dungeons until after Asima Na," Knot-head replied. "And there are only two catacombs still to be opened."

"And after Asima Na?"

"The masons are to spend eternity down here with Abador's ancient rulers," Knot-head said, grinning.

Seeing Croatalus step toward the catacomb where he was hiding, Lucian dropped to a crouch, catching his knee on the bottom sarcophagus.

"What was that?" Croatalus asked, peering into the catacomb.

"Probably just a rat." Knot-head shrugged. "This place is full of 'em."

"How many catacombs?" Croatalus asked again, his gaze still focused on the shadows. "One more after the one the men are working on," Knot-head replied.

Croatalus continued staring beyond the tomb for several heartbeats before finally turning away. "Then the amulet will soon be in my Lord Nikobar's possession. Now, regarding the other matter, Lord Dreyfus has assured my Lord Nikobar that everything has been arranged for when the princess speaks to the High Council."

Lucian couldn't believe what he was hearing. Was Lord Dreyfus the traitor who betrayed Avicus?

"And what of the lad, Lucian?" Croatalus asked, wrenching Lucian back to the present.

"His bedchamber is empty," Knot-head replied. "The kitchen servants saw him pass through there into the courtyard earlier. I have men making a search of the palace. We'll find him soon enough."

Croatalus again stepped to the catacomb where Lucian was hiding. "The sooner we rid ourselves of that meddlesome youth, the happier I'll be. Do we understand each other?"

"My men will find him, I assure you," Knot-head replied. "He won't leave the palace with the princess here."

Croatalus was still staring into the catacomb. "Have one of the men fetch two of the masons from the dungeons," he said. "Have them start with this one. We wouldn't want any rats lurking in there making a nuisance of themselves."

****

Croatalus had remained in the crypt, and Lucian was convinced the Valessian commander suspected someone was in the catacomb. He had to warn Princess Rhiana of Lord Dreyfus's treachery before she set off for the meeting with the High Council. To do that, of course, he had to figure out a means of getting out of his current predicament or face sharing the same fate as the unsuspecting stonemasons.

Lucian was suddenly aware of voices. He assumed it was the Black Crow returning with the two masons.

"Start gathering up the brickwork from the other vault and bring it here," Croatalus told his fellow Valessian before addressing the anxious-looking masons. "This catacomb requires sealing. My Lord Nikobar regrets having to place you in the dungeons, but you will be rewarded for your hardship. I can assure you in his name that you will live like royalty for the rest of your days."

The Black Crow arrived with the first barrowload of stones. Croatalus and Knot-head watched in silence as one of the unsuspecting masons busied himself sorting through the stones while the other began mixing the mortar.

The thought of being entombed alive was more unnerving than being at the mercy of the Sister Witches. For a maddeningly crazed heartbeat, Lucian contemplated shouting out to reveal himself. It was still all he could do to hold his nerve, watching on as the masons affixed one row of stones after another.

The masons were experts at their craft, and the rows of resealed stones were soon up to head height. Lucian could have wept when a Black Crow arrived to inform Croatalus and Knot-head they were to report to Nikobar immediately. Knot-head ordered the Black Crow ferrying the stone to ensure the catacomb was sealed before hurrying after Croatalus.

It was then that Arkan Sula's voice sounded within the gloom.

"*Feed their superstitions.*"

Lucian wasn't wholly sure what Arkan Sula was intimating, but the masons were fitting the last row of stones in place when the Elkai repeated his warning.

"Old King Megras will save you."

Lucian hadn't thought to consider which of Abador's one-time rulers resided in the catacomb he was being entombed within. If he remembered rightly, Old King Megras had survived Queen Xenela, so His Majesty was interred in the upper sarcophagus.

Resting his hands on the remains of Abador's first ruler was eerily reassuring, and he suddenly knew what to do. Mouthing a prayer begging Old King Megras' forgiveness for what he was about to do, he cupped his mouth and gave a low lingering moan.

The masons stopped what they were doing. "Did you hear that?" one of them gasped.

"Get on with your work!" a voice barked. Lucian assumed this to be the Black Crow.

"It's Old King Megras," the second mason whimpered. "He's cursing us."

"It was just the wind, you fool!" the Valessian scoffed.

Picturing the scene beyond the resealed stonework in his mind's eye, Lucian visualized the Black Crow approaching the stone. He hurriedly positioned himself against the back wall and gripped Old King Megras' sarcophagus before heaving with all his might, bringing the stonework crashing down on the Valessian.

Emerging from the catacomb, Lucian scrambled over the collapsed stone. Ignoring the cowering masons, he set off for the stairwell. He was halfway up when an idea came to him.

Retracing his steps, Lucian paused to assure the masons he was of flesh and blood. While relieving the unconscious Valessian of his jupon, he hurriedly told them his name and explained what was afoot in Abador.

The masons needed no further bidding and helped Lucian with the Valessian's breeches, boots, and helmet.

Lucian was tugging on a boot when Valessian began to stir. One of the masons grabbed up a mallet and brought it down hard on the Valessian's head to silence him once and for all.

"I suggest you place him in there," Lucian told them. "Rest assured; Old King Megras will forgive you for the very future of Abador is at stake."

Chapter Twenty

The High Council

The Black Crow's livery was somewhat baggy on Lucian. With one hand cinching the breeches to stop them slipping down about his knees, he hurried across the courtyard and through an archway that would ultimately lead him up to the mezzanine gardens temple. Continuing through to the stairwell, he cautiously edged his way up the steps and peered along the corridor. A Black Crow was standing guard in the entrance to the archway leading through to the mezzanine gardens. Fortunately for Lucian, the Valessian was slouched against the wall with one elbow resting on the rim of his shield, idly scraping the dirt from under his fingernails.

The princess's chambers lay at the other end of the corridor. Again, fortunately for Lucian, the corridor arched slightly in the middle. If he could reach the bend before the guard glanced up from his nails, he could hide out in the princess's chambers until her return.

Having seen the Black Crows strutting about as though they were superior to Abador's soldiers, Lucian stepped out of the stairwell onto the corridor with as much confidence he could muster. He'd advanced about ten paces, however, when the Valessian called out tersely, demanding to know what he was doing.

Lucian's heart was racing, but imagining how a Black Crow might react, he threw up a hand dismissively and continued along the corridor without breaking stride. His quick-thinking paid off, for the Valessian retorted with an insult but remained at his post. Arriving at the princess's rooms, Lucian gave a quick knock should Varna or another of her royal highness's ladies be inside before trying the door. Finding the door unlocked, he slipped inside and quickly shrugged off the Valessian livery. He was looking for somewhere to stash the livery when Princess Rhiana entered with Varna close behind.

"Forgive my being here, Your Highness," Lucian blurted out, offering a hurried bow, "but I've much to tell you."

"How many times must I insist you have earned the right not to bow to me?" the princess chided him.

"I should think always once more, Your Highness," Varna interjected, smiling at Lucian.

Princess Rhiana momentarily eyed Varna with mock-reproof before returning her attention to Lucian. "What's happened now?" she asked him.

And so, Lucian revealed all that had happened in the royal crypt.

"We might be powerless to prevent Nikobar from finding the amulet you speak of," Princess Rhiana said once Lucian had finished his tale. "But we can at least play my Lord Dreyfus at his own duplicitous game."

****

Word of Princess Rhiana's return to Abador had naturally quickly spread beyond the city's walls. One of those who'd set forth to Abador upon receiving the news was General Thuldor. The amiable Thuldor had at one time commanded the Centaurian Guard.

Lucian remembered Varos saying the general would still command the Centaurian Guard had he not lost the use of his left arm in battle. In gratitude for his many years of service, General Thuldor had been awarded the Order of Abador and elevated to the rank of Council Elder. Lucian also remembered Varos saying how Thuldor, who was still referred to as "General" as a courtesy, kept a small yet highly-trained bodyguard at his villa high up in the Thalesian Hills, paid for out of his own purse. He'd brought two dozen men from his private bodyguard to Abador. Lucian was grateful to have them here, for they were unsullied by either Nikobar's gold or sorcery.

Walking beside General Thuldor with Princess Rhiana as they made their way to the High Council chamber, Lucian estimated the general to be of a similar age to that of his grandfather. However, whereas his grandfather's thinning hair was as white as an early-morning frost, the general's hair was a mass of reddish-brown curls, graying slightly at the temples.

Council Elders were required to wear the burgundy and pale blue silk robe of office, but General Thuldor was wearing his old uniform.

"I still can't believe the Xaviers are gone from us," the general said. "I remember Avicus coming through to the Guard as though it was yesterday. Raynor and Kadian also. And I swear to you, Lucian, all those who played any part in the Xaviers' downfall will pay the highest price. And please again accept the gratitude of an old soldier for saving Abador's most radiant flower."

"Ridding Abador of Nikobar and his Black Crow mercenaries, as well as those who have sold themselves to Nikobar's gold, will be thanks enough, General," Lucian replied.

Princess Rhiana had insisted they say nothing of Asima Na or Nikobar's ongoing search for the Amulet of Meshtar to General Thuldor. He was a soldier to his core, so insinuating Nikobar had devised the princess's abduction and made it appear as though Agnar was responsible and bringing about a war between Abador and Varnia had sufficed.

The princess had also gotten word of Lord Dreyfus's treacherous scheming to Lord Colwyn, Old King Obelus's former Chief Consol. Though Lord Colwyn was now over eighty years old, his mind was said to be as sharp as a sickle come harvest time. Colwyn was rarely called upon to attend High Council meetings anymore, but his word still carried immense weight within the Senate.

Since returning to Abador, Lucian had learned of mounting unrest within the Senate. Prince Tarvel had been dead for over a year now, and yet King Ocwan hadn't thought to proclaim Princess Rhiana his rightful heir. Queens became Queens through marriage, not through lineage, and a kingdom without a King was seen as a cursed kingdom. Should His Majesty fall to a Huskenbach spear or arrow, then the princess' right to her father's throne would be open to challenge by any ambitious rogue with gold enough to raise an army.

But, of course, Lucian kept such dark thoughts to himself.

Every Abadorian had heard tell of the opulence of Abador's High Council Chamber, but few ever got to see its grandeur.

The chamber was circular in design with a domed

ceiling and supported by a ring of ornate marble pillars, which served to form an inner circle housing the table where King Ocwan and the Council Elders sat to conduct Abador's affairs. Ornate tapestries and bronzed engravings hung from the walls, the nearest of which depicted His Majesty's great-grandfather Old King Xelsus slaying the three-headed Vordra.

The domed ceiling was covered with a magnificent fresco depicting a banqueting scene within the Great Feasting Hall on Mount Herros.

The High Council Chamber also housed Abador's library, which detailed the city's rich history.

Lucian's grandmother had taught him to read and write. He'd hated being stuck indoors trying to make sense of letters and ciphers and would have much preferred to be helping his grandfather with the nets. He'd since come to appreciate the importance of the written word, however.

Lucian was still taking in the chamber's splendor when Lord Colwyn arrived. Though stooped and frail, Lucian sensed a steeliness behind the venerable elder's pale-gray eyes.

General Thuldor insisted on assisting Lord Colwyn to the council table as the other elders, all stern-faced and dressed in burgundy and pale blue cotton belted robes came bustling through the door.

Lucian had never met Lord Dreyfus, but he readily sensed him to be the tallest of the elders. Dreyfus had graying hair swept back from a prominent forehead and an aquiline nose. It was his eyes that Lucian noticed, however, for they were lifeless. He was pondering what intrigue Dreyfus was conspiring against Princess Rhiana when the doors suddenly flew open, and

Nikobar entered flanked by Knot-head and another Valessian who was unfamiliar to Lucian.

****

Lucian had only a vague understanding of the protocols surrounding the High Council yet knew only those called upon to speak before the Council were permitted inside the chamber. He was only there because Princess Rhiana had called upon him to speak before the High Council.

Nikobar hadn't been called on to speak, so had no reason for being there. Yet here he was.

Princess Rhiana was clearly taken aback at seeing Nikobar take the seat beside Lord Dreyfus. "Forgive me, Lord Nikobar, but what business have you here today?" she asked him.

"I received special dispensation to attend today as per my Lord Dreyfus," Nikobar replied matter-of-factly.

Lucian saw the princess bridle at Nikobar not calling her by her rightful title, but General Thuldor and Lord Colwyn were the only elders to express annoyance.

"And what pray might this 'special dispensation' be?" the princess asked of Lord Dreyfus.

Glancing up from the table, Lucian saw Kalt and the other Valessian had taken up positions beside a bronze engraving depicting Valkyar slaying Gazankulu. Was there any significance to their doing so, he wondered?

Lord Dreyfus sat gazing into the middle distance for some time before responding to Princess Rhiana. "I gave my Lord Nikobar special dispensation to attend the Council because he wanted to hear what Master

Lucian has to say…Your Highness," he added, more as an afterthought.

"But my Lord Dreyfus, you know as well as I that—"

"We took a vote earlier today," Lord Dreyfus interjected brusquely. "The vote was in accordance with the protocols as laid down by your father, His Majesty," he continued, as though reading from a preprepared script. "My Lord Nikobar wishes to question Lucian as to why he would wish to spread false rumors of the Galyaks being involved in your abduction. We have experienced no trouble of late with Kirgus Khan, whereas Agnar has made no secret of coveting your father's throne."

Lucian had kept his eyes on Nikobar as Lord Dreyfus spoke. He and the princess had told only General Thuldor as to what occurred aboard the Cassiope while fleeing Necros. Nor had they made any mention of Arkan Sula revealing himself to Lucian and the Xaviers on Galtar. He didn't remember seeing the raven at the time, but if the raven was serving as Nikobar's eyes as Arkan Sula believed, it stood to reason he would be aware of Kirgus Khan's death. And yet Nikobar had shown no response on hearing Lord Dreyfus say Khan's name.

"Agnar will have trouble keeping his own throne once Jarl Laurik has united the northern clans against him," Lucian said, glancing about the table before returning his gaze to Nikobar. "For Prince Ærin lives…"

"I fear Master Lucian is allowing his imagination to run away with him again," Nikobar said, silencing the murmuring. "All I ask today is that I be allowed to address the High Council before Master Lucian is called upon to speak."

"You may address the High Council, my Lord Nikobar," Lord Dreyfus intoned.

Nikobar got to his feet. "I am not of Abadorian blood, as you all know, but His Majesty King Ocwan has entrusted me to rule Abador in his name. As such, it would be remiss of me to accept the word of a mere youth—"

"But—"

"My Lord Nikobar has the chair," the elder facing Lucian cut in.

"Thank you, my Lord Selin." Nikobar nodded before continuing. "I confess being at a loss as to why Master Lucian insists Her Royal Highness the Princess Rhiana was being held by the Galyaks on some obscure island in the Gidean Sea when the proof of Varnia's guilt in her abduction is overwhelming."

"The 'obscure island,' as you put it, my Lord Nikobar, is the island of Necros," Princess Rhiana said. "And I would be there yet had it not been for Lucian and the Xavier knights."

Nikobar shrugged his shoulders in mock apology. "I assure you no one is making light of your horrifying ordeal, Your Royal Highness, but Master Lucian has admitted to having never seen a Galyak before the day he claims to have witnessed you being given over to the Galyaks. And he has also stated that he'd just awoken from a nightmare when he saw a young lady that he somehow knew to be yourself even though he'd never previously met or seen you. And what of the slain Huskenbachs found in the Thalesian Hills among the bodies of Your Royal Highness's escort?" he added

241

hurriedly before Lucian could interject. "Those Huskenbachs were put on display in the main square for all to see. If you had remained in the city—" He paused to glance at Lucian again. "—instead of allowing your head to be filled with fanciful tales spun by traitors then—"

"The Xaviers were not traitors!" Lucian snapped, his temper spilling over.

"But we are agreed the warriors found at the scene of Her Royal Highness's abduction were Huskenbachs…?" Nikobar said, glancing to General Thuldor.

"They were Huskenbachs," the general conceded begrudgingly.

"The Huskenbachs you speak of were from Jarl Laurik's retinue," Lucian said. "The Jarl was himself abducted by brigands and left to rot in the Eramian Wasteland along with Yanek of the Xaviers."

"Could it not be that Agnar and Kirgus Khan formed an alliance against Abador?" Lord Colwyn offered.

"Then let them come," General Thuldor bellowed, bringing his hand down on the table. "Our walls have stood for a thousand years and will stand for a thousand more."

Nikobar was about to speak but fell silent when Croatalus came bursting through the door.

"What is the meaning of this?" General Thuldor challenged as Croatalus approached the table and whispered something in Nikobar's ear. Knot-head and the other Valessian were already making for the door.

Without offering a word of explanation, Nikobar got up and followed Croatalus out of the chamber.

"It would seem my Lord Nikobar has more pressing matters to attend to," Lord Colwyn said with a wry smile.

Lucian suspected Croatalus had come to inform Nikobar that the Amulet of Meshtar had been found.

"I think we would be best served by hearing Lucian's testimony," Lord Colwyn said. "What say you, my Lord Dreyfus? That is why we are gathered here today, after all."

The chamber doors burst open again. Lucian feared it was Nikobar returning, but it was Captain Giffin.

"His…His Majesty—" Giffin panted, struggling to catch his breath, "—is returned to the city."

****

Lucian's elation at King Ocwan's return to Abador had rapidly soured. His Majesty had traveled with a small retinue, leaving the army in a state of readiness for an invasion of Varnia, which meant Nikobar's Black Crows remained in control of the city. More disturbing still was the news of His Majesty being holed away with Nikobar and Lord Dreyfus discussing who knew what.

Little wonder Nikobar was so anxious to take his leave from the High Council Chamber, Lucian thought to himself while pacing frustratedly about his bedchamber. His deliberations were suddenly interrupted by a forceful knock at his door. It was General Thuldor come to say His Majesty had at long last concluded his meeting with Nikobar and Lord Dreyfus and now wished to speak with Lucian in the Temple of Xavius.

"Will Princess Rhiana be with His Majesty?" Lucian asked the general as they descended the stairwell leading to the courtyard.

"Her Royal Highness has apparently been taken ill and has retired to her bed," General Thuldor explained. "I'm sure it's nothing serious. I should imagine she's simply overcome at His Majesty's return."

"I should imagine the whole city is overcome at His Majesty's return," said Lucian. "I only wish he'd thought to bring a cohort of the Centaurian Guard with him."

"As do I, lad," the general replied somberly. "As do I."

"Has His Majesty disclosed any of what was discussed with Nikobar and Dreyfus?" Lucian asked.

"All I know is His Majesty has announced a celebratory banquet in the Feasting Hall tonight," the general revealed. "Her Royal Highness was strongly opposed to the banquet, but I hear Nikobar convinced His Majesty a celebration was in order. It was Varna who told me about Her Royal Highness's objections," he added.

"So, Princess Rhiana objected to the banquet and is now feeling unwell?"

"You think Nikobar is responsible for whatever ails the princess?" General Thuldor asked as they emerged into the courtyard.

"I think it's too much of a coincidence to be otherwise," Lucian said distractedly, glancing over his shoulder to watch a covered wagon come trundling through the palace gate.

"Must be part of tonight's celebrations," General Thuldor said, following Lucian's gaze.

"And on such short notice as well," Lucian said, eyeing the wagon with suspicion.

****

The Temple of Xavius was circular in design with a triangular pediment and raised on a high podium. The temple was constructed of Carystian marble and white limestone, with a six fluted column portico. Between the two central columns was a bronze sculpture of Xavius clutching a thunderbolt.

This was the first occasion Lucian had to visit the temple. Upon passing through the temple's ornately decorated ivory doors, he gazed about in wide-eyed wonder at the decorative arches, colonnades, and vaulted ceiling.

Lucian was suddenly aware he and General Thuldor were no longer alone in the temple. Turning toward the open doors, Lucian saw King Ocwan, swathed in an intricately folded ivory-colored robe, flanked by a half-dozen of the palace guard.

Lucian knew King Ocwan's regal profile from the coins his grandfather brought home from the market. But His Majesty was much thinner than Lucian had anticipated. This was perhaps to be expected given the turmoil of recent weeks, of course. Though still a relatively young man, the stresses of kingship had taken a toll; the sad, wise look of his lined face made him seem much older than his forty-one years.

Lucian and General Thuldor bowed their heads as His Majesty advanced toward them.

"So, this is the young man who saved my daughter and foiled Agnar's intrigues," His Majesty said, smiling at Lucian.

Ordinarily, Lucian would have been too tongue-tied to speak, but with Asima Na approaching and Nikobar soon to own the Amulet of Meshtar if he wasn't already, this was not the time for such docility. "Forgive me, Lord King, but it isn't Agnar's intrigues that threaten Abador," he said. "I assure you the Huskenbachs played no part in Princess Rhiana's abduction. It was the Galyaks who were holding the princess in the Temple of Hadeas on Necros."

"Lucian is convinced it was the Galyaks holding the princess, Your Majesty," General Thuldor added.

His Majesty glanced from the general to Lucian. "My Lords Nikobar and Dreyfus have explained why you might be confused, Lucian, but—"

"But it was the Galyaks, Lord King," Lucian said forcibly. "Surely, you've spoken to Her Royal Highness…?"

"Of course, I have spoken with her." His Majesty's irritation showed. "She says she doesn't remember anything about her ordeal, which the gods be praised, is just as well."

It was Lucian's turn to look confused. "But she remembers everything about what happened, Lord King." A disturbing thought suddenly reared its ugly head. "Has Princess Rhiana been alone with Nikobar since your return?"

"I received word my daughter was suffering from agonizing pains behind her eyes, and as I was in consultation with my Lord Nikobar I bid him see visit with her to see what he might divine," His Majesty replied. "He administered a potion that he keeps close to hand for he also occasionally suffers from similar head pains."

Lucian now had assumed Croatalus had arrived at the High Council Chamber to alert Nikobar that His Majesty had returned to Abador. But what if he'd gone to concoct a potion to affect Her Royal Highness's memory? "I need to know all that Nikobar said when you spoke with him and Lord Dreyfus, Lord King," he said.

The King was taken aback at being spoken to in such a manner.

"Forgive the lad his impetuousness, Your Majesty," General Thuldor said hurriedly. "But it was such recklessness that saved Princess Rhiana."

"I understand your grievances against my Lord Nikobar," His Majesty replied. "He is a Cygian, but he also saved my daughter's life."

"Nikobar is merely passing himself off as a Cygian, Lord King," Lucian blurted out. "He was behind Princess Rhiana's abduction. He intended to sacrifice her to Gazankulu on Asima Na. If you won't accept my word on it, Lord King, then I beseech you to visit the royal crypt. Nikobar's Black Crows are desecrating the catacombs in search of the Amulet of Meshtar as we speak."

"You say you want to know what was discussed during my audience with my Lords Nikobar and Dreyfus," His Majesty retorted. "My Lord Nikobar was singing your praises for leading Captain Giffin to the island where Agnar was keeping my daughter. It was he who proposed a celebratory banquet in your honor."

Lucian was struggling to keep his temper in check. "I didn't lead Captain Giffin anywhere. He helped Varos and I free Avicus from—"

"My Lord Nikobar has advised me of these delusions of yours where you believe you freed Avicus and rode with the Xaviers," his Majesty cut in forcibly.

"But I did ride with the Xaviers, Lord King,"

Lucian spluttered. "And we met with Arkan Sula on the Rock of Galtar. It was he who told us about Nikobar's true intentions and of Asima Na."

"I see these delusions of yours are as vivid as my Lord Nikobar says," His Majesty said, softening his tone. "My Lord Nikobar says he can prepare a potion to rid you of this malady of the mind."

"This is no malady of the mind, Lord King," Lucian pressed. "What I say is the truth. You need to cast Nikobar and his infernal Black Crows into the darkest of your dungeons. Arkan Sula said every Galyak on Barrati will make for Necros to witness Nikobar perform the ritual of Asima and—"

"Enough!" His Majesty barked. "You say the Elkai speaks to you? Then call upon him now. Have him tell you the words he spoke to me the day I ascended to the throne."

"I can't call on Arkan Sula, Lord King," said Lucian.

"Just as my Lord Nikobar predicted." His Majesty nodded. "Abador has enemies enough without the need to devise imaginary ones," he said with solemn finality. "Now, General Thuldor, I would like to speak with you in private."

Finding himself dismissed, Lucian bowed to His Majesty before retreating from the temple.

Chapter Twenty-One

The Feasting Hall

The sun had set long ago, and yet with the Drago Constellation approaching its zenith, the skies above Abador were a portentous blood-red. Lucian's mind was in turmoil as he made his way across the courtyard toward the Feasting Hall. The banquet was in his honor, which meant he was expected to wear the ceremonial belted robe that still lay on his bed untouched.

Varna had mildly scolded him for shunning royal protocol, but with King Ocwan seemingly lost to Nikobar's sorcery, Princess Rhiana remained in grave danger, and hiding the dagger wedged in his jerkin in a ceremonial robe would have been impossible.

Carrying weapons into the Feasting Hall was against royal protocol, but Lucian was beyond caring.

Arriving at the towering doors leading through into the Feasting Hall and finding Knot-head, whose name he now knew to be Kalt, one of Croatalus's men-at-arms, with twenty or so Valessians standing guard served to heighten Lucian's unease. He could feel Kalt's baleful stare as he came past but purposely ignored him.

The Feasting Hall's doors were of stout Abadorian oak and stood twelve feet tall, with each of the doors requiring six servants to open or close. As with the

High Council chamber, the Feasting Hall was decorated with exquisite tapestries and bronze carvings depicting scenes from Abador's illustrious history. The floor was laden with an exquisite mosaic depicting a scene from Mount Herros. A score or more silken crimson and pale blue banners bearing Abador's rampant unicorn hung suspended from the ceiling.

This was the first occasion Lucian had had cause to step inside the Feasting Hall. He saw the tables closest to the royal dais where King Ocwan and Princess Rhiana would sit, as would he, of course, were taken up by sophisticated-looking men in fine robes and their elegantly dressed women. Lucian supposed these men to be either senators or nobles. He heaved an inward sigh of relief on seeing General Thuldor making his way onto the dais to take his seat.

The general was wearing a ceremonial robe and looked distinctly uncomfortable.

Lucian made his way through the circular space within the hall's center. He assumed it had been cleared of tables for the evening's entertainment. He hopped onto the dais.

"Not one for following conventions, are you, lad." General Thuldor chuckled as Lucian settled into the seat beside him.

Before Lucian could respond, a fanfare of trumpets sounded to herald the arrival of His Majesty and Princess Rhiana. Directly behind them came Nikobar, Lords Dreyfus, Colwyn, and Selin with the other elders that had attended the High Council meeting of earlier.

His Majesty looked resplendent in a crimson and pale-blue belted silk robe. Princess Rhiana was wearing a long-flowing dress of shimmering pale-blue silk embroidered with golden petals, with a jewel-encrusted tiara nestled in her auburn curls. She looked truly radiant, but Lucian sensed something amiss with the princess's eyes. As she approached the dais, Lucian saw the same lifelessness in her eyes like those of Lord Dreyfus.

Lucian watched His Majesty acknowledging the tables where the senators and nobles were seated and couldn't help but wonder which of these men had allowed themselves to be seduced by Nikobar's gold.

Nikobar was dressed in a jewel-encrusted silk gown similar to the one that he'd worn that morning. Lucian had wondered how His Majesty might react on seeing him again and was mildly surprised when the King offered him a half-smile.

Lucian could see from Princess Rhiana's lifeless stare that she was still suffering the effects of whatever potion Nikobar had concocted, his anxiety deepening when she ignored him as she came past to take her seat. Nikobar and Lord Dreyfus' show of ignoring him was so ludicrously obvious that at any other time, Lucian would have laughed out loud. For a heartbeat, he contemplated grabbing up the carving knife that lay within hand's reach and plunging the blade deep into Nikobar's foul heart.

As soon as His Majesty, Princess Rhiana, Nikobar, and all the other elders were seated, a procession of servants came bustling into the hall brandishing silver platters laden with an array of roasted game, poultry, fish, vegetables, fruits, and freshly baked bread. A score of girls in gold-colored robes went about with carafes of wine and water. The aromas of wild boar and venison were mouthwatering. Lucian, however, had little appetite. But rather than risk displeasing His Majesty further, he plucked a hunk of venison from one of the trays and dropped it onto his plate.

Lucian was absentmindedly glancing about the hall when General Thuldor leaned into him.

"I don't know what good it will do, lad, but I've sent for the rest of my bodyguard," he whispered. "After you'd left the temple, I suggested to His Majesty that he should perhaps visit the royal crypt to inspect the work the stonemasons were supposedly carrying out. His Majesty informed me he had already done so and that the damage to the outer wall was merely superficial. May the gods forgive me, but I defied my Lord King and visited the crypt to see for myself. You were right in everything you said. Each of the catacombs has been defiled. It was obvious to a blind man. Something is obviously ailing His Majesty's mind."

"Nikobar's sorcery," Lucian muttered, glancing past the general to where Nikobar was huddled in conversation with Lord Dreyfus. The urge to grab the carving knife was suddenly all-consuming. He was reaching for the knife when a sudden commotion sounded out in the antechamber.

The Feasting Hall fell silent, and all heads turned toward the doors as a dozen servants came through the doors pulling a covered wagon.

It seemed the entertainment was about to begin.

****

Lucian couldn't be sure, but he thought the wagon was the one he'd seen arriving while he and General Thuldor had been making their way to the palace temple earlier. He watched on as the servants

252

maneuvered the wagon into position so that the tailgate was facing the royal dais.

The servants retreated from the hall as six figures cloaked in hooded robes with their faces hidden behind theatrical masks came out from behind the wagon.

The masks were devised to represent the two basic human emotions of joy and sorrow. As the majority of Kracian plays were either comedies or tragedies, such masks were commonplace. Three of the figures wore masks depicting joy, while the others wore masks of sorrow.

One of three depicting joy shuffled forward. "Your Majesty, Your Royal Highness, my lords and ladies and members of the Senate," he began, offering a sweeping bow. "My name is Ralok, leader of this humble theatrical troupe you see here before you. We normally perform acts from antiquity, but this day, we have been called upon to recount a tale of treachery and false intrigue surrounding the adventures of a modest young man and of a noble quest to save the life of a beautiful princess."

Lucian sat bemused. His confusion stemmed not so much from the entertainment having been kept a secret from him but rather who might have provided the troupe with sufficient detail to enable them to fashion a reenactment. And would the troupe dare to mention the Xaviers in His Majesty's presence? Glancing along the dais, however, Lucian saw Ralok and his troupe now commanded everyone's attention—especially Nikobar's. It wasn't only those on the dais who were captivated, of course, for the hall was deathly silent.

"The young hero of our tale lived in a small village called Kalimar with his grandparents," Ralok continued with the tale. "One fateful afternoon, our hero ventured to a secluded cove with his pet Varnian wolfhound, Lykka, who, in reality, was a wolf. Fearing the reaction should the people of his village realize Lykka to be a wolf, our hero's wily grandmother suggested they engage in a minor deception.

"Our young hero was at the cove in defiance of his grandmother…but that's a tale for another time," Ralok said, bringing the hall to laughter.

Lucian felt his stomach spasm on hearing Lykka's name and mouthed a prayer in the wolf's honor.

"But wait," Ralok shouted loud enough to wrench Lucian from his reverie. "Perhaps I may be so bold as to call upon our young hero, who we are here to pay homage to after all—join us in our humble reenactment."

Calls of encouragement erupted about the hall as Lucian gingerly made his way from the dais toward Ralok. Seeing Varna watching from the doorway, he sheepishly offered her a wave.

"You can move closer, for I don't bite," Ralok said, bringing another ripple of laughter about the hall. He then came behind Lucian, placing his hands on his shoulders. "I call upon you all now to close your eyes and allow our hero to set the scene for us." The rest of the troupe paraded about the wagon in synchronized movements.

"Where would you like me to start?" Lucian asked over his shoulder, momentarily distracted from seeing Croatalus appear within the mezzanine directly above the dais.

Ralok made a theatrical show of cupping a hand to his chin while resting his elbow in his other hand as

254

though contemplating Lucian's question. "Well, I usually find the best place to start any tale is at the beginning.

"Could it be that our hero, who thought nothing of entering the Labyrinth of Kamar or the Serpent Queen's subterranean lair, suffers from stage-fright?" Ralok mock-announced as the three thespians representing sorrow gathered about him.

This brought on further peals of laughter about the hall, leaving Lucian feeling slightly foolish. The fate of Abador hung in the balance, and His Majesty was sitting through a play seemingly without a care in the world with the architect of the city's downfall seated next to him. Lucian was suddenly reminded of a tale his grandmother had told him about the emperor of a faraway land who'd played the fiddle while his kingdom burned.

"Then allow me, my young friend, to paint the picture as I believe it to be," Ralok said, pausing again for effect. "Our hero had fallen asleep within the ruins of an abandoned fortification at the cove close to Kalimar, which, if memory serves—and my memory isn't what it was once, alas—lies on Kracia's northeastern coast. How am I doing so far?" he asked, resting his chin on Lucian's shoulder, eliciting more laughter about the hall.

"It was on waking that our hero saw something he never thought to see," Ralok continued as the thespian who'd hurriedly come beside Ralok to lay at his feet made an exaggerated show of stirring from his slumber and suddenly recoiling. "It was a Galyak Drakkar making for shore."

The mood within the hall changed immediately. "Is

it possible I have erred in our tale?" Ralok called out while the rest of the troupe made a theatrical show of apology. "But I surely can't possibly have got this part of the tale wrong," he continued, stepping toward the wagon and reaching for the pin that would release the tailgate, "for it was told to me word-for-word by another who was at the cove that night. Someone who can tell us who is truly behind Princess Rhiana's abduction."

And with that, Ralok released the pin and stepped back as the tailgate came crashing down.

The murmuring grew ever-louder as the surviving Valessian from the fight at the stable emerged from the wagon's shadowy interior.

Croatalus bellowed an order to Kalt to arrest Ralok and his troupe, but not before the Valessian pointed an accusatory finger at Nikobar. In that same eyeblink, Ralok's robe crumpled to the floor. The other thespians also cast off their masks and robes, revealing familiar tunics underneath.

The six Xaviers drew their swords to meet the advancing Black Crows. For the first time in Abador's illustrious history, the sound of clashing steel reverberated about the Feasting Hall.

****

The hall descended into a confused melee as those unsuspecting nobles loyal to Abador hurried their women to the doorway while terrified servants ran screaming hither and thither. Lucian's only concern was reaching Princess Rhiana. Turning to the dais, he saw His Majesty, Lord Colwyn, and General Thuldor slumped unconscious in their chairs. Princess Rhiana was nowhere to be seen. Nikobar and Croatalus had also disappeared.

Lucian was pushing his way to the dais when Arkan Sula spoke to him, telling him to make for the Colossus of Abador with all possible haste. He set off toward the entrance to the archway closest to the dais, only to see Kalt rushing across to block him.

Lucian only had the dagger that he'd secreted in his jupon, so he grabbed up a toppled candlestand and charged at Kalt. The Valessian man-at-arms had had time enough to steady himself, however, and effortlessly deflected the stand, dislodging more of the candles.

Kicking one of the candles aside, Kalt attacked, hacking at the candlestand to force Lucian away from the archway.

While fending off Kalt, Lucian frantically looked about him for anything that might serve as a weapon. His eyes fell on a carving knife lying atop a silver platter amid an assortment of spilled food beside an overturned bench.

Kalt, however, had seen the carving knife and had second-guessed Lucian's intentions. The sergeant was so focused on Lucian, however, that he failed to see Captain Giffin leap down from the mezzanine.

Kalt's sword tumbled from his hand as he and Giffin tripped over the upturned bench.

Lucian paused long enough to grab up Kalt's sword before charging through the archway, all the time praying the corridor led to a place from where he might get his bearings.

The gods were with him, for he soon arrived in the courtyard. Racing across the courtyard, he ducked into the archway he knew led to the first of the winding stairwells built into the Colossus's circular hollow base. Taking the steps two and three at a time, Lucian emerged dizzily out onto the decorative dais through an opening between Valkyar's bronze feet to find Princess Rhiana precariously perched at the edge with Croatalus' whip coiled about her throat. Nikobar was stood his back to Lucian, his face upturned to the Draconis Constellation.

"Your youthful zeal is to be commended, my interfering young friend," Nikobar rasped without lowering his gaze. "I confess I was slow in realizing Arkan Sula was guiding your hand," he said, turning to face Lucian at last. "And where is the lord of inconsequence? For it was surely he leading the pitiful charade in the Feasting Hall? I had hoped he would dare face me. But no, he continually chooses to hide away in the shadows like the…Ahh, more meddlesome guests," he said on seeing Avicus and Varos come vaulting out onto the dais. "Only six of you now?" he mock-intoned. "Kirgus Khan was of some use after all."

"Raynor still lives, Cygian," Avicus said. "And Arkan Sula has been watching your every move."

Nikobar threw back his head and roared with laughter. "The Elkai saw what I allowed him to see. Show yourself, Elkai!" he challenged, his eyes darting about the night sky. "Once the Dragon Lord is returned to the sunlit world, we will see which of us is the stronger."

A thunderous explosion shattered the silence as the star within the Draconis Constellation that Lucian had imagined being the dragon's eye imploded to illuminate the night sky. "Had Arkan Sula not been so ignorant, Xaviers." Nikobar sneered, fishing what Lucian assumed to be the Amulet of Meshtar from inside his robe, "he would have known Asima Na is now at hand. Bring her to me," he commanded Croatalus.

Before Lucian could react, Nikobar threw out a hand, and he and the two Xaviers were ensnared within a ring of fire.

Lucian could only watch on helpless as Nikobar plucked the dagger from Croatalus's sword belt, using the tip to prize the amulet open. He then grabbed Princess Rhiana's hand and dragged the blade across her palm. Turning her hand over, he allowed a single droplet of the princess's blood to fall onto the blood-encrusted scale while reciting the ancient ritual of Asima Na.

An otherworldly threnody sounded on the night air as Nikobar was enveloped within tendrils of crimson-tinged black smoke cascading from the amulet. The thickening tendrils rose into the air, rapidly intertwining until forming a swirling maelstrom.

Lucian stood utterly transfixed as a monstrous winged beast with slit-yellow eyes slowly took form within the maelstrom. Unable to tear his gaze away as Gazankulu unfurled His latticed wings, Lucian was oblivious to everything around him until a blinding flash released him from his stupor.

Epilogue

Lucian hurried into the Feasting Hall just as a fanfare of trumpets heralded the arrival of His Majesty King Ocwan and Princess Rhiana, with Lords Colwyn and Dreyfus, General Thuldor, and the other elders on the High Council following behind.

A month had passed since the celebratory feast, and yet Lucian was still none the wiser as to what had happened atop the Colossus of Abador that night. As with Princess Rhiana, Avicus, and Varos, all he'd been able to say with any certainty when he'd appeared before His Majesty, and the High Council was there being a dazzling white flash that left each of them blinded for several minutes. When everything came back into focus, Nikobar was nowhere to be seen. It was as though the Cygian enchanter vanished into thin air. There had been little point in interrogating Croatalus, for the Valessian's mind was gone

What Lucian and the two Xaviers had decided to keep to themselves, however, was of their seeing something forming within the maelstrom just before the blinding flash. They agreed to this simply because Princess Rhiana had made no mention of it. Lucian remained convinced that it was Arkan Sula's doing, just as he believed it was the Elkai who'd called upon Kia to guide the Cassiope's safe return to Abador. Hearing the Xaviers explain how the butte had come alive to seal the Galyaks within merely confirmed his suspicions that Arkan Sula only made them think he was returning to Abador when they parted company on Galtar.

The Xaviers had also explained how Jarl Laurik sailed to Necros with some three hundred Huskenbachs. Having put any Galyaks they happened upon to the sword, they scoured the island for Kia before setting sail for Kracia. On arriving in Abador posing as the thespian troupe, the Xaviers gave Kia to Lanum for safekeeping. On being reunited with Kia, Lucian took princess Rhiana to the secluded cove.

The feast was in honor of the Xaviers now that Raynor was well on the way to making a full recovery from his wounds.

Lucian was again breaking with royal protocol. He'd been awarded the Order of Abador and so should have accompanied the royal party into the hall. He had, however, begrudgingly given in to Princess Rhiana's insistence that he wear the burgundy and pale-blue belted robe he'd been expected to don at the celebratory feast. His Majesty was dressed in a pale-blue belted silk robe replete with crimson sash, while the elders were in their ceremonial robes of office. All eyes were on Princess Rhiana, of course. To Lucian's mind, she looked as radiant as the sun in her gold-colored flowing gown.

His Majesty had readily pardoned Lord Dreyfus and those elders, senators, and nobles who'd fallen prey to Nikobar's sorcery. Croatalus and the dozen or so Valessians that had survived the fight in the Feasting Hall had their foreheads seared with a branding iron to forever mark them as landless brigands before being cast into the Gidean Sea.

Lucian's grandparents had traveled from Kalimar

for the ceremony as His Majesty's guests of honor. Since arriving in the city, his grandfather had apologized profusely for not believing his tale about Princess Rhiana, while his grandmother had fussed over him endlessly. He'd enjoyed reintroducing his grandmother to Varna, and it had proved especially pleasing watching the two women huddled by the fire in conversation as in days gone by. He'd also enjoyed seeing his grandfather engrossed in conversation with Èinor and the other Xaviers. When he'd asked his grandfather why he'd chosen to hide his meritorious service with the Centaurian Guard, the old man had said he was merely abiding by his grandmother's wishes as she abhorred all talk of war. Of course, that hadn't stopped him reliving the battle of Humran with General Thuldor over several mugs of warm mead.

****

Once everyone was seated within the hall, His Majesty spoke of his determination to restore Abador's prestige as the "Kingdom of Conscience". Kings should never be called upon to apologize for their actions. Yet His Majesty proceeded to astound the gathering by asking the Xaviers for their forgiveness.

A commotion suddenly sounded, and all eyes turned to the doors.

Arkan Sula came bustling through into the hall, flanked by Rojan, Jarl Laurik, and several fierce-looking Huskenbachs. The Elkai came to a halt and thumped the butt of his staff hard on the mosaic floor three times. "I bring good tidings, Lord King," he announced, approaching the dais. "Agnar has fled Varnia."

The hall fell silent as everyone absorbed the news.

"And we have you to thank for this, Jarl Laurik?" His Majesty asked.

"It is true we owe a debt of thanks to Laurik for getting the northern clans to rise up against Agnar," Arkan Sula acknowledged. "But it was the news that Prince Ærin lives that ultimately forced Agnar into exile."

The hall rippled with murmured gasps.

"Prince...Prince Ærin lives?" His Majesty spluttered.

"And seeing as he will soon be of age to become Wulvran," Arkan Sula continued, "I come here today to propose a union between Prince Ærin and Her Royal Highness—" He paused to offer Princess Rhiana a curt bow. "—to ensure a lasting peace between Abador and Varnia."

"Then I heartily agree to the union you propose," His Majesty announced to the hall amid raucous cheering.

Arkan Sula suddenly turned to Lucian as though only just noticing him. "The robe suits you." He smiled, coming across. "How's the shoulder?"

"It heals well, thank you, lord," Lucian replied.

Arkan Sula turned toward the dais. "Did you have your physician soak the thread in cat's urine before the sutures were applied, Lord King?" he asked. "Ideally, it should be the urine of a black cat, but I suppose any cat would suffice."

"I honestly couldn't say." His Majesty frowned.

"Well, let's see," Arkan Sula said, tugging at Lucian's robe. "Come, come, no need to be shy."

Lucian felt his cheeks reddening as he slipped the robe from his left shoulder.

"Your Majesty is to be commended," Arkan Sula said.

King Ocwan was bemused. "I am?" he asked, glancing about the hall.

"Why yes," Arkan Sula said, turning toward the dais. "You consented to the union without demanding proof Prince Ærin lives. Which is more than I can say for Laurik's fellow chieftains." He harrumphed while glancing to the Huskenbachs.

"I wouldn't presume to doubt your word," His Majesty replied.

"Do move into the light," Arkan Sula chided Lucian while handing him his staff. "Might I trouble you for some wine, Lord King?" he called out.

"When might we anticipate Prince Ærin's arrival at court?" His Majesty asked.

"Hmm, what was that…?" Arkan Sula said, looking up from examining Lucian's shoulder on seeing Varna coming through the throng with a goblet of wine.

Jarl Laurik and the Huskenbach chieftains suddenly dropped to bended knees.

"Your Majesty," Arkan Sula said, snatching his staff back from a bemused Lucian. "Lord King," he announced loud enough for all to hear. "I have the honor of presenting Queen Gwenyd of Varnia."

Silence descended once again.

"Long have I yearned for the day I could call you by your rightful title again, Your Majesty," the Elkai continued. "Now, if you'd be so kind as to inform His Majesty how you would know your son, Prince Ærin?"

"I would know him by the mark he carries on his left shoulder," Queen Gwenyd said, stepping toward Lucian and sending his world upside down.

Raucous cheers erupted about the hall as Lucian and his mother embraced.

Jarl Laurik and the other Huskenbach chieftains were on bended knee again, but Arkan Sula impatiently motioned them to their feet before approaching Lucian. "I saw from your bewildered gaze when I entered the hall with Rojan, you thought him to be Prince Ærin." He smiled at Lucian.

"I did, lord." Lucian nodded.

"Well, there's no denying Rojan is special," the Elkai continued. "With my help, he will become a true adept in time." He took hold of Lucian's arm and set off toward the dais again. "Forgive me, Your Highness," he said to Princess Rhiana. "I trust you have no objection to the union now…?"

"None, lord," the princess replied. "Though it may take time to familiarize myself with my future husband's true name."

"There's no need, Your Highness," Arkan Sula replied. "For Lucian is the name your father gave you." He turned to face Lucian. "With your mother's consent, I proposed deceiving Agnar by calling you 'Ærin' for it means 'Rightful One' in one of the ancient tongues. I forget which now. Careless of me, most careless. Everything is again settled, for the time being at least, but I will be calling upon you and the Xaviers once you've been proclaimed Wulvran, my prince. After the honeymoon, of course…" Arkan Sula gave Lucian a playful dig in the ribs.

"Might I ask why you'll be taking my husband away so soon into our marriage, lord?" Princess Rhiana asked the Elkai, glancing coyly at Lucian.

"I have been called upon to return the Spear of

Lixivior to its rightful resting place, Your Highness," Arkan Sula replied, rapping his staff on the mosaic. "It has served its purpose, after all," he added, giving Lucian a knowing smile.

Lucian now knew what had caused the blinding flash atop the Colossus of Abador.

"And we shall hear no more of Nikobar," the Elkai said to the gathering, "for Gazankulu didn't return to Orbelium alone."

"I need to ask your forgiveness, lord," Lucian said.

"Whatever for?"

"I was angry with you for sacrificing Lykka to Vulturna in my stead," Lucian explained. "At least I now understand why."

"What you witnessed was no sacrifice, my prince," Arkan Sulu said. "For Lykka was no mortal wolf."

"Then what was he, lord?" Varos asked.

"Surely you've not forgotten telling Lucian the name you would have given Lykka had he been yours…?" Arkan Sula replied with a mischievous smile. "For Lykka," he announced to the hall, bringing his staff down hard on the mosaic, "was Valkyar Himself! And He wishes to reward you, my prince, for all you have done to restore order to Kracia."

In that same heartbeat, a familiar yowl sounded, and Lykka came bounding into the hall.

A word about the author...

Mick O'Shea was born and raised in Accrington, Lancashire, but has been living in Surrey for the last 13 years. He is 59 years old.

While working in the finance sector Mick penned articles for leading UK magazines including Amped, Wired, and Record Collector, before attempting his first manuscript, Only Anarchists Are Pretty (a semi-biographical account of the Sex Pistols' early career), which was published by Helter Skelter in October 2004. He made the switch from numbers to letters on a full-time basis in 2008 and currently has some 20 published titles in print with several other titles in the pipeline.

www.ingramcontent.com/pod-product-compliance
Lightning Source LLC
Chambersburg PA
CBHW060531260626
47161CB00003B/848